WE COULD BE
VILLAINS

MISSY MEYER

The characters and events portrayed in this book are fictitious. Any similarity to real persons, living or dead, is coincidental and not intended by the author.

WE COULD BE VILLAINS

Published by Rocket Hat Industries
Copyright © 2014 by Missy Meyer
All rights reserved.

Cover Art by Missy Meyer

ISBN-13: 978-0-9862399-0-8

WE COULD BE
VILLAINS

ONE

I remember the day I met Nate; we ran into each other as we were escaping my office building, since the building was on fire at the time.

Well, to be fair, the entire building wasn't on fire, just the far corner of the top floor, but we all had to evacuate anyway. I'd run down the stairs along with everyone else from the upper floors, because the elevators were off-limits in an emergency. I had just rounded the corner at the ground floor, passing in front of the elevator bank, and ran straight into someone coming up the stairs from the basement.

Because I'm graceful that way, I promptly fell on my butt.

People were rushing past on both sides, but the person I ran into stepped in front of me and offered a hand to help me up. He was a scruffy guy in a T-shirt, with a wide smile on his face. I took his hand and he helped hoist me up off the ground.

"Thanks," I said as we were both bumped and jostled by other people trying to get out.

"My pleasure," he said as the crowd of people rushed between us. I followed the flow and went out to the wide lawn in front of the building.

The second thing I remember about Nate was seeing him again outside the building. He was off by himself, standing in one of the patches of grass, while most of the other office drones were clustered on the sidewalks or in the parking lot. As for me, by then I had my sensible flat shoes in my hand and was enjoying the feel of the grass between my toes. It was late enough in the morning that the sun had dried up the usual morning dew, but the ground under the grass was still cool. I was just happy it wasn't raining, since springtime in Seattle can be a bit damp.

It was nice to have an unscheduled break from work, even if it came at the expense of having part of our office burn up. The fire was on the top floor of the building, so I wasn't too concerned that it would make its way to my desk—the building was six stories tall, and my cubicle was on the third floor, near the other end. At least I hoped the firefighters would keep the flames from spreading, since my purse and keys were still upstairs.

Nate was typing away at something on a smartphone—I figured he was just texting friends about the fire, or posting something to a social media site, like a lot of other people around us. I found him strangely compelling, but I couldn't put my finger on why. He had a rumpled look the way that a lot of guys did in my building, like he'd just rolled out of bed, threw on the nearest clothes, and come in to work. WonderPop was, after all, a software company—it started out making educational products for kids, and over the years appeared to be trying to take over the universe by branching out into every type of software known to man.

Nate wore the standard tech company uniform: slouchy jeans, a T-shirt with a clever geek joke printed on it, and Chucks on his feet. He topped it off with the usual disheveled programmer hair, a few weeks late for a trim, a pair of thin wire-rimmed glasses, and just enough stubble to read as laziness with a razor instead of an actual attempt at a beard.

Still, he was fascinating. I was off to the side, so I could only see part of his face, but what I could see looked like an expression of sheer determination as he tapped away on the on-screen keyboard of his phone. Finally, he poked at the phone with a dramatic flourish and looked back up at the building. Then he glanced around at the rest of the evacuees, finally looking my way. He caught me looking at him, so I gave him a big smile. He grinned back, and even his smile was charming.

He started walking my way just as Amy, who sat in the next cubicle over from me, walked delicately across the grass toward me. She shaded her eyes from the rare Seattle sun as she watched the firefighters swarm around the building. Amy was nice, though we weren't particularly close. And she was irritatingly perfect—around five feet four, tiny frame, blond hair, blue eyes, with an enviable sense of fashion, even though it included high heels. As opposed to my own medium height, medium brown hair with a medium curl, medium brown eyes, and an extra five to ten pounds I figured were just part of the price of sneaking up on age thirty. I was the exact same height my mother was, who at five feet six had always referred to herself as "too short to be a model, too tall to be a jockey." Not that I had the looks for the one job or the athletic ability for the other, but still.

Amy finally made it over to me, being careful of her high heels in the grass. "A nice break from work, lots of firefighter eye candy, and a sunny day to boot. Can't go wrong."

"I just wish I'd brought a snack," I said. "Who knows how long we'll have to be out here?"

Nate sauntered over just as I asked the question. "Shouldn't be too long," he said. "The fire's pretty small and should be easily contained." He stuck out his hand. "Nathan Anderson. Please call me Nate."

"Sarah Valentine," I said. We shook; his handshake was firm and dry, which was a delight—both attributes seem to be lacking in this day and age. It's as if people go to a class to learn to give sweaty, limp-fish handshakes. Amy introduced herself and shook his hand, holding her hand up in a delicate (and limp) fashion. She threw in one of those patented hair-flips that cute, perky girls seem to specialize in.

"Are you new here?" Amy asked. "I haven't seen you around before. Sarah, have you seen him around?"

I shook my head. Nate answered, "I'm temping, just started last week. I'm not surprised we haven't met yet; this place seems to be packed with people."

I started to say something back, but the bulk of the crowd suddenly let out an "Oooh," which made us turn to see what was going on. Over at the far corner of the building, most of the firemen were aiming their hoses at the top floor of our building, but a few of them had started running over toward someone dressed in bright orange.

"Holy crap!" Someone behind us shouted. "It's Firewolf!"

Sure enough, there was Firewolf, a member of the illustrious Ultimate Faction. I didn't know all that much about the group, except for that there were maybe a half dozen prominent members, each with some sort of superpower or ability. For some reason, they chose to set up shop in Seattle instead of a more hustle-bustle city like New York or Chicago. The fact that there were already established hero organizations in those cities may have had something to do with it. For all I knew, we had the superhero B-team. Or even the Z-team.

The Faction used to be called the Omega Faction, until a few years ago when a particularly critical reporter called them out on the fact that omega was technically the last letter of the Greek alphabet and that the group probably picked the name just because it sounded cool. The reporter was fired the next week, and the Faction changed the first part of their name but threw on the tag line "The last group you'll ever need to call." It was an interesting lesson in both image recovery and the power the Faction had behind the scenes of the city. I have to admit, the new "Ultimate" name felt a little like overcompensating to me.

The ladies in the crowd behind us were all tittering about how glamorous it was to have one of the Ultimates out to our little office fire. I heard Amy give a happy, gentle sigh beside me. I glanced back at the crowd and noticed that it was growing; people from some of the other buildings on the WonderPop campus had come out to watch either the firefighters or Firewolf, or both.

"So we have a fire in our building, and Firewolf shows up to help?" I asked. "Doesn't that strike you as a little bit . . . I don't know, useless?"

Amy wrinkled her brow in an adorable way. "What do you mean?"

I looked at Nate, and I saw him smile with understanding. "The guy starts fires," I said. Nate nodded.

"So?" Amy said. "Then he's perfect for a fire."

I shook my head. "No, he's the exact *opposite* of perfect. He can start them, but he can't put them out. Well, I guess he could, but he'd need a fire hose or a bucket, just like the firefighters."

Amy sighed, this time in frustration instead of hero worship. "Sarah, you really need to lighten up." She teetered back across the grass to some of our coworkers who were standing on the sidewalk, walking mostly on her toes so she didn't sink into the turf.

Nate chuckled next to me. "Of all the choices of supers to come by, Firewolf does seem a bit rude and insensitive. Anyone else might be able to actually help fight the fire. This guy is useless for us today."

I looked at Nate. "Yeah, it's almost like he's rubbing our faces in this fire. You know, you may be the first person I've ever met who isn't completely dazzled by everything the Ultimate Faction does."

He smiled at me. "Well, I like to think for myself. Not a lot of people seem skilled in that area."

Back over with the firefighters, I could see Firewolf talking in an animated manner, illustrating some point by flailing his arms all over. The firefighters were dazzled. Firewolf came to the end of his story, and the men around him burst into laughter and applause. There were still a few men fighting the fire, but there were no more flames to be seen, and the smoke had gone down from a billowing cloud to a misty trickle.

Firewolf started into another story, and the men who were clustered around him fell silent again. I looked at the example of what our city considered someone super. He was dressed in skintight orange with a yellow and red flame pattern, and the costume revealed that he wasn't exactly in the best shape. A few parts of him jiggled in a way that you don't want your superheroes to jiggle. His half mask hid most of his features; when you got down to it, he could have been anybody's slightly bloated uncle, dressed in an inappropriately tight outfit, who just happened to be able to make fire shoot out of his hands when he thought about it hard enough.

"I wonder how he found out about the fire," Nate said. "Do you ever think they just sit around and listen to the police scanners and wait for some cool event to go to?"

"Wow, I thought I was cynical, but you totally have me beat."

"I'm actually a very positive person," he said with a grin.

"Really? Because I kind of like the snark," I said.

"Well, the positivity is still usually snarky."

"Good." We watched as the firefighters started packing up their equipment. One of them walked over toward our group.

"Folks! May I have your attention!" The people who had been chatting quieted down. "The fire is out, but we'll still have to do quite a bit of inspection to make sure the building is safe, so we're going to close it down for the rest of the day. Since the fire didn't touch most of the building, we fully expect everything to be up and running tomorrow. If your offices are here on this side, we'll have men escort you up in groups to gather your personal belongings. If your offices are on any floor in the southeast corner, please meet over in that parking lot so we can go in for you and retrieve anything you need." He waved his hand toward the parking lot where Firewolf was still holding court.

A number of people started walking that way, including people I knew worked in my nonburned section of the building. They probably just wanted autographs.

Our department leader stepped out and shouted his own orders at us. "All right, everybody, you heard the man. We'll go up together so you can get your stuff and go home; you'll all be paid through the rest of the day. We'll see you all tomorrow. Make sure you have your ID card in hand; you'll still need to swipe in at the door." I clutched at the ID I wore on a lanyard around my neck, just to make sure I still had it with me.

I looked at the groups gathering to go in and get their belongings. "I better go and get my purse and keys," I said.

"I have all of my things already," Nate said. "I guess I'll just head home from here."

I held out my hand. "Nice to meet you, Nate."

He gave me another delightfully firm handshake. "The pleasure was all mine, Sarah Valentine. Maybe I'll see you around."

TWO

Of course, the building was just fine the next day. Gossip made its way around that only a tiny section of the sixth floor had any damage; even the floor below the fire stayed untouched. It probably helped that the building was constructed out of mostly concrete.

I got back to work and had a busy day catching up from missing most of the day before. I did graphic design at WonderPop—cover art, marketing materials, anything with images. But I'd been roped into a few emergency copywriting assignments when our usual writing staff was unavailable or out on a group bonding retreat or just not answering their phones because it was beer o'clock. For some reason, their type of artistic production was held high as important, while my brand of artistic production was distilled down to "drawing pretty pictures" and "putting colors together."

Since we weren't writing code, we were near the bottom of the software company food chain. My department had been moved to our current building a couple of months before; whenever someone else needed more space, we got shuffled around. Typical corporate America.

Amy, in the next cube over, also worked in graphic design. Her domain was the home-office types of software; the packaging she designed was more bold blocks of color and simple icons. My assignments trended more toward the games, so a lot of my work was artistically rendered in-game footage or paintings (or photographs carefully filtered to look like paintings) of warriors, elves, dwarves, dragons, or whatever else was fighting in that particular game.

"I called my mother last night," Amy said, poking her head around the dividing wall between our cubes. "Told her all about how Firewolf came to rescue our building." I searched her expression for any sign of sarcasm, but I think she was actually serious.

"Yeah, it was . . . pretty exciting." Watching the guy stand around and tell stories to the actual people working to fix the problem. What a hero.

"Of course, I kind of wish it had been Commander Alpha. That guy looks like he's sculpted out of marble! Or even Action Alex—he's kind of cute. I wish I could meet guys like those. But still, what an amazing day!" She tossed her blond hair back over her shoulder, and I fought the competing ideas that it was both adorable and incredibly irritating. It also made me think of how my vaguely uncontrolled shoulder-length hair would never flutter and flow like that.

"Yeah, it sure was. Hey, I have to get back to this cover design."

"Okay," Amy said. "Oh, would you have a chance to look at something I'm working on a little later?"

"Of course," I said. We frequently looked at each other's designs; it's helpful to have a second set of eyes, since when you've been working on something long enough, another person can sometimes see things that you don't. "Just let me know."

Before lunch, I fished my shoes out from under my desk where I'd kicked them off, and headed to the break room to grab the sandwich I'd packed that morning. Halfway there, I sidestepped a cart being pushed down the aisle and looked up to see that the cart pusher was Nate. He was dressed in another variation of the tech-slacker uniform: different jeans, different clever T-shirt, different-color Chucks.

"Well, if it isn't Sarah Valentine," he said. "How are you today? Less excitement in your day? No rude heroes?"

I smiled. "Fortunately, today has been a whirlwind of the ordinary and mundane. And no, I haven't been visited by any oafs in masks yet today." I rolled my eyes.

"Perfect," he said. "I think I may have something here for you." He looked down at his cart, which was full of mail, packages, and interoffice envelopes. He ran his fingers over the top of the neat row of interoffice envelopes, stopped near the middle, and pulled out two with my name on them.

"Impressive organization," I said as he handed me the envelopes.

"I've always believed that no matter what you do, you should try to be good at it," he said.

"Too true," I agreed. "Thank you."

"My pleasure." I watched him roll his cart down the hall, pausing at offices and cubicles and immediately pulling the appropriate mail out for each recipient. I didn't care that he was delivering the mail; I was fascinated by how organized he was. Good at what you do, indeed.

I got my sandwich, threw the envelopes on my desk to look at after lunch, and went outside to eat. There wasn't an outdoor lunchroom per se, but we did have a ragtag collection of picnic tables out near one of the parking lots for the smokers in the building. I wasn't the only nonsmoker out there with a lunch bag; we get few enough beautiful spring days in Seattle, we try to take advantage of them as often as we can.

Nobody really had much to say about the fire itself; all anyone wanted to talk about was Firewolf. Though I did manage to pick up a couple of bits of gossip about the sixth floor. People weren't sure what they actually did up there as part of WonderPop, but I heard a couple of people talk about extra security. Government stuff, maybe. Someone mentioned satellites, but they weren't sure.

I finished up my lunch and went back upstairs early; I just didn't have it in me to hear more about how amazing it was that a superhero came to watch our building burn. I had time to kill, so I dropped off my empty bag at my desk and then went exploring.

I was familiar with the third floor, where my department was, and could make my way around the first and second, but in the couple of months since we'd moved into that building, I'd never had a reason to go to the other floors. I decided to try and find out what went on up on six, since the gossip had been so mysterious.

I took the stairs, each flight making a lap around the elevator shafts. The main part of the sixth floor didn't look too different from the rest of the building, mostly offices and gray-fabric cubicles. Like our floor, it was deserted for lunch. I found a wide hallway that went back toward the southeast corner of the building. I hadn't really thought about how large the building itself was, since I mostly kept to my little area, but the burned area was a surprisingly long distance away.

Before I even got close to the corner that had been burned, there was a security checkpoint—a desk that blocked most of the hallway, and a tough-looking guy in a uniform sitting behind it. Which was kind of weird, since we had a checkpoint down in the front lobby. I walked up to the guy at the desk.

"Hi," I said.

"How may I help you, ma'am?" he asked.

I didn't want to explain that I was being nosy about what they did in that section, so I went with the more obvious nosiness instead. "I was wondering how much damage there was. How long will it take to recover?"

"Unknown, ma'am." He wasn't the most talkative guy, that was for sure.

"Oh, okay, cool," I said. "The rest of the building just wonders, you know?"

"Is there anything else I can help you with, ma'am?"

I glanced around. There was a weird metal track on the wall. I looked up to see a strip of metal on the ceiling over my head.

"No," I said. "Nothing. Thanks. Have a good day."

He nodded but didn't return the pleasantry. Nice. I walked away, then looked back and waved at him. When I looked, I checked out the strip of metal in the hallway ceiling. Now that I wasn't standing under it, I could see that it was one of those metal grate doors, like you see on the front of stores at the mall. The metal track on the wall was for the door to slide down.

Why they would have extra security up there was beyond me, unless the lunch gossip was true and the company was developing some secret government software over there. I made up a few possible scenarios in my head, each one feeling more cool and exciting and intriguing than the last.

Though in reality, it was probably something totally mundane. Because I worked there, and nothing exciting or intriguing ever happened around me.

I got back to my desk and opened the top envelope of the two that Nate had given me. Inside were proofs of some cover art I'd done for an upcoming game, *Battlefield Fortress.* There were sticky notes with comments in a few places: mainly our marketing department asking for this elf to be moved over there, and for that dragon to be put on this side so they'd have a spot to put review quotes.

The changes would be easy enough, even a little mind-numbing. That's the problem with a job that you don't think of as a career: it's hard to really get excited about it. Of course, I always did the best work I could, but thinking about Nate's ultra-efficiency with something as dull as the mail, I figured I could probably always push myself and try to do a little better.

I opened up the second envelope, pulled out the single sheet of paper inside, and laughed out loud. Good thing everyone else was still out at lunch. The sheet was a photocopy of Nate's face, pressed up against the glass of the copy machine. He'd used a marker to scribble a half mask on himself, and written at the bottom in surprisingly tidy handwriting: "May I save you from a boring dinner sometime?"

Yeah, definitely an interesting guy.

THREE

I didn't see Nate at all on Friday, and then it was the weekend. I had pretty exciting plans, as usual—a little laundry, a little grocery shopping, a lot of loafing around. Saturday morning was back to the usual Seattle weather: cloudy and drizzly and a little cooler than you'd expect. I made a cup of coffee, threw on a pair of thick fuzzy socks to battle the chill of my hardwood floors, and fired up my computer. After checking my emails, I finished up a freelance project I'd been working on and sent it off to the client. Then I looked around my living room and pondered my morning.

My apartment is one of those loft spaces converted from an old factory, in an area just south of downtown Seattle known as SoDo. Which used to stand for "south of the dome," but the Kingdome was torn down years ago to make way for a more modern and stylish sports stadium. I suppose they'd repurposed the name SoDo to stand for "south of downtown," which was also geographically accurate, but I stuck with the dome reference out of sheer stubbornness.

The loft was small, but pretty cool, with exposed brick here and there and a nice modern kitchen. Not a lot of space to entertain, but then again, I didn't really entertain. Which was probably a side effect of not having all that many close friends. Most of my college friends had moved away in pursuit of their careers, some to cities in other states, a couple as far away as Japan and Belgium. We all kept in touch over various forms of social media. As for me, I'd hopped around jobs a bit before settling in to WonderPop a couple of years ago, but I've just never been good at making friends at work. Maybe it's because I spend so much time around those people already.

I bet Amy of the hair-flip made plenty of work friends.

I didn't mind too much, since I've always been more of a homebody. I'd rather sit on a comfy couch and read an exciting book, going on adventures in my head, than stand around listening to small talk and trying to dance at a party. I did have other hobbies, more active ones—I went to a local gym a couple of days a week, where they specialized in kickboxing. And during the fall and winter, I was a referee for the Emerald Wheels, one of the local roller derby leagues. But that rainy morning wasn't one for leaving the loft as far as I was concerned; it was meant for a cozy breakfast in. I curled up with a bank heist book I'd read before but really loved.

By lunchtime, I was ready to get out of the house, and the drizzle had turned into more of a sprinkle. Some days in Seattle, a sprinkle of rain is as good as it's going to get. I grabbed a quick burger for lunch and went to the grocery store. It wasn't too crowded, even though it was a Saturday. I was able to get everything I needed (and a few things I really didn't) and make it to the check stand in near record time.

The local newspapers stacked near the cash registers had a story about Commander Alpha on the front page, big surprise. The magazines had the usual combination of movie stars, celebrities, and superheroes. The cover of *People* had those twins from New York with vision powers—I think one of them had X-ray, while the other could maybe see in the dark? Whatever it was, I felt like their creepy pale eyes were watching me as I waited.

I was behind a lady with a baby in the seat of her shopping cart, so I made funny faces at the kid while I stood in line. Fortunately, the baby thought I was funny and smiled. They don't always.

On my way back to the apartment, I thought about babies. Definitely my mother, were she still alive, would be nagging me nonstop to get married and give her grandbabies already.

Especially since I was sneaking up on the big three-oh, with no prospects in sight. I wasn't even sure I wanted babies of my own; I'd never spent any time around them and didn't really see what the big deal was. I'm sure Mom would have a number of choice things to say on the issue. I wish I still had her around so she could give me a hard time—both she and my father passed away in a car accident when I was in college.

Come to think of it, that probably also adds to why I spend most of my time alone. It was only the three of us while I was growing up; a small number of extended family members lived several states away, and they didn't seem particularly interested in any of us. When my parents died, I was already fairly used to a quiet existence without too many people around. I'd often wondered what it would be like to have a huge family. Seemed so alien to me.

That evening I poured myself a glass of wine and fired up my biggest addiction—my gaming console. Yeah, not only do I design covers and posters for games; I love to play them, too. I even consider it socializing, since I've cultivated a select group of strangers who like to play the kinds of games I like to play and are the rare sort who don't send me private messages calling me fat or ugly. Or requesting that I send them topless photographs. The group consists of fewer than a dozen people, half of them other women.

I put the disc for *Secret Ninja II* in the machine and booted up the system. I checked my messages on the console first, seeing that Gladiolus had wished me a happy weekend, and xXStormChaserXx wanted me to ping him if I ever felt like doing some multiplayer runs at a shoot-'em-up game we both enjoyed.

As I loaded up *Secret Ninja II* so I could play, another message popped up from Gladiolus: "Getting near the end of Ninja??"

I opened up the messaging system and wrote back: "Close, I think. Last few missions?"

She wrote back: "No spoilers, but the ending . . . WOW."

I sent back a smiley face and loaded my saved game. I'd been taking my time playing through, trying to stretch the game out as long as possible, because I'd heard the designers who made *Secret Ninja* and *Secret Ninja II* had moved on to a new kids' title and weren't planning on making a *Secret Ninja III*.

I launched the game and felt like I'd had my fill of social interaction for the day. It wasn't dinner out with a friend, but a few messages with an acquaintance were good enough for me. Plus, I'd gone out and talked to the cashier at the grocery store and made faces at a baby. As far as an introvert is concerned, I'd already had enough social interaction for the entire weekend.

I jumped my little ninja around the screen. If I couldn't have any adventure or excitement in my own life, at least I could live vicariously through characters on the screen. Because really, even though I'm a quiet and reserved person who doesn't have many friends, I've always thought that if adventure showed its face in my vicinity, I'd grab that sucker and hold on tight. But since the life of a graphic designer for a software company isn't exactly ripe for thrills, I play games. I kickbox. And thanks to the fact that roller derby refs had to learn to play the game itself, I know how to skate around, avoid getting hit, and fall down strategically in order to not damage myself. I definitely want to be at least a *little* bit prepared for adventure when it comes my way.

* * *

Saturday turned into Sunday, which turned all too quickly back into Monday. I made my way back across the freeways and bridges to WonderPop (who liked to say they were a Seattle company, even though they were a freeway and a bridge away from the city proper) for another exciting week of castles, orcs, dragons, and whatever.

There was an interoffice envelope on my desk when I got in, which started my day off with a smile. I figured I knew who put it there. I opened it up, and sure enough, another photocopy from

Nate. This time, it was of his arm and wristwatch. He'd doodled some extra controls around the watch, making it look like some sort of communication device or something the Ultimate Faction might use. In his neat handwriting, it read, "Time for lunch today?"

I took a red pen and drew both a big hand and little hand on the face of his watch, both pointing up at the "12." Then I scribbled out my name from the front of the envelope, wrote in "Nathan Anderson—Mailroom" underneath, and took it over to the mail drop slot near the elevator.

I almost felt like a secret agent passing notes to a mysterious contact. I'm not gonna lie, it felt kind of cool.

At noon on the dot, Nate was there at my desk. He was dressed in what I had already started to think of as his uniform: jeans, tee, Chucks. I wondered how many different colors of those shoes he owned.

"Do you have any preference for lunch?" he asked.

"I'm an easy date," I said. "Soup, salad, sandwich? They actually have pretty good stuff over at building four."

We swiped our ID cards on the way out and strolled across the lawn toward the nearest street. We crossed over to the other side of the road and went into a sizeable cafeteria in one of the other WonderPop buildings. About half the buildings on campus had places to eat, but some of them were small, or the food wasn't as good. I was lucky to work across from one of the better places.

It was a little crowded, but I could see plenty of tables that were still free as we got in line.

"So," Nate said, "did you have an exciting weekend?"

I laughed. "My weekends are usually anything *but* exciting. No, the usual for me. Groceries, laundry, reading, some video games."

"Really? What do you play?"

"Right now I'm near the end of *Secret Ninja II*. I have a copy of *Badlands Wars* waiting to go after that."

"Oh, man. *Secret Ninja II* was great, but the ending—"

"Stop right there," I said, holding up my hand. "No spoilers."

"Of course not! I was just going to say, I thought about it for days afterward."

"Those are the best," I said. "I love any kind of story that really gets into your head."

"Then you're going to love *Badlands Wars*."

We got our trays of food, hit the beverage station, then cashed out and found a little two-seat table near the window. As we sat down, I noted with amusement that I had a club sandwich while Nate had a chef salad with bacon. It was almost the exact same meal, although mine was between bread and his was in a bowl. But he made up for the healthiness of the salad with a side of french fries. We dug in.

"So, what brings you to WonderPop?" I asked.

"Oh, you know. It's every man's dream to work in the mailroom of a huge software company."

I laughed. "It's honest work."

"And I appreciate you saying that. I can't imagine every woman wants to go to lunch with the new guy who works in the mailroom."

"Well, you didn't question the fact that I'm a chick who's playing a game where I use stealth to assassinate a lot of people and am excited to move on to a game where I shoot a lot of people. So we're probably even."

"We'll call it squaresies, then."

"Done."

The conversation turned back to our topic from the previous week, namely the group of differently skilled folks who claimed to protect our region of the country.

"Firewolf was all over the news again this weekend, did you see?" he asked.

"No." I grimaced. "I try to steer clear of the news, and that goes double for superhero news."

"Oh, you'll like the irony of this one." He paused dramatically. "He went to help out, just like he did with us . . . at a burning ice-skating rink."

I choked on my sandwich, managed to swallow the mouthful I had, then laughed until a couple of tears squirted out of my eyes. The people around us looked at me like I was a freak, but I didn't care.

After I gasped for a little bit and finally started breathing right again, I asked, "So, did he do anything to help?"

"What do you think?"

"I wouldn't be surprised if the guy is actually afraid of ice."

"Probably true," Nate said. He took a sip of his drink and looked thoughtful.

"What?"

"Do you ever wonder . . ." He shook his head. "Nah, maybe this is too heavy for first-lunch-date conversation."

"Oh, come on. You can't leave me hanging. Spit it out."

He twirled a french fry around and said, "Well, do you ever wonder why they call those guys the good guys?"

"I . . . well, I . . ." I paused and thought for a second. "You know, sometimes it doesn't make all that much sense, does it?" He nodded, so I continued. "Look at that Commander Alpha. Leader of the Ultimate Faction, supposed to be the hero of the city and all that. But what does he really *do*?"

"Smash things?" Nate offered. "When your power is superstrength, it's pretty much all you can do, isn't it? It's not like the poor guy can even fly or anything."

"I don't know, maybe they're really nice people if you get to know them."

"They're more famous than some movie stars. You really think they're down to earth, humble, or kind?"

I thought about it. "You're probably right. But what can we do about it? You'll never get anyone to change their minds about how great those guys are, even if you had proof that they were giant jerks."

Nate nodded again and looked up at the clock. "Oh, wow, look at the time. We should really get back."

We cleaned up our lunch mess and wandered back across to our building. We passed our IDs over the scanners at the door, waved at the security guard behind his desk, and went down the hallway to the elevators and stairs.

"I'm down this way," he pointed.

"I think I'm going to take the stairs up," I said. "Work off a little bit of that lunch."

He turned away, then turned back. "How about dinner sometime?"

I grinned. "I'd love it. You know how to get in touch with me."

He grinned back. "Lucky me, I have an endless supply of interoffice envelopes. I'll be in touch."

He turned away again and started down the hall.

"Hey," I said.

He turned back toward me. "Yeah?"

"If you've only been here a week, how do you deliver the mail so efficiently? How do you know the building so well?"

He laughed. "I've been studying the blueprints all month." He turned back and went down the stairs to the basement.

I went toward the stairs headed up, smiling. It wasn't excitement or adventure, but for the first time in a while, my life had a little bit of fun.

FOUR

My first real dinner date with Nate was that next Friday, arranged through photocopies and interoffice envelopes. We went to a seafood place downtown I'd heard about at work, and the food was great. The nice part was that the company was even better; it was like Nate and I shared the same opinions and ideas about almost everything.

He asked the awkward question about what my family did, and I told him that my parents had both died when I was in college. Turned out he'd lost his parents too—a plane crash when he was in high school. We traded stories about the things we'd accomplished or the things we hoped to do that they'd never be around to see.

The conversation turned lighter, and we talked more about video games. It was delightful to be able to discuss my favorite games with someone who understood just how fun the escapism could be. I told him about my kickboxing, and he told me about his failed attempts to learn to ride a unicycle, which made me laugh.

Dinner turned to dessert, which turned to coffee. We lingered a good long time and then finally made our way out to our cars. Nate said good-bye and ran his hand gently over my arm.

I would have been okay with a kiss, but it was also kind of nice that he didn't push.

Our second and third dates happened over the next couple of weeks. For both, Nate asked what I wanted to do, and I told him to surprise me. Indeed he did, and the surprises were much more interesting than dinner and a movie. On our second date, Nate took me to a rock-climbing place down by the lake. It was a huge indoor facility, with several sheer walls covered with handholds and footholds that looked like chewed-up wads of bubble gum. We climbed one of the walls side by side, shouting encouragement to each other all the way up, and I was delighted to beat him to the top by a hair. Though he may have let me win.

On the way back down from the top of the wall, my rope got tangled somehow. I was stuck twenty feet in the air, dangling a good ten feet from the wall, while Nate quickly zipped back down to the ground. The employee who was down below holding the slack end of my rope called for someone to get some gear, so somebody could climb up and give me a hand. While the guy who had belayed for Nate was putting on a harness, I decided to see if I could figure it out myself.

I leaned my weight backward and forward, and started to slowly swing my way toward the climbing wall. After a couple of minutes, I had enough momentum that I could reach out and grab hold of one of the chewing-gum handholds. From there, I got a foot in place, and climbed up far enough so I could reach the tangle in my rope. I looked down and saw Nate watching me intently. I gave him a wave, then tugged at the loops of rope until I got the knot loose.

The employee who'd been sent up to rescue me was fast; I'd just let go of the rope when he made it up to where I was.

"All good?" He asked.

"I think I got it," I said. "But thank you for coming up." The guy belaying me on the ground tightened up the slack rope and slowly lowered me back down to the ground.

"Nice job," Nate said. "You stayed cool under pressure."

"Thanks," I said. "But I wasn't too worried—I had professionals looking out for me."

"Still, I'm impressed." He raised an eyebrow, then helped me off with my harness so we could go get some dinner.

On our third date, we went to a huge indoor games complex. We took swings in the batting cages, shot up zombies in a video game, raced around in go-carts, and played laser tag against some kids half our age. I didn't feel bad for the kids when we beat them.

I did feel bad for another reason: I offered to pay my way for everything, but Nate insisted on paying the tab everywhere we went. Despite the fact that he surely made less money than I did, he acted like it was no big deal. It kind of added to his mystery.

Dates two and three both ended with a kiss on the cheek and an invitation for another date. I was starting to get antsy; I'm as human as the next girl.

On our fourth date (indoor skydiving, which was amazing, then dinner at my favorite steakhouse near my loft, which was delicious), just about two weeks after we'd met, I approached the delicate subject of seriousness.

"I have a question for you," I said.

"Shoot," Nate said.

"I don't want to be pushy or anything, but it's probably a good idea to get on the same page about what we're really looking for. How serious this is."

He blinked at me. "Well, where do you stand?"

I laughed. "My mother, were she still around, would have me find someone willing to marry me as soon as possible and start having babies. I'm definitely not ready for that. I don't even know if I want kids."

Nate sat back in his chair. "As far as marriage and babies, I'll admit, I don't feel anywhere near ready for that myself. I'm never around kids, so I don't know how I even really feel about them."

"Exactly," I said. "I probably don't get to see all of the . . . magic, I guess? It just looks like a lot of eating and crying and pooping."

"I know, right?" he said. "As far as seriousness . . . I mean, serious relationships are great and all, but . . . you see where I'm working. I'm kind of in a complicated, in-betweeny place right now."

"Oh, sure, of course," I said. "I wasn't saying we should jump into anything, or anything."

"But I like you, Sarah. I really do." He ran his hands through his hair. "And also, I'm not seeing anyone else right now, and I don't see a reason to start."

"Cool. Okay. Good." I looked down at my empty plate and played around with my fork.

He laughed. "Okay, so, we both appear to also be awkward and strange when serious things come up. Just another thing to throw on the crazy-similarities pile."

"Yeah," I said. "True."

"But we should always talk about this kind of stuff, I think," he said. "The best married couple I know, the guy is a buddy of mine from way back. And they talk everything out, all the time. I never see them fight. That's something to learn from."

"Look, we have all the time in the world," I said. "We can take things totally slow and figure it all out together as we go. Why not just have fun and let things happen as they will?"

"Sounds good," he said. "I'm always in favor of fun."

We finished up dinner and decided to stroll around the neighborhood, with the goal of a drink somewhere. The formerly industrial area near my apartment was slowly gentrifying; what was once barred doors and graffiti had, over the last couple of years, turned mostly into small cafés, bars, cute shops, and more ice cream joints than seemed appropriate for a place that was cold for over half the year. The businesses served the residents who'd all moved into converted buildings like mine, or the ultramodern buildings constructed where old brick heaps like mine had been torn down.

We linked arms and made our way to a nice little craft-beer place around the corner from my building.

"Nice night," he said, looking up at the moon.

"A weird spring," I said. "Usually it would be raining and cold."

"Have you ever thought of leaving Seattle?" he asked.

"Kind of? But not really," I said. "Only in an abstract way, I guess. I haven't really had a reason to think about it. I grew up in the suburbs, went to college near downtown. Every time I've been looking for a new job, one presented itself nearby."

"That's work, though. Do you ever get the itch to travel, just to see what's out there?"

"Sure," I said. "But then my practical side takes over and nags me that there's no way I could move anywhere else without a job lined up. And wouldn't job hunting in different states be amazingly hard? While I have everything I need right here, including a job that I find tolerable."

"Just tolerable? That's hardly high praise," he said.

We made it to the craft-beer bar and found our way to a little table in the back. "Are there exciting jobs out there?" I asked. "I've never been able to come up with one. Seems like we all have to tolerate our jobs, don't we?"

"So you're looking for an exciting job? Or just excitement in general?"

"Oh." I flopped my hand in the air with uncertainty. "I don't know. Maybe a combination of both. Doesn't everyone want a little bit of excitement or adventure in their lives? I've just never really figured out how to get it."

He tapped the table in thought. "What if an opportunity just presented itself? The perfect chance for adventure, with no obvious downsides?"

I shrugged. "Hypothetically? I'd like to say I'd grab the opportunity with both hands and give whatever it is a shot. Realistically? I have no idea. I can't even imagine what that kind of opportunity would be."

"Well," he said, "you never know. Keep your eyes open, I guess."

We had a couple of delightful beers; then Nate offered to walk me back to my apartment. We took our time.

"Do you think it's easier for people like the Ultimate Faction?" I asked.

"Is what easier?" Nate asked.

"Knowing what you want to do with your life. Embracing a

life of adventure. You're born with a crazy weird power, or develop it after falling into a pit of acid or getting bitten by a radioactive bug or whatever. Just like the obvious choice for me was to get a degree in something I found vaguely interesting and go work in that field, maybe the obvious choice for them is to go get a fancy outfit and run out to save the city."

"Or go the other way, go get a fancy outfit and run out to overthrow the city," he said.

"Sure, sure. But, sometimes the choice is obvious, right? You look at your skill set and what you bring to the table, and you realize, yeah. This is the thing for me. This is what I've been waiting for."

Nate shook his head, laughing. "I don't know if choices that obvious fall into our laps all that often."

"But they sometimes do, right?"

"I like to think so, yeah."

"Good." We made it to the front door of my building, and I turned to face him. Made bold by good beer and good conversation, I said, "The obvious choice here is to kiss me, so I suggest you grab that and run with it."

He did, and he did.

FIVE

I was ready for the next interoffice envelope to come in the next couple of days and was totally disappointed when the week came to a close without one arriving on my desk. My disappointment turned to confusion when I called Nate that next weekend and got a recording that his number had been disconnected.

My confusion turned to worry when my text message bounced back and he didn't respond to an email. Then my worry turned to a little bit of beating myself up, because my inner critic told me that a phone call, text, and email all on the same weekend was a little smothering.

I tried to tell my brain that neither the call nor the text actually went through, but my brain would have nothing to do with it. So I spent the weekend fretting. It wasn't like I could go by his house to see if he was okay; I only knew which neighborhood he lived in, not the address. I searched for him on the Internet but found nothing. I even dug out a physical copy of the phone book from the dark, gloomy place in the back of a cupboard where I'd shoved it, since they refuse to stop delivering the things, and it pains me to throw them away, *just in case.*

Well, in this case, it still didn't help.

Bright and early on Monday, after a restless night of worry and fret, I made my way into work. I dropped off my purse and keys at my desk, started up my computer, then went back downstairs to the basement. I'd been to the mailroom once or twice, so I found it without much trouble.

Everyone was hustling and bustling down there, and I didn't see Nate anywhere. A woman passed me by, then stopped and turned back.

"Can I help you with something?"

"Yeah," I said. "I'm looking for Nathan Anderson."

"Oh, sorry," she said. "He quit on Friday."

"What?" I asked, probably a little more shrill than expected.

"Yeah, he didn't even give two weeks' notice. Can you believe it?"

Disappointment, which had turned to confusion, which had turned to worry, turned a fascinating corner and made its way right around to anger.

"Unbelievable," I agreed. "What a dick move."

"You got that right." She blew out a sharp breath. "Well, we're shorthanded down here. Anything else I can help you with?"

"Oh, no, nothing. Thank you. You've been very informative."

I made my way back upstairs, fuming. Yes, we'd only been going out for a couple of weeks, and I guess despite the fact that I'd really felt a connection, I didn't know him all that well. But he really didn't seem like the type to quit his job, disconnect his phone, shut down his email address, and not tell me anything about anything.

I tried to keep from stomping back to my desk, but I probably still walked a little more forcefully than usual. At least I didn't need to fret anymore, so that was something.

* * *

The week went by surprisingly fast; it seems like having something like that happen to a person would make time crawl. Nevertheless, it was the weekend again before I knew it. I'd had a busy week, with a number of revisions to assorted projects. (And let me tell you, it was no fun receiving those interoffice envelopes with changes from the marketing department that week. It also didn't help that the new mail guy was a fumbling, disorganized mess.)

I kicked around my apartment on Saturday, tried to play some games, but they felt a little tainted somehow. Everything seemed a little more boring and ordinary since I'd been hit with such a weird bombshell. I went to the rink where the roller derby teams practiced, to try skating away my thoughts. But even a couple of hours of rolling in circles really fast with aggressive music playing in my ears didn't make me feel any better.

By Sunday, I was more than a little tired of my brain telling me over and over that it was something I'd done, and that I'd be single and alone forever, and that I might as well start accumulating a collection of cats to give meaning to my life. I poked around a couple of online sites to see if there were any quick freelance design projects that sounded interesting, but nothing inspired me.

I decided to go in to the office to tackle a few leftover tasks from the week and hopefully turn that nagging portion of my brain off. That was one nice thing about my job: the flexibility to work odd hours now and then, and then shave the time off another day of the week.

I threw on a glamorous outfit of yoga pants, a T-shirt, and a beat-up pink hoodie. I always tried to dress a little nicer than we were required to at work, but on a day like that one, feeling the way I did, I was going to be as comfy as possible.

The commute was a dream, since it was the weekend. It was a nice change to not have to fight all the other drivers on the freeway or the bridge. I was able to coax my little car up to the speed limit for once. I don't think it liked the feeling much. The poor thing was over ten years old and mostly held together with bumper stickers and hope.

The parking lot was also a vast wasteland, which was a delightful rarity. I even splurged and swiped my card at the entrance to the underground garage; normally the spots down there were all full by the time I got in, taken by the crazies who worked from six in the morning until who-knows-how-late at night.

That Sunday, there was just one other car down in the garage. The emptiness was luxurious. I got out of my car and ran a few laps around it, then spun around and sung about the hills being alive with the sound of music, because how often does anyone get the chance to be a total goof like that in a place with such great acoustics?

I took the elevator up from the garage to the main floor, which was that particular elevator's only route. Even those who get the luxury of parking underground still have to go through the security zone and swipe their ID.

I got out of the elevator and went down the only available hall, to the security desk. There was one lonely guy there, probably the owner of the other car in the garage, slouching behind the desk with all the TV screens. He straightened up when he saw me. I scanned my card and saw him glance at one of the screens.

"Good morning, Miss Valentine. Getting some work done?"

"Going to try. I was bored and have plenty to do here."

"Well, you'll be all alone up there; even the cleaning crew has come and gone. Please take care of yourself. And call me here at extension one thousand if you need me."

"Thank you," I said. "I'm sure I'll be fine."

I went up the stairs instead of taking the elevator—no sense in being lazy, when I'd gone to the trouble to hike all the way into work. Plus, it made me feel a little better about wearing exercise clothes. I dropped off my purse and keys in the bottom drawer of my desk and fired up my computer.

While things booted up, I decided to take a little field trip. I remembered the second security checkpoint at the end of the hallway up on the sixth floor and wanted to see what it looked like on the weekend.

I hoofed it up the stairs and down the hallway, and my suspicions were confirmed: the piece of metal was a big grate, which slid down on the tracks on the walls. The lights were all out behind the grate, so I couldn't see too far down that way to see what was back there or if the fire damage had been repaired.

The grate didn't reach all the way down; the big heavy edge was about a foot shy of the floor. Seemed like shoddy workmanship to me. I went back to my desk, feeling vaguely unsatisfied with what I'd seen.

After fiddling for a while with a photo of a muscle-bound dude with a sword so that he matched the lighting and shadow of the castle in the background, I figured it was time for a break. I saved the work I'd done on my computer, fished a dollar out of my purse, and headed down to the vending machines on the second floor of the building. I put the dollar in the pop machine, punched the button for a diet cola, and watched as the button flashed red and my dollar slid back out at me. The little screen flashed "Out of Stock" and I sighed. This was definitely not my week.

I checked out the rest of the pop machine, and the snack machine too, since I had a dollar in hand. Nothing else looked that good, so I trudged back upstairs. I stopped short when I turned the corner into my cube.

There was an interoffice envelope on my desk.

Then a whooping alarm went off in the building, and I jumped and let out a little scream.

The alarm was deafening, the same shrill and piercing tone as the fire alarm that had caused us all to evacuate a couple of weeks ago. I glanced at the envelope again, then went over to the windows. I looked everywhere, but didn't see any activity or any sign of danger. No fire, no police, no nothing. I went back to my cube and grabbed the phone, looking at that envelope on my desk as if it was a snake, coiled and ready to spring.

I dialed the security desk.

It didn't even ring; I just got a wah-wah-wah sound, which told me that something was seriously wrong with the phones. Which wasn't all that surprising, since the blaring alarm told me that something was also seriously wrong with the building.

And then it got even seriously wronger, because the building started to shake. It didn't quite feel like an earthquake, which I'd experienced more than once. But that was my only frame of reference, so I figured that's what it was. Except that the alarm had gone off before the building shook. And the phones were out beforehand, too.

I tried to breathe steadily. I closed my eyes tightly to try and center myself and told myself not to panic. Then I opened my eyes again and went back to the window. There was definitely something out there now.

That something was Commander Alpha.

And he was punching the side of my office building.

Now, what I don't know about Commander Alpha could fill a room, but I knew that his big power was superstrength. He was bulky but not in a fat or bloated way (like Firewolf). He was just a really big guy, who looked even bigger. His outfit was mostly white with some blue highlights, and it never seemed to get dirty. Probably some space-age polymer or something. He was too far away for me to see his face, but I'd seen it plenty of times on the news. Square-jawed, sort of handsome, but with a kind of permanent arrogant sneer, which subtracted some points.

Anyway, that was the guy who was currently punching the first floor of my office building, just to the right of where I was.

He stopped punching for a second and turned around to reach for something behind him on the ground. I knew I should probably get away from the windows and get the hell out of the building, but it was kind of too fascinating to stop watching. He turned back around and had in his hands, of all things, an electric bullhorn.

He put it up to his face, and then his booming voice rang out. "I have you trapped, so you might as well give up. Don't make this harder than it needs to be."

I was pretty sure that message wasn't meant for me, which meant that the security guard and I probably weren't the only people in the building.

He put his bullhorn down and went back to punching my poor building some more. I heard a crumbling here, and a cracking there, and realized that the time had definitely come to get the hell out.

I leaned down and pulled open the bottom drawer of my desk. I grabbed my purse and keys, kicked the drawer shut with my foot, and heard something make a crunching noise above me. Then the back of my head hurt. Then everything went black.

SIX

I woke up slowly, real thoughts slowly taking over from hazy and easily forgotten dream images. I stretched and lay in bed for a moment, my eyes still closed, trying to figure out why everything felt a little strange.

I lay there and went through my personal inventory. I couldn't sense any light beyond my closed eyelids, so either it was night or I was in a dark room. The back of my head hurt a little bit, and I pondered that for a moment. It didn't take me long to get to the last thing I remembered: standing at my desk, blaring alarms, and a sharp pain on the exact same spot on my head.

I opened my eyes to see where I was. Sure enough, it was a dark room, although there was some moonlight coming in through a window. So, nighttime. My pillow and sheets were white, which meant I definitely wasn't at home—my collection of bedding ran the gamut from gray to blue and back again to lighter gray. And the cheap sheets I bought were nowhere near this soft and cozy. I blinked the sleepy bleariness from my eyes, and I was able to look around the room.

At first glance, it was clearly a hospital room. There was another empty bed next to mine and a machine up next to my head with some softly glowing lights. I turned my head to look past my feet and saw a guy dressed in white scrubs sitting behind a desk, with a soft lamp glowing next to him. He had his head propped on his hand and was poking his finger at the desk's surface. Which was weird. I decided to avoid drawing his attention until I figured out a little more about where I was.

I continued my personal inventory, from wiggling my toes up to twisting my neck. The only pain I had was the dull ache on the back of my head, and I was pretty sure that something had fallen on me when Commander Alpha was punching my office building. Other than that, everything appeared to be in working order, which was a relief.

Feeling around to find out what I was wearing, I discovered that I wasn't in one of those awful open-backed hospital gowns, at least. I was wearing a T-shirt and some sort of drawstring pants. Both were as soft as the sheets, which was nice. The thought that someone had changed me out of my clothes wasn't so nice, even if it had been medically necessary.

I couldn't feel any IV needles in my hands or arms, but I had something around one of my wrists and figured it was a hospital bracelet. I felt it with my other hand; it was way too big and kind of lopsided. I moved my arm up in front of my face to see what it was. The thing wrapped around my wrist was white, and kind of shaped like a stylish ladies' watch, but without a face. There was a soft blue light pulsing on the front of it. I watched it for a minute, then put my other hand to my chest. The blue light was keeping time with my heartbeat.

If I was in a hospital, it was like no other hospital I'd ever seen. And since hospitals are all pretty much the same everywhere, I figured there was a possibility that I wasn't actually in a hospital.

I looked over at the guy behind the desk; he was still poking at the desktop and hadn't noticed that I was awake. I took a chance and shifted myself around so I could get a better view of the room, and he didn't even look up.

There were a bunch of cupboards, and a door off to the right side. I looked around to the left, but there wasn't much off that way besides a couple of other beds. Then there was the wall beyond the desk guy. There was something that might have been a door behind him, but I wasn't sure. It was just a door-sized rectangle that was a different shade than the wall, but I couldn't see a doorknob, just a panel off to the side.

I thought about my options. If I wasn't in a real hospital, this was a pretty interesting facsimile. And since police, firefighters, and building security would have taken me to an actual hospital, it was a strong possibility that I'd been carried away to wherever I was by one of two parties: Commander Alpha and his Ultimate Faction, or whoever was inside my office building that Alpha hated so much that he tried to punch the building down around them.

I could stay where I was and wait for someone, like the guy at the desk, to let me know where I was, or I could wait for an opportunity to get out and try to figure out whether I was in the clutches of the good guys or the bad guys.

The man behind the desk stretched and stood up, which pretty much made my decision for me. Either he'd come over to check on me or I'd get a chance to escape.

He poked the desk one more time, then went over to the door on the right. He opened it up and flipped a light switch, and I could see a mirror and a sink in a small room beyond him before he closed the door. So since that was the bathroom, then maybe the door-shaped object just beyond the desk was my way out.

I pushed the sheets off, sat up, and swung my legs over the side. I felt a little bit dizzy but not too bad. I stood up and the dizziness increased, then faded back again. I wanted to give myself enough time to adjust, but I also wanted to be quick enough to make it out the door before the guy finished up in the bathroom.

I took a couple of tentative steps while holding on to the bed and figured I had decent enough balance to make it. I walked as quietly as I could toward the desk. I looked at the surface that the guy had been poking, but it was just an ordinary desk. Weird. Then I looked at the door-sized section of wall beyond. It wasn't a trick of my distance vision—there was definitely no doorknob to be had, only the small panel on the wall next to what I figured was the door. There was a green button, larger than any of the others and centered in the panel, so I took a chance and poked it.

The door slid open without making a sound, which I thought was pretty damned cool. I was more nervous than scared, since whoever had brought me in clearly cared that I got medical attention. I wasn't even against being there, necessarily, but I wanted to know where I was and who had brought me there.

I went out the door into the darkened hallway beyond, and the door slid shut behind me. To my right was a short bit of hallway and a window. I went over and looked out and was surprised to see some palm trees swaying in the breeze, the sky behind them a dull pink color that meant the sun was just about to rise.

I crept down the hallway in the other direction, away from the windows. There were a number of other sliding-panel doors along the way, with nothing to identify what was inside them— each one only had a number. I looked back at the door I'd come through, which was numbered "12." The numbers got smaller as I made my way down the hall. I tried pressing the buttons next to some of them, but since they were red instead of green, I didn't think I'd get them to open. I was right.

At the end of the hall was a set of what were clearly sliding double doors, like at a grocery store. I crept up toward them and looked through, but due to the darkness outside and the tint on the glass I couldn't see much.

I took a deep breath and stepped up to the doors. They opened for me, just as silently as the door to the weird hospital room had.

I had just a moment to realize that it was surprisingly warm for nighttime, before I saw that there was a man just outside the doors, standing in the shadows. I froze.

He stepped forward and I saw him tap his wrist with his opposite hand. Soft lights came on around me, illuminating the front of the building. The hallway behind me lit up as well.

The man was wearing a beautifully cut suit, with a casually open shirt and no tie. He had a kind of blond windblown-surfer look. He held his hands out to each side, palms open toward me, and smiled. Even though my nerves were on high alert, his entire demeanor was nonthreatening and weirdly comforting.

"Hey, Sarah Valentine," he said. "Nice job getting this far."

"Thanks?" I said.

"May I fill you in on where you are and what you're doing here?"

"Yeeeeess?" I said.

"Great. Then let's get you back in bed before the doctor kicks my ass too hard," he said, and held out his arm.

It was probably crazy to take his arm, but that's what I did. My head hurt, I had no shoes, I had no idea where I was, I kind of had to pee, and really, I figured more answers would only make my next attempt at escape that much easier.

* * *

The mystery man led me back down the hall to the hospital room and escorted me inside. The overhead lights were on, and the guy who had been sitting behind the desk was standing next to my empty bed, straightening the sheets. He glanced at me, then at the man in the suit, then blushed and shuffled away.

The man in the suit helped me back into bed. "I'm going to call the doctor to have a look at you, and go grab something from my office, okay? Then I'll be back to explain where you are." I nodded. He pulled back his sleeve to reveal what looked like a big clunky digital watch and tapped on the front of it a few times. I realized it was the same thing he'd tapped outside to turn the lights on. Then he turned back toward the desk.

"Make sure she doesn't leave again, Jake?" He said to the guy behind the desk. Jake just nodded his head.

"Hey," I said.

"Yes?"

"You said you going to call a doctor?"

He held up his wrist, showing me his watch, then smiled his big smile again. "Just did."

I watched him go back out through the door. Jake rolled his chair out from behind the desk and parked it in front of the door.

"Dude," I said, "I'm not about to sneak out when you're watching me." Still, he folded his arms and stared at me. I twiddled my thumbs for a few minutes, looking around the room now that the lights were on. I recognized a few standard hospital items, but there were other things that baffled me. But one thing I realized was that it was a really beautiful room. Soft gauzy curtains in front of the windows, clean modern lines, colorful abstract art on the walls. It was pretty pleasant for a hospital.

The door opened behind Jake, startling him so that he almost fell over in his chair. A woman was standing behind him in the doorway, looking down at him in confusion.

"Jake," she said, "she's not going to sneak out again with you in the room."

"That's what I said," I said.

Jake quickly rolled his chair back behind the desk, and the woman came over to me.

She sat on the edge of my bed. "Hello, Sarah. I'm Dr. Adams, but please, call me Adina. How are you feeling?"

"My head hurts a little, but other than that, I think I'm okay."

She quizzed me on my name and how many fingers she was holding up. She asked questions about the year, and the city where I lived, and what I last remembered. She prodded the back of my head, which hurt, and shined a light in each of my eyes. Then she flexed all my joints and gave me that awful reflex test where they hit you in the knee with a tiny hammer. Finally, she smiled and stood up from the bed.

"Good?" I asked.

"Very good," she said. "You're doing just fine. No signs of permanent brain injury. I'm glad we took a little extra time to make sure everything was all right."

I nodded, then thought about what she'd said. "What do you mean, a little extra time?"

Her smile dimmed. "I really should leave this for Mark to talk to you about."

I wondered if Mark was the guy in the suit, who said he'd be coming right back. "You're the doctor; this sounds like a doctoring thing," I insisted. "How long have I been here?"

She put her hand on top of mine. "We've kept you asleep for three days," she said. "But with a head injury, that's completely normal. We were monitoring your brain activity the entire time."

I thought about that, then figured, what was done was done. "Okay, cool."

Her eyebrows went up. "You're fine with that?"

"Does it matter, since I'm awake now?" I said. "Plus, it's not like I suddenly woke up out of a ten-year coma. Three days, no big. Sometimes I've felt like sleeping that long after getting home from work on a Friday night."

Dr. Adams smiled again, more amused than before. "You *do* have an interesting outlook," she said. She got up and went over to the desk and tapped around on the surface just as Jake had. "We'll see about getting you some broth, something easy to eat. I'd like to keep you here overnight, just to keep an eye on that head of yours. Ask Jake or any of the other nurses for anything you need; we have a library of books, if you'd like to read something."

She pulled back the sleeve of her white coat to reveal a big wristwatch like the guy in the suit had worn. She tapped the face of it a couple of times.

"So that guy . . . Mark? Is coming back?"

"Yes," Dr. Adams said. "His office is right down the hall. I'll let him know that you'll be good to go tomorrow."

"Unless I sneak out of here again tonight," I said. Which, of course, fat chance of that happening. They'd undoubtedly be on high alert now.

"Wait until you talk to Mark," she said. "You seem like the type that might stay put after that."

SEVEN

Sure enough, Mark was the tall blond guy in the suit. He came back in carrying a manila envelope, accompanied by an older woman dressed in the same white scrubs as Jake; she was carrying a tray with a covered dish on it. She sat the tray down on the desk and tapped on the surface of the desk. Jake quickly got up and took the tray, bringing it over to my bed and moving a rolling table over so that I could eat. At least the weird hospital from the future had some standard equipment. He lifted the cover to reveal a bowl of chicken broth, speckled with spices.

Jake went back to the older woman, they spoke for a moment, and then he left the room. I guess the nurse shift was changing. I turned my attention back to the tray in front of me— the broth smelled fantastic, and I was torn as to whether I wanted food or answers first.

"I can talk while you eat," he said, which solved the problem. "However, if you would be so kind, I do have something for you to sign before I start explaining." He opened up the envelope, pulled out several sheets of paper, and handed them to me. At the top of the first page, "NONDISCLOSURE AGREEMENT" was printed large and bold.

"Seriously?"

"It's our standard NDA. You're welcome to read the entire thing, if you like. In fact, if you have a case of insomnia, it's really helpful reading. But as you may have guessed from what you've seen so far here today, we have a pretty interesting operation going on, with lots of company secrets. I can only tell you about them if your paperwork is in order."

I skimmed the pages; it all seemed pretty standard, actually. I'd filled out a few NDAs in the past, promising not to give out any top-secret information about projects people were working on. Usually, the project wasn't even worth blabbing about (even though I never felt the urge to blab). I had a feeling that some of the things I'd find out here might be pretty blab-worthy. The agreement named Mark's company as Predictive Solutions, a group I'd never heard of.

Mark handed me a pen, and I initialed each page at the top and scrawled my name on the last. Mark took all the pages, put them back in the envelope, and then tossed it on the foot of my bed. He pulled up a chair and sat, then nudged the rolling table with its bowl of broth closer to me.

I tried to pace myself with the broth, since it had been a couple of days since I'd had food, and Mark started to talk. And despite the fact that I thought things were weird, well . . . they got weirder.

"My name is Mark Scarborough. Some people around here call me Scar, and you're more than welcome to. I wanted to give you a brief overview of where you are, before we move you out of the hospital wing, so that things aren't too much of a shock to you."

I nodded, spooning the delicious broth into my mouth as fast as I could without making myself sick. I liked the idea of a guy without visible scars being called Scar, so my brain instantly labeled him that way.

"You're not in Seattle," he said. I nodded again as I ate. Of course not, since there were palm trees outside the window and it was warmer. I was probably somewhere in California, but I had no idea why they would have taken me there.

"I can't tell you exactly where we are, but you're on an island in the Pacific Ocean," he said.

I stopped with the nodding and the soup. "An island?"

He went over to the gauzy curtains and pulled them aside so I could see the view out the window. It was all blue sky and green landscape outside, with a big palm tree right in the middle of the view. A lush tropical landscape, obviously closer to Hawaii than California, now that I was seeing it in daylight. Stranger and stranger.

Mark let the curtains drop and sat back down. "You were at WonderPop at a very bad time," he said. "The building was supposed to be empty except for the guard, and unfortunately, nobody double-checked the parking garage after the mission was in motion. That was a terrible mistake, and I'm very sorry that it happened."

"The guard, he's okay?"

"Yes, he made it out of the building just fine. That's kind of you to ask."

"Sooo . . . you were there? When the alarms went off?"

"I myself was not there, although I've been filled in on what happened. It appears that when Commander Alpha punched the building enough times, some of the concrete fell and hit you in the head. Our team was there, found you, and pulled you free. They made sure you were stable and opted to bring you here instead of dropping you off at a local hospital."

I felt my nerves come back a little. "So you're not part of the Ultimate Faction? Who's your team? And why bring me here?"

"To answer your last question first, just look around you. Our facility is far more advanced than most hospitals, and we knew we'd be able to offer you a far superior level of care."

I swirled the spoon around in my broth. "And your team?"

"That's a bit more complicated, and I'd like to ask that you try to stay as calm as possible when I tell you."

I set down the spoon and leaned back against my pillows. "Okay, Mark. Scar. Dude. Hit me with it."

He reached into his pocket and pulled out a white card, about the size of a playing card. He flipped it over to show me the logo on the back side. It was sort of medical-looking, with a caduceus—that pair of snakes twining around a staff with wings at the top—but instead of a plain ball at the top of the staff, it was a flaming orb.

I looked at it for a long moment, then started to laugh. Almost hysterically. Scar stared at me as I gasped, my laughter finally easing up.

"I take it you know this logo?" he asked.

"Know it? I designed it," I said.

Now it was his turn to be confused. "What?"

"Yeah, it was a design contest about ten years ago, right? The guidelines were something medical and mystical combined. I won a fifty-dollar gift card for that thing, which was pretty handy for a college student."

"And you know who you designed it for?"

"Well, I did afterward, of course. Wished I'd held out for a couple more gift cards. You can spare the cash, am I right?"

He seemed genuinely taken back. I think I spoiled his big dramatic surprise.

"So, then, I guess it isn't really a surprise to tell you that you're currently a guest of Doctor Oracle," he said.

"Yeah, I figured that out."

"And that doesn't concern you in any way?"

I pushed the rolling table off to the side. "Well, from what I've heard, this is about the best possible option for being captured. Oracle never kills anyone, does he? Plus, you're taking care of me in an ultramodern, sparkling medical facility on a tropical island. I tried to escape and you didn't shoot me or taze me, or even manhandle me."

"Not our style," he said.

"I know," I said. "I don't keep up much with the whole battles of the supers, but from what I've heard of Doctor Oracle, he's one of the better baddies. No offense," I added. I had no idea if the bad guys were sensitive about being called the bad guys.

"None taken."

"Are you Doctor Oracle himself? I always thought he'd be shorter. Plus, it would be weird if you had two nicknames."

"No, I'm not Doctor Oracle. I'm the concierge here at the facility. You'll meet him in due time." He pushed the rolling table back up against the wall, and the older nurse came over to pick up the tray.

"So I'm here in the hospital overnight, according to doctor's orders. Then what?"

"Well, there's where we have an issue," he said. "I'm delighted that you're taking all of this so well, so perhaps I can speed up my spiel and get to a more important subject."

"Please, do."

"Well, you've been here over three days. Part of the WonderPop office was destroyed by Commander Alpha, and unfortunately, right now you're all over the news. Your purse and keys were found in the rubble, and your car was in the garage."

"Did my car get damaged?"

"No, your car is fine. The garage stood up fairly well to the abuse."

"Damn," I said. "Guess I can't get a new one out of this, then."

"Anyway," he went on, "your ID card was scanned as entering the building, but not exiting. They haven't been able to find any . . . um . . . body parts in the rubble. So right now it's a mystery as to what happened to you, if you're dead or missing or what. We're more than happy to broadcast that Doctor Oracle has kidnapped you."

"Which is true."

"In a way, yes."

"Why not just let me go?"

"On doctor's orders, you're here for at least one more night, and we'd like to get something out today. But more importantly, do you *want* to go?" He leaned back and looked at me.

I thought about it. I was being well cared for, the place was obviously really nice—and possibly much larger than the little building I was in. They'd had me sign legal documents, which meant they probably weren't in a hurry to kill me. Plus, Doctor Oracle supposedly never killed anyone. And I was curious as hell.

"What's the upside of letting the world know I was kidnapped by an internationally known criminal?"

"Your friends and family would know that you're alive. Then they don't have to mourn; they'll just worry."

I thought about that. "What are my other options?"

"I was really hoping you'd go with the kidnapping thing," he said. "We don't really want to raid the medical examiner's office for spare body parts we could plant in the rubble."

"Ew," I said. "Yeah, no. Let's go with kidnapping. Not that I have all that much in the way of friends, and even less in the way of family. But I like the idea of being involved in something exciting, as opposed to a missing-person mystery."

"Great," he said. "I'll have Doctor O send out a press release."

I laughed. "Seriously? A press release?"

He put on a comically stern face. "We're high-tech here, Sarah. Nothing but the best."

I was starting to feel tired, and my head was hurting a bit. After all the excitement of the morning, and apparently three days asleep, my adrenaline was wearing off fast and I was ready to crash.

"Ugh," I said, slumping down in bed. "I want to know more."

Scar got up and put his chair back where he found it. "I promise, I'll be back tomorrow to tell you anything you want to know. And I'll drop off some reading material for you a little later. You should take a nap; you've been through a lot."

"I'll agree to that, on one condition."

"What's that?"

"Doughnuts for breakfast tomorrow."

"Deal. See you in the morning."

He left, and I slumped down farther on the bed. The older woman came over and lowered the bed so I could lie down. "My name is Louise," she said. "Let me know if you need anything."

I napped for a bit, then woke up to find that Scar had brought in a binder full of articles and stories about Doctor Oracle, including a couple of interesting op-ed pieces that described how Oracle's deeds were closer to the actions of "good guys" than any other criminal organization.

I read through them as I had another bowl of fantastic broth, though they would have been better accompanied by a sandwich. Of course, there were a ton of articles condemning Oracle as a monster as well. But it was interesting to note that the most vicious articles also had nothing but glowing things to say about the Ultimate Faction, a group whom I already thought weren't the most glowing people around.

Definite food for thought.

* * *

As promised, Scar returned in the morning with doughnuts—a beautiful selection from a maple bar to a chocolate with sprinkles, and everything in between. I took a dense, crumbly old-fashioned. Scar took a simple glazed doughnut, and he then offered the rest of the assortment to the nurses as they were changing shifts.

Nurse Louise was taking over for poor Jake, who told me when he came on shift the night before that he got in trouble for letting me escape, but he assured me that he didn't blame me. He let me know that he wasn't going to be punished, but he was awfully embarrassed about the whole thing. I found it interesting that a supposed prisoner tried to escape, and the person who was supposed to be watching that prisoner didn't get punished, but instead seemed to be punishing himself with guilt over letting down his supervisors.

I tried to go slow on my doughnut, but after three days conked out cold and a day of broth, it was hard to not inhale the thing.

Plus, it was a *really* good doughnut.

Scar pulled his chair back up and handed me a manila folder and a second doughnut. "Here's your press release." He ate his doughnut as I opened up the folder to read the brief paragraph, which was short on details and long on declarations of world domination and demands for ransom.

It was a little worrying; I had no idea who on earth would have the inclination or the funds to pay the kind of ransom that was being demanded. Scar must have sensed my unease.

"Don't worry," he said. "You're actually free to leave at any time."

"Really?"

"Really. Though I hope you'll want to stay and learn more."

"So why all this?" I waved the sheet of paper at him.

"Appearances." He took the paper, put it neatly back in the folder, and set it aside. "Every opportunity to rile up the so-called authorities, we have to take. Otherwise, they'll think we're weak. Or having problems. Or that someone else has been taking over our enterprises. Actually, you've helped us out a great deal; a couple of folks had already tried to take responsibility for the destruction at WonderPop. By being able to identify you by name, we've let the police and the government and the supers know that we're the true responsible party."

"But . . . you're not responsible for the destruction at WonderPop. Are you? I thought Commander Alpha had broken the place up."

"Ah, true. Yes, he did punch the building down. Unfortunately, he doesn't have to take responsibility for that."

I shook my head. "Wait, what? Why not?"

"Because he, and the supers as a whole, are generally above the law. If you really studied the news stories I left you, and read between the lines, you'll see that they're the cause of damage or injury a large percentage of the time. But the blame is always shifted to the villains, the bad guys—anyone on the other side of the law."

"I can totally see that," I said.

"Really?" His eyebrows shot up in surprise. "You agree with that method?"

"No, no," I said. "But I can totally see why they can get away with it. I'm sure they'd make the argument that if you weren't there, trying to . . . I don't know, steal something or break something or take over something, then they wouldn't be forced to take action against you. Or against an office building, as the case may be."

He leaned back and smiled. "Precisely, Sarah. That's the exact argument they make."

"Believe me, I've seen these guys in action my entire life. I'm sure they'd say that they have no choice in the matter. After all, what are they going to do, let you go scot-free? Never. They've sworn an oath to king and country. Or to government. Or to whoever pays their bills."

That made Scar laugh. "You're amazingly cynical," he said.

"I'm also a pessimist," I said. "That way, when good things happen, it's always a pleasant surprise."

He laughed again. "Fantastic. I like that outlook."

"It's always served me well."

Scar glanced down at his giant watch, which I'd already guessed was also a communications device. He looked up at me with a genuinely glum look. "I'm so sorry, but I have to go get this press release out and take care of a couple of other pressing matters."

"I thought I was going to get a question-and-answer session," I said.

"That you will," he said. "How about this. Dr. Adams should be in a bit later to give you a look. If she clears you to leave the hospital wing, I'll come get you for lunch. If not, I'll bring lunch to you. Cool?"

"All right. Though people may think I'm just using you for food."

"I've been used for worse," he said, smiling. "See you around lunchtime, either way."

"If it's as good as those doughnuts, I'll be happy, whether it's here or somewhere else."

"Oh, I think you'll be pleasantly surprised," he said. He put his chair back in its proper corner, spoke for a few moments with Louise, then went back out through the futuristic silent door. A door I hoped I'd be able to go back through in order to get to lunch.

EIGHT

As expected, Dr. Adina Adams came by midmorning to kick my tires and check under my hood. Or at least to prod the back of my head and make me recite more facts and figures. Everything checked out all right, and my head barely hurt at all.

"I understand that Mark will be coming by at lunch." Nicknames clearly didn't fly for Dr. Adams. "I'm fine to let you go, but please check back in or call us here if you experience anything strange. Headaches, blurred vision, forgetfulness. The brain is still a fairly mysterious thing, so we can never really be sure what's going on up there."

"I promise I'll let you know if anything gets weird. Well, weirder than usual. This whole situation is pretty weird."

"I'm sure it is. Mark said he was going to take you for a tour around the building, but make sure he doesn't wear you out too much. Sleeping for three days can make you oddly tired."

"Yes, ma'am," I said, though I was feeling pretty close to fine.

"Oh, and one other thing," she said. "Mark said he would send up some clothing for you. I'm guessing you don't want to go around the island in hospital pajamas."

"Too true," I said. "What about the clothes I came in with?"

"I believe they were sent off for cleaning, but I can see if we can find them. Though Mark will likely bring in something new."

"Eh, those were my third-favorite yoga pants anyway. I might as well get something out of this whole ransom-demand thing. I'll see what he brings."

"Wonderful." She offered her hand, and I shook it. "I hope to see you again, but not in this room," she said.

"That makes two of us."

At half past eleven, a young man showed up with a shopping bag. He handed it to Louise, who brought it over to me. I turned the bag over and dumped a surprisingly large variety of clothing onto the bed. One of those cards with the Doctor Oracle logo fell out. On the back was a message in small, tidy writing: "Louise made a note of your sizes, but we weren't sure about your style. It's all yours to keep. –Scar."

A girl could get used to this kind of hostage treatment.

I slid my legs over the side of the bed and stood up. Louise watched me to make sure I was steady, but I'd already been out of bed a couple of times, both for my escape attempt and a couple of trips to the restroom. I was pretty steady.

"There's a call button in there if you need anything, dear," she said. I thanked her, grabbed the stack of clothes, and made my way into the bathroom. I stood there, looking in the mirror.

I guess I didn't look too awful, if you consider the fact that I'd been unconscious for a couple of days. A little pale, a little tired. My hair was a mess, but that was nothing new. I gently prodded the back of my head and felt a much smaller lump than expected. There was no scab, so whatever rubble hit me on the head hadn't broken the skin. All in all, I guess I was pretty lucky that my head didn't get smashed wide open.

I took care of business in the bathroom, then tried on the clothes. Fortunately, everything was relatively soft and roomy and easy to get in and out of. There was even an embarrassingly large variety of undergarments, from a sports bra to lacy boy shorts. I was delighted to find a pair of yoga-style bottoms, although they felt like a much better quality than anything I owned. I paired them with a tank top and a slouchy sweatshirt and figured I had the perfect just-out-of-hospital look going.

As I found the clothes I wanted to wear, I thought about my escape attempt. It seemed like the perfect choice when I was totally in the dark about where I was, but I didn't think I'd try again anytime soon. Not when I'd found out so little about where I was, with the promise of finding out so much more. I didn't feel like I was in any danger; instead, it was exciting.

I wet my fingers in the sink and combed them through my hair as best as I could, and it ended up in a rough approximation of my usual hairstyle—wavy and kind of all over the place. Oh well.

I opened the bathroom door and found Scar already there, chatting with Louise. He made his way smoothly around the desk and offered his arm again, in a funny echo of the previous night when he'd caught me trying to get away. I looped my arm in his.

"I'm told that you've been set free," he said.

"That's what I hear."

"Excellent. Now, just one more thing before we head to lunch."

"What's that?" I asked.

He led me over to the desk and picked up another bag off the floor. Inside were three nice pairs of comfy-looking shoes. "Can't have you going to lunch barefoot," he said.

I hoisted myself up to sit on the desk, and put on a pair of ballet flats. They were the softest and most comfortable pair of shoes I'd ever worn, and looking at the label, they probably cost more than all my own shoes combined. Though Oracle probably stole them. Or they fell off a truck.

While I was putting the shoes on, I took another good, hard look at the surface of the desk, which both the nurses and the doctor had tapped on as if it were a keyboard. Nothing—it was a smooth, flat white. I was clearly missing something.

Scar helped me back down off the desk. I stood there with one hand braced on that glossy white surface as he popped a piece off the side of his wristwatch doodad and put it in his ear. He tapped the front of the watch a few times, then said, "Hi, Bobby! Scar here. Could you get back up to the hospital wing and grab the rest of Miss Valentine's clothes and shoes, and take them to her room?" A pause. "Perfect, thank you." He disconnected and put the earpiece back into the side of his watch.

Here I'd thought the watch was just for texting, but no. It was ten times cooler.

"I have *got* to get me one of those," I said.

"That can be arranged," he said. "Do you have a color preference?"

"Orange," I said. I loved the heck out of orange, but so many things only came in red, blue, or green.

"You got it," he said. "I'll get it to you later today."

"You'll bring it by . . . my room?"

"That's right. We have a spot with a really nice view set up for you. I'll show you where and give you a tour, but right now, I think lunch is probably our first order of business."

"Agreed." He pressed the button next to the door and it slid open. "So they aren't automatic?" I asked.

"Some of the public doors are, those that are unlocked all the time," he said. "Like the double doors at the front of the building, as you saw yesterday. But doors to living quarters, offices, that sort of thing, all have a variety of privacy settings. Just like this one. If the door is locked, instead of opening, pressing the button will sound a chime." He demonstrated by closing the door again, pressing a second button above the first to lock the door, then pressing the green switch again. A soft, gentle note sounded throughout the room, easy to hear but not jarring.

"Nice," I said. He unlocked it again and we went through.

The wide hallway outside the door was brightly lit this time, full of sunlight from the window at the end of the hall. I turned away from the window and saw a fascinating vehicle. It looked vaguely like a golf cart and yet almost completely not like a golf cart at all. It was round and had what looked like three black rubber playground balls instead of four tires. There were two seats and a steering wheel, with a couple of switches on what could be described as a dashboard. No other controls, no gas pedal.

"I . . . What the hell is this thing?"

"Transport ball," he said. "Terrible name, but it got the most votes."

I poked at it, and it rocked slightly on its three black balls.

"You voted to name it?"

"We do that with a lot of things here," he said. "So you'll find some things with clever, brilliant names. Then you'll find a transport ball, and you'll just shake your head in sadness."

He helped me get in. I grabbed around for a seat belt, but there was nothing.

"Don't worry," he said. "These don't go terribly fast. And if anything does happen, the shell will erupt into multiple air bags." Still, I gripped the sides of my seat. We were pointed toward the end of the hall and the window with the nice view, so I figured he'd have to do some fancy backing up and forth to get us turned around.

He pressed one of the buttons on the area where a dashboard would be, if the transport ball had been a normal vehicle. I heard the softest electric whine, which quickly faded. Then he pressed a button in the middle of the steering wheel, and the body of the transport ball spun smoothly around so we were pointed the other way down the hallway.

"That . . ." I looked behind us, then forward again. "That was *so cool*."

"You ain't seen nothing yet," he said.

* * *

Scar tackled part of the promised tour before lunch, simply because we had to travel past interesting things from the hospital wing to where the food was. We rolled down the hall in our tiny little ball, and he pointed things out along the way.

"This area is mostly administrative offices, finance and such, and of course, the hospital wing. The building is centrally located among everything else, so it made the most sense to put the hospital here." He drove slowly toward the glass double doors; now that it was light outside, I could still see through them despite the tint on the glass. The doors slid open quickly and silently when we approached in the transport ball.

"It's like something out of *Star Trek*, but way cooler."

"That's actually where the idea came from," he said. "One of our techs was a huge fan and made the doors his pet project."

"Do they have a name? That the committee voted on?"

"No," he laughed. "We just call them doors."

"Boring," I said.

"You're riding in a transport ball. Be careful what you wish for."

"Right, right. You don't want to go through . . . I don't know, *whoosh portals* or anything."

As soon as we passed through the doors, we were into new territory for me. There were two paths next to each other, one a little wider than the other. We rolled down the wider path, and I looked over at the narrower path as we separated from it. The smaller route looked like it curled around underneath the one we were on. Our path ended in a T-shaped intersection with two options: left or right. A beautifully manicured hedge lined the path on the far side.

Scar brought the ball to a halt at the crossroads. Pointing to the right, he said, "Down that way are a lot of the laboratories, tech, maintenance, vehicles. Basically, most of the work."

"Will I get to see that?"

"Probably, depending on how long you choose to stay here with us. But it's not really a first-day-tour kind of thing."

"Good thing this is my fourth day here. Or is it my fifth?"

He smiled and turned the transport ball down the left path. "This way we have all of the residential areas, as well as dining, shops, entertainment, anything people might want to enjoy in their off time." I could see a long white building up ahead of us, surrounded by more blue sky and greenery.

"Where is everyone?"

"We have different paths for walking, so you won't see any pedestrians out here with the transport balls. Like the narrower path that led away from the administrative building. It passed under our path, then connected with the main walking thoroughfare." He brought the ball to a halt in the middle of the path we were on, hit a couple of buttons, then stepped out and came around to my side. He offered me a hand and helped me out of my seat.

Standing up, I could just barely see over the top of the hedge. On the other side and a bit below us was a walkway with a number of people strolling both toward and away from the long residential building. And beyond that path was a gorgeous wide beach that looked like it was covered in sugar instead of sand. Beyond that beach, of course, was the ocean. Bright and greenish blue, it was absolutely beautiful. There were a number of colorful umbrellas on the beach, lots of lounge chairs, and lot people in swimwear who looked as if they were on a holiday.

"Scar, I'm going to have to demand that I get to go on the beach," I said. I'm from Seattle, after all. Our beaches are mostly made up of pebbles, rocks, and grit. Oh, and lots of stinky washed-up seaweed.

"That I can guarantee," he said. "But definitely after lunch."

We got back in the ball and continued along toward the residential building. It had another pair of glass doors that silently opened for us. "This building has always been residential; it started out as a resort, which went bankrupt. For all outward appearances, it's still a fully functioning island vacation spot."

Scar was driving us along a wide paved path inside the building, which felt like a maintenance tunnel. "So I'm not exactly getting the scenic tour right now?"

"No, sorry. The vehicle paths aren't exactly in the glamorous areas. We'll get you out on the walking path soon enough, and you'll be able to check everything out from the angles they're meant to be seen."

He brought the ball to a stop in front of what looked like an elevator. Again, he hit some buttons, got out, and came around to the passenger side to give me a hand.

"So where are we now?"

"The elevator," he said.

"Oh, good. At least those haven't changed here in the future."

He tapped the button, and the elevator softly chimed. The doors opened (whisper-quiet, of course) and we got in. There was a panel, just like every other elevator ever. Scar tapped the button next to the number "1" and a star. The floors above went up to four, and there was an SB below where we'd gotten on at B. I guessed they were for basement and subbasement.

"We're not actually that much more advanced than the rest of the world," he said. "We're just not that good at sharing some of our advances with the rest of the class."

I didn't feel any movement, but the elevator chimed again and the doors slid open. We walked down a short hallway, which opened out to a huge atrium, with a ceiling made of a few support beams and a lot of glass, letting in tons of natural light. It was like a mall food court, but the most beautiful mall food court you could ever imagine. And like a mall food court, there were dozens of little tables with umbrellas artfully scattered around the room. Around the perimeter of the room were a number of different service windows, each one advertising a different cuisine and painted a different distinct color.

"I know what you're thinking," Scar said.

"Yeah?"

"Mall food court," he said.

"Yeah." I couldn't believe that this was the secret lair of an evil genius. Or whatever Doctor Oracle was.

"Well, we have futuristic this, and ultramodern that, but when it comes down to it, people still really like things that are familiar. So why freak them out with something that's so important for personal comfort—their food? We even just call it the food court. No vote necessary on that one."

"Makes sense," I said. Several great smells competed in my nostrils, and my stomach growled. "What are my options here?"

He pointed to the left and swept his hand around to the right. "Red is Italian, blue Asian, purple Mexican, yellow is comfort foods, green is the salad bar, brown for burgers, and the gray one on the end rotates through a variety. The schedule says that today is Indian, and I know for a fact that the curry is fantastic."

"That might be a little bit too much for me right now," I said. "But I'd love to investigate the comfort foods."

We went across the atrium toward the area painted yellow. I'll admit, I gawked like a tourist at everyone and everything along the way. Some people wore what looked like uniforms made up of khaki pants and a polo shirt with my logo on the pocket. Some were dressed up a little nicer, the men wearing ties and the women wearing skirts. Still others were dressed as casual as could be. We passed a trio of women wearing beach cover-ups and flip-flops, who were talking with a woman in medical scrubs. It was definitely a fascinating mishmash of people, made up of a wide variety of shapes, sizes, and ethnicities. At a rough guess, I figured there were around forty or fifty people in the seating area.

"How many people do you have here?" I asked.

"Three hundred and twelve on the island," he said. "You're lucky number three hundred and thirteen."

"That's about my luck," I said. We reached the counter, and as soon as I saw and smelled what they had, my stomach cranked up the grumbling to a growl. A woman behind the counter wore an apron and had a hairnet on, and I was reminded of the lunch ladies in grade school. She smiled widely when she saw Scar.

"Well, if it isn't old Scar. Been a while since I've seen you at my window," she said. She turned to me. "And I don't believe I've had the pleasure of meeting you yet, young lady. I'm Nancy."

"Sarah," I said. "Just got here a few days ago."

"Well, I hope you love it like we all do. Now, what can I get you? Everyone always goes on about the macaroni and cheese, but I have to say I'm most proud of the meatloaf today. Broke out my grandmother's secret recipe for it."

I looked at everything, then at Scar. "I don't have any money; how much are things?"

Nancy laughed, but in a kind way. "Oh, honey, you *must* be new."

Scar put his hand on my shoulder. "We don't deal with money here, Sarah. Get whatever you like."

You don't have to tell me twice about free food. I asked for small portions of the macaroni and cheese, the meatloaf, and the lumpy mashed potatoes. Which I chose over the creamy mashed potatoes, because Nancy had both.

"About fifty-fifty, those," said Nancy. "We could never just go with lumpy or smooth, or half the place would go on strike."

Scar got a plate of food for himself; then we stopped by a condiment bar with every sauce and spice under the sun, a silverware station, and a beverage station with several of those machines that have a hundred kinds of cola. Loaded down with a plate of hot food and an ice-cold drink, I let Scar lead me to an empty table.

The food was as good as advertised, and I had a hard time going slow. But I knew if I ended up back in the hospital wing with a stomachache, Dr. Adams would never let me hear the end of it.

Scar checked his wrist gadget for the time, then looked around. He spotted someone across the room and waved. An Asian woman about my height, wearing blue coveralls, made her way across the room toward us.

"Sarah Valentine, this is my wife, Jin Scarborough," Scar said. I shook Jin's outstretched hand.

"You're looking much better than when I last saw you, Sarah," she said.

"Have we met before?"

"Well, you were unconscious at the time. I was with the team that brought you back here."

I blinked at her. "Were you at the WonderPop building?"

"Not in the building, but nearby. I was the driver that day."

"Well, thank you. I'm glad I didn't get left behind."

"Oh, when the team found you, there was no chance of that," she said.

"What do you mean?" I was puzzled. "You could have left me for the police or someone to pick up."

Scar put his hand on his wife's arm. "I haven't *quite* told her everything yet," he said.

Jin looked at him, then at me, then back at him. Then she grinned. "Oh! Well, then, you better get to telling. I have some of my grease monkeys to join for lunch anyway." She looked back at me. "A pleasure to meet you now that you're awake, Sarah."

She walked away toward the purple section that served Mexican food, and I turned to Scar.

"Okay, so what aren't you telling me?"

"Finish your lunch, Sarah. You need to regain your strength. Really, there's just still so much to tell."

"And I feel like you aren't telling me a really important part of things," I said.

"I'll tell you if you eat."

"Fine." I scooped up a mouthful of the delicious macaroni and cheese and looked at him.

"Okay. There was a three-person team in the WonderPop building at the same time you were, doing a job. Which I'm not going to go into the details of right now, because it's really not important, and you don't have the security clearance yet anyway."

I swallowed my food, replaced it with a piece of the divine meatloaf, and nodded for him to continue. I'd noted his use of the word *yet* regarding my clearance but opted not to question it.

"We needed at least one of the team members to be really familiar with the building so the team would be able to find what they needed without a problem. That meant studying the blueprints in depth, but also getting inside the building in a way to become familiar with all parts of it."

I chewed on my meatloaf and thought about that. An insider who had studied the blueprints and had access to the entire building. I swallowed, put my fork down on the side of my tray, and said, "You have *got* to be kidding me."

Scar looked up at me; then his eyes shifted above my head. I felt the presence of someone standing behind me.

"Hello, Sarah," Nate said.

NINE

I turned around in my seat, and sure enough, there was Nate standing behind me. At least he had the good grace to look a little bit embarrassed. I almost didn't recognize him for a minute, even having heard his voice. His face was clean-shaven, which made him look five years younger than he had with the scruffy beard. He was also massively cleaned up from when I'd last seen him—he had much nicer and better-fitting clothes, and he'd had a great haircut. He was now wearing a pair of hip glasses with heavy black frames.

He stepped around and pulled out one of the chairs at our table and sat down. "I know this is probably a shock," he said.

"Seriously?" I said.

Scar pushed his chair back. "I have a feeling you two have a lot to discuss."

I turned to him. "You don't have to go."

Scar put his hand on mine. "You'll be fine." Then he leaned down and whispered in my ear, "Don't be afraid to be as mad as you need to be." He gathered up all our lunch dishes and trays. "Nate, I haven't shown her to her room yet."

"No problem," Nate said. Scar left, carrying our trays with him. Leaving me with the great disappearing man.

"So, at least your name is actually Nate," I said.

"I understand if you're angry," he said.

"You saying that really doesn't help me be less angry."

"No, but I guess if I tick you off even more, you can blow through the anger faster."

"Nice." I turned away and watched some of the people make their way around the food court.

"Can I have a chance to explain everything?"

I thought about it. We'd talked about not taking things too seriously. He'd told me straight out that things were complicated, and they were definitely turning out to be that. "How much of what you told me was true?" I asked.

"Almost all of it," he said. "Everything about my parents was true. The things I love, my opinions about politics and the supers, what foods I like. My personality. Really, I just fudged the job part. Oh, and my last name."

"So Nathan Anderson doesn't exist."

"But Nathan Hart does." He held out his hand for a shake, tilting his head to the side like a puppy. I couldn't help myself: I shook it.

"You are not forgiven, but I'll hear you out," I said.

"Fair enough. Want to stay here, or can I continue the tour and show you to your room while I explain things?"

"Taking me to the beach would probably move you a little farther up the apology meter."

"You got it," he said. We got up and he led me out a side door, which of course opened silently for us. We were on a wide walking path, which hugged the side of the building.

"We'll go slow; I know you're just up and around today," he said.

"And thank you for asking me how I'm feeling," I said.

His eyebrows shot up, and he held up his hands. "I've been getting regular reports on your condition for the last four days, Sarah."

"Yeah, well . . . that still doesn't account for how I *feel*," I grumbled.

He stopped walking, and I stopped with him. "You're right. I'm sorry. I'm sorry about how this whole damn thing played out, and you have every right to be angry with me. I know we can't start over again, but I promise that I'll be completely honest with everything from here on out."

"All right, then. Start explaining." I crossed my arms.

He swept his arm toward the ocean. "After you."

We went down a path toward the beach, and we both took off our shoes before stepping onto the sand. It felt as great between my toes as I thought it would—soft and powdery and warm from the sun. We walked over to a pair of chairs underneath a big blue umbrella, far away from anyone else, and sat down facing the water. The view was beautiful. I tossed my shoes down onto the sand, and he did the same.

"Why does the name Nathan Hart sound familiar?" I asked.

"I'm the owner of the Hart Corporation," he said. "Real estate, manufacturing, shipping, and a bunch of other arms. It's a gigantic business octopus."

I blinked at him.

"My grandfather started the company in real estate, and my father expanded it far beyond. And when he and my mother passed away, I took over. I'm pretty hands-off for the most part; I let people run the business who are actually interested in running that kind of business."

I stared at him some more.

"We're doing good work here, too. Great work. But it's the kind of work that could never be done under the umbrella of the Hart Corporation. They have too many government oversights, too much transparency and publicity."

"So instead you infiltrated WonderPop to do something for Doctor Oracle?"

"In a manner of speaking."

"What does that mean?"

"I don't work for Doctor Oracle."

"So, what, you're a contractor? Just helping out? If you don't work for the guy, why are you here?"

"Sarah, I *am* Doctor Oracle."

Maybe it was the head injury, but I really didn't see that one coming.

I held up my hand for him to pause so I could stare out at the ocean for a bit and think about what he'd told me. So he wasn't the cool, geeky slacker I thought he was. He was the owner of a huge freaking corporation, one that was probably worth a lot of millions or even billions of dollars. But not only that, oh no. He was also one of the biggest supervillains around, running what was apparently a much larger and more intricate operation than I'd ever thought.

"This is going to take a while to really sink in," I said.

"Of course," he said. "It's a lot to throw at you all at once."

I swept my hand around at the few people on the beach and those going to and from the residential building. "How do they all deal with it?"

"Well, most people don't know the entire story," he said.

"What do they know?"

"They know that they work for Doctor Oracle, but he's a very reclusive guy. Most of them never really see him."

"But . . . you're out in the open around them. Right now."

"Well, they don't know that he's me. That I'm him. As far as most people know, I'm one of the department supervisors here, nothing more."

"And do they know that Doctor Oracle and the Hart Corporation are connected?"

"No. Fewer than ten people in the entire world know that."

"And now I'm one of them."

"And now you're one of them."

I looked out at the ocean some more, processing. "So what if I went around and told everyone here who you really are?"

"Well, I'm really hoping you won't do that. Plus, you did sign a nondisclosure agreement. If you think regular lawyers will shut things down fast, imagine how the lawyers for a notorious criminal organization could keep people from spilling their guts. The world is afraid of supervillains, but even supervillains are afraid of lawyers."

I imagined it, and it wasn't pretty. Not that I had any intention of blabbing to anyone at that moment; despite still being angry with Nate over his disappearing act, I was crazy intrigued. "I signed that NDA with some company called . . . what, Predictive Solutions?"

"That's one of our various business umbrellas. Oracle, predictive . . . same stuff."

I burrowed my toes farther into the sand. "Even with the NDA, you're telling me an awful lot of stuff that could really damage you, Nate. And you seem pretty confident about it. Lawyers or not, I could get information out there if I wanted to. How are you so sure you can get me to stick around?"

He looked down, then back up at me. "I guess if I'm going to make you more angry, now's the time to do it." I just looked at him until he continued. "We've already run all of our full background checks on you. Without your consent, I know, and I'm sorry. But it's standard for anyone we bring to the island."

I looked out at the ocean. "I guess it makes sense, to do that when you brought me here."

"Actually," he said, "it's a lengthy process. We started running them two weeks ago."

I blinked and looked back at him. "Like, right after we met?"

"Did you see the envelope on your desk on Sunday?"

"Yeah, it startled the crap out of me. I didn't open it."

"I figured you hadn't. If you had, you would have seen that we were trying to feel you out about a possible job offer out here."

"Wait," I said. "So . . . we'd barely met, we went on a couple of dates, and you were ready to offer me a job here on your supersecret private island that's like a Bond villain's lair and a Ritz-Carlton had a baby? Are you crazy?"

"We see talent, we jump on it fast, Sarah. You're a great graphic designer, and we've been planning for a while to bring one on board. Right now, all of our stuff is being done by outside agencies, through a chain of cover businesses. It's a pain in the ass. Plus, you have your eyes open about the supers, which is the biggest thing we look for."

I looked out at the ocean a bit more. "I think I need to walk and think on all of this," I said.

"Of course," Nate said. He picked up our shoes and we slowly made our way down to the waterline. From there, I could look back up and see the huge residential wing, four stories of living space with the big glassy dome of the food court tacked on the side. It was like a cruise ship had beached itself.

We walked along the water's edge in the harder-packed sand. I could see why the original builders had put their hotel here: the water was crystal clear, the waves were soft and gentle, and there was a protective reef a few hundred yards out to sea keeping the bigger waves at bay.

"Topic change," I said. "I've seen pictures of Doctor Oracle, haven't I? I don't recall him looking like you. And doesn't he have some sort of big nasty scar?"

"You've probably seen him; he's given a number of video ultimatums. But he wears a mask, and there are some prosthetics involved, including the forehead scar."

"Fancy. You called yourself 'he,' as if he's another person."

"Well, a number of us have played the part, as the situation demands. I guess in the grand scheme of things, Doctor Oracle isn't even one person; it's more the entire organization. But people like to have a figurehead, someone to look up to."

"But really, it's you?"

"Well, I started the whole thing. And I'm the money guy, because, well, I have more money than any one person would ever need in ten lifetimes. I guess you could say I'm in charge in a nominal way, although the department supervisors pretty much have free reign to develop whatever they want, as long as they run it by the rest of the team first. Plus, I do the extra-deep voice that everybody knows. A couple other members of the team are working on imitating it, but nobody's quite there yet."

"So explain to me what makes you different than the Ultimate Faction guys," I said, although I thought I had that figured out.

He looked at me. "I'm pretty sure you know there's a difference," he said.

"I want to hear it from you," I said.

"Well, you've seen the way the Ultimate Faction operates. You could make an argument that they're lapdogs for the government, or you could also make the argument that the government is *their* lapdog. They're tied in together. But have you ever seen any of the Ultimates—Commander Alpha, the Green Lady, Professor C, Firewolf, any of those guys—actually strive to make a difference? They're great at stopping a mugger on the street. But they're absolute crap when it comes to education and a support system to keep that kid from becoming a mugger in the first place."

"And that's what you do," I said.

"Hell yeah, that's what we do. I'll show you some of the things we're working on, some of the things we've done. But we figured out a long time ago that the government that supports all of us also wants to keep us as controlled as possible. They don't want big, sweeping changes for us, because that might mean big, sweeping changes for them, too. They can talk all they want about making things better, but I've yet to see them do much about it, besides a few small measures here and there, enough to make the people happy and thinking that things are improving. We just want to make those measures larger. And more frequent."

We slowed down on our walk, and I turned to see how far we'd come. It was going to be a long hike back, and even though I was still full of a great lunch, I was feeling tired from three days of unconsciousness and an afternoon of information overload.

Nate raised his wrist; he had one of the same communicator watches I'd seen on almost everyone. His was a nice shade of blue. He put the earpiece in his ear, then tapped a couple of times on the face of the watch.

"Hey, Scar, we made it pretty far down the beach. Could you come out with a ball?" He nodded as he listened to the response, even though I was the only one who could see him. I found it charming, which clued me in right then that I couldn't be mad at Nate forever. I just liked him too much. But I figured I wouldn't let him off the hook too easily, especially since he was suddenly a fountain of truth. And that truth was fascinating as hell.

Nate put his earpiece back. "Scar will be here in a couple of minutes," he said.

"Why do you call him Scar instead of Mark? Seems like I've heard his actual name about fifty-fifty so far."

"Scar's a really old nickname," he said. "I've known him since we were kids. It's based on his last name, Scarborough."

"You grew up together?"

"In the same house," he said. "His father worked for my father, in . . . well, as similar a role as I guess there is to what Scar does here. Not so much butler as personal assistant. He calls it concierge, which works for everyone. The man is an organization machine; he keeps this whole place running smoothly."

"So then he knows who you are."

"He and his wife both know, yeah. And Dr. Adams, of course, but she has one of those doctorly oaths of privacy and stuff. Also all of our department heads, who you'll meet in due time."

I looked at the residential wing and saw one of the transport balls leave a path and start trundling over the sand toward us. It seemed to handle sand just as well as paved paths. It also really showed me how far we'd walked, as it looked absolutely tiny.

"You're still so sure I'll stay around for a while."

"Won't you?" He turned from watching Scar's progress to look me in the eye. "You already know that the supers are little more than show ponies. I know how much you enjoyed rock climbing, and laser tag, and skydiving. We talked about adventure and excitement, Sarah. I know you want that. I wanted it, too, and I found it. Is it cocky to think you'll stick around here at least long enough to check things out and see what we do? I don't think it is."

I sighed. "You're an ass, you know that?"

He laughed. "I do."

"I'll think about staying," I said. "For a while. And as long as you don't sic the wolves on me, since according to the stories, that's all you crazy evil geniuses do."

"No wolves here, although we do have some pretty vicious bunnies living behind the residential wing. And I'm not really all that evil, nor am I a genius. How about scoundrel? I like the sound of that."

"Only if you add in *dastardly*. Dastardly scoundrel has a nice ring to it." Scar rolled up next to us in the transport ball, the smooth rubber balls that served as tires having no problems getting traction in the sand. Very cool.

I got into the passenger seat beside Scar. He turned to Nate.

"Want me to pop open the jump seat in back?"

"No, I'll walk back," Nate said. "Sarah's probably had more than enough of me for today."

Scar punched a button on the dash, and the ball turned another perfect half circle so we were facing the other way.

"We're not even in a hallway," I said.

"You have a sweet ride like this, you want to show it off," Scar said.

Nate came around to my side and touched my arm. "I'll see you tomorrow," he said. "Think about any questions you want to ask. I'll answer them all, no matter what they are." He handed me my shoes, and we motored off.

"A lot to take in for one day, right?" Scar asked.

"You have no idea," I said.

TEN

Scar drove the transport ball back up the beach to the pavement but didn't drive it back into the building. He parked just outside, where the little road we were on crossed a wide walking path. Where the two intersected, I could see that the walkway and the vehicle track were different shades of gray and had different patterns of stones set in along the edges. I asked Scar if that was the indicator of what the paths were used for.

"Good eye, Sarah. Yes, the blue swirly pattern along the sides means a trail you can walk on without fear of being hit by a transport ball, or any other vehicle. The darker-colored roads with yellow geometric patterns are the ones you shouldn't walk on."

"Got it."

"Oh, and they're lit with yellow and blue at night, too, so you can still tell what kind of path you're looking for. Now, it's just a short way inside; I wanted to take you in through the front instead of the driving tunnel so you'd be familiar with how to get around."

"Great, good." He came around to the passenger side of the ball and offered me his arm again. "Scar . . . Mark, thank you for being so courteous and kind. Whatever Nate's paying you, he should double it."

"I'm taken care of just fine here, don't worry." He led me inside, through a pair of the automatic doors that were already getting familiar. A large lobby sprawled out in front of us, like a fancy resort hotel but without the check-in desk. It was a beautifully done room, full of squishy-looking chairs, potted plants, and soothing art on the walls. We walked across to a bank of elevators on the far side of the room. "There are stairs too," he said, "and we encourage everyone to use them. But since we have you up on the top floor, I think we'll hitch a ride."

"So you said this was once an actual resort?"

"Indeed it was," he said. "They went out of business, but their loss was our gain. When we were looking for a place to build this facility, it was the perfect choice. We gutted everything down to the bones, of course, and built it back up to be more like apartments and less like a hotel. We have two guys running the residential side of things; one of them worked in cruise lines, and the other was a hotel bigwig at Disney World. After all, we have residences here, but also shops, restaurants, a gym . . . It's like a very small city under one big roof."

We got in the elevator and rode up to the fourth floor. Scar led me down the plush carpeting to a door near the end of the hall marked with the number "404."

"We have rooms available on both the beach side and the jungle side, but I figured you'd want a beach view. Though a lot of people prefer the mountains, so if you'd rather switch tomorrow, please let me know."

"Beach view is just fine by me," I said.

The door was another of the flat rectangles with a panel next to it. Scar pressed his thumb against a square on the panel. The light in the middle of the panel glowed white, then turned green. The door slid open just as silently as all the rest, and we went inside.

"Take a look around; then we'll set the door to your thumbprint," he said.

It was, as advertised, a small apartment. We entered an open-plan room with a living room and a small kitchen, both designed and decorated in a simple and ultramodern style. The kitchen had a two-burner stovetop, a small oven, a microwave, and a refrigerator that wasn't quite full-sized that looked vaguely

European. All the appliances were gleaming stainless steel, surrounded by white cabinets and speckled granite countertops. The living room had a bright red couch, a deep and comfortable-looking blue chair, and a flat-screen TV mounted on the wall. At the far end of that room was a sliding door, and I could see a balcony beyond. Of course, I made a beeline for that door. For once, it didn't open automatically for me.

I slid the door open (still, it was the nicest sliding glass door I'd ever opened, smooth and light, without a single shimmy or squeak) and went out onto the balcony. The view was amazing; I could see beach in front of me and way off to both sides. I leaned forward; it was all beach curving out of sight to the left. Off to the right, I could see the hospital wing and the much larger structure beyond it, and a generous slice of mountains and jungle back behind those buildings. Beyond that, my view was blocked by privacy walls on each end of the balcony, to keep me from seeing into the other balconies.

It was beautiful, and I felt like I was on an amazing vacation. It was hard to keep in mind that I'd been brought here without my permission and that a press release had gone out to the world announcing that I'd been kidnapped by someone that most of the world thought was a pretty nasty piece of work.

Didn't feel too terrible just then, though. Plus, the nasty piece of work wanted to offer me a job, if I was open to taking it. I just needed to decide if I was.

Scar followed me out, then pointed out that the balcony ran the length of both the living room and the adjacent bedroom. We went back inside, and I checked out that bedroom; it had a door out to the balcony too, this one with a superfine mesh screen door in addition to the glass door.

"In case you want to sleep with the door open, you can keep out the bugs," Scar said.

"So you haven't managed to eradicate bugs from your private paradise?"

"We wouldn't even dream of trying. Some of them are pests, but some of them are also beneficial to the gardens."

That surprised me. "You have gardens here?"

"It helps us limit our dependence on shipments. We have an extensive system of gardens and fields, as well as a thriving livestock program. Around seventy to eighty percent of what we eat comes from right here on the island."

The tour of the apartment concluded with the bathroom, which was just as deluxe as the rest of the place. Separate soaking tub and stall shower, a kind of waterfall-like faucet on the sink, and one of those electronic toilets from Japan I'd heard about.

"With both a shower and bathtub here, I'm guessing water supply isn't an issue?"

"We have a proprietary desalinization technology, with a facility on-site. As long as there's seawater in the ocean, we'll have plenty of fresh water for everything we need here."

"Wait, so how does that work? And when you say it's 'proprietary' . . . I mean, the rest of the world could really benefit from something like that. Does that mean you don't share?"

"Sarah, I really don't want to overwhelm you with information on what really is your first day," Scar said. "But don't worry, we're sharing that particular technology with a lot of other partners around the world. We can get into patents and licensing at a later time. But I want to assure you that there are millions of people right now who have fresh water available thanks to this technology."

"But why haven't I heard about it?"

He led me back into the main living area. "I think you're going to find out a lot of things are going on around the world that you haven't heard about, unfortunately. Seems like the government thinks if you see other nations are having hard times, you'll feel better about your own. So they're not going to tell you all about the clean drinking water and efficient farming methods people are using on the other side of the world, because if they instead tell you that those people are starving and miserable, you'll look at your own life and say, 'Hey, things aren't so bad here.'"

"That's a cynical point of view," I said. "So I totally get it."

Scar helped me set the panel next to my door with my thumbprint. "After you scan your thumb, you'll get a pop-up menu of options on this little screen here; you can leave your door unlocked, or set it to allow certain people immediate access, or require everyone to ring the bell. It's up to you."

He opened up the small refrigerator, and I saw that it was stocked with a little bit of food already. "I wasn't sure what fruits or veggies you like, so I put in a basic assortment. There are also a couple of boxes of cereal in the cupboard here, and milk in the fridge."

"Don't tell me you make cereal here."

He laughed. "No, we get that shipped in. People will eat fruit and vegetables from anywhere, but they get a little obsessive about their cereal brands. But the milk is from our small dairy here on the island. The cows are totally grass-fed, and it's the best milk I've ever tasted. Most of the fruit is grown here, although the apples are from Washington. This isn't really an apple climate."

"Fantastic, it all looks great. Thank you."

"Oh, and before I forget." Scar reached into his pocket and pulled out one of the communicator watches, in a really cool shade of orange. "As requested, orange for you. We call it the ChatterBox, or CB for short. It has a kinetic battery, so it recharges itself just from the movements of your wrist as you go about your day."

"That's amazing! Is that another proprietary technology?"

"Nope, Seiko came up with that one," he said. "We just tinkered with it a little bit. You can also set up your front door to recognize you by your CB, so you don't even have to put your thumb on the panel. It will just sense when you get close, and open for you."

He showed me the earpiece that separated out, then tapped once on the face of the ChatterBox. "I've put in a few numbers already for you. It's easy to add anyone else you like: just tap the face of your CB against the face of theirs, and you exchange numbers."

"You're in here?" I looked at the face of the thing, which seemed like a tiny smartphone screen.

"Yep, here," he said. He tapped on the icon of an old-style telephone handset. It occurred to me that it wouldn't be much longer before that kind of phone didn't exist anymore, but we'd probably still use that icon forever.

Scar was listed in there as "Mark—Concierge"; Nate's entry was "Nathan—Admin." There were also entries for "Dine,'" "Food," and "Shop."

"These three are hotlines. The 'Dine' one dials the food court, while the 'Food' one dials the grocery, which actually includes the pharmacy. Shop will connect you with a general number for both clothing and any other nonfood goods you might want. You're free to go down to the first floor and check all of that out on your own, or I can come by tomorrow and show you."

I was still feeling pretty tired. "I think I'll rest here for a while and see how I feel later."

"No problem," he said. "There's also a guide on the TV that tells you what hours things are open and where they're located on a map. And you can find most current TV programs and recent movies on there."

"Great," I said, my head practically spinning from all the information of the day.

"Oh, and we have a library on the first floor, too," he said. "If you'd rather read. We have a pretty great selection, including a few novels from our own employees here." He said his good-byes and left, and I was finally alone after a day and a half of strangers and crazy new information.

I flopped on the couch (unsurprisingly, soft and cozy) and switched on the TV. As advertised, there were interactive guides to the shops and food options, and a huge catalog of shows and movies to watch. I used the remote to flick around the map of the first floor, from the food court to the clothing stores to the bowling alley. Everything a person could want, all in one place.

I wanted to go look around, especially now that I was footloose and fancy-free without a chaperone, but I was feeling tired. I slouched down into the cushions on the couch and lodged the TV on a movie that sounded dry and boring. It certainly was—within five minutes I was asleep.

* * *

I snorted myself awake, and looked around in a moment of panic until I remembered where I was. I blinked the bleariness away and looked out the window. It wasn't full dark yet, but it was close. I'd missed the sunset, which was a shame: I figured the room would have a great view of the sun setting over the ocean.

Checking my new orange ChatterBox, which displayed the time up in the corner, I saw that it was around half past seven. I'd slept hard for a good couple of hours. I went into the fancy bathroom, unwrapped a toothbrush and brushed my teeth, then took a shower that could have been faster, but the fancy rain showerhead and hot water were just too great to use in a rush. There was no need for any hustle anyway—I had nowhere to be and nowhere I needed to go. I washed my hair, being gentle with the back of my head, but it barely hurt at all and the lump was smaller.

As I looked in the closet and found the few other clothes Scar had picked out for me, my stomach told me I needed to go find myself some dinner. Even though the apartment had some food in the fridge and a full set of cookware and plates, I didn't feel like making anything for myself. Especially when there was a food court full of options, and I'd only tried one.

I put on a pair of shorts and a T-shirt, then put my hoodie back on over the top. There were a couple of pairs of shoes in the closet, and I grabbed the easiest possible thing—flip-flops. Orange, which I thought was a nice touch. I turned on the TV to make sure nothing had closed yet. Poking around the food court map, it looked like most of the options stayed open until ten, and the comfort foods window was open twenty-four hours. Perfect.

Strapping the new ChatterBox back on my wrist, I pressed my thumb to the panel next to the door, selected the option to lock the door behind me, and headed out to explore.

I opted to take the stairs down but gave myself permission to take the elevator back up after dinner. I was still recovering from an injury, after all. From the lobby, there were several options to get around the main floor. There were large passageways to the left and right; more people were heading toward the right side, so I figured there'd be more action down that way. Heading right, I discovered immediately that most of the people were friendly and happy, or at least faked being happy enough to smile and say hello.

I also got the feeling like I'd just moved to one of those small towns where everyone knows everyone else. I know I got the eyeball from more than one person, but they were all still friendly about their gawking. I tried not to care, since I had no idea how long I was going to stick around.

Which was food for thought. Everyone thought I'd be eager to stick around, and I didn't really disagree with them. I was fascinated by the operation they'd put together and was already impressed at some of the good works they were doing. The potential job offer was also a bonus. And, being honest, for the time being it was a delight to get a break from work, in a place where I didn't have to pay for anything. It was like a vacation from my mind-numbing job and life, but without the downside of a vacation price tag.

I passed the clothing boutiques, the drugstore, and the grocery store, which looked smaller than a supermarket but larger than I thought it would be. Then I was into familiar territory, passing the hallway that led to the service elevator Scar had brought me up in. Straight ahead was the food court, and the smells coming out were all amazing. I decided to try Italian, so I headed over to the red window on the left. Another incredibly friendly woman was behind the counter, and patiently waited while I debated pizza versus pasta. On her advice, I got both. Iced tea and silverware, and I was set.

I found a table by myself and told myself I'd only eat half the pizza and half the pasta, to make up one full meal. I then proceeded to eat everything on my plate. It was all just as good as lunch had been.

I pushed my tray away and sipped on my tea, watching everyone milling around. There were more people than when I'd been there for lunch, but the area didn't feel full at all. There was plenty of room for everyone, and it still felt almost empty. There were groups of people chatting and laughing. At one table, two people were playing a game of chess. Next to them was a foursome playing a card game.

I looked around and noticed a woman walking toward me. She looked familiar, but it took me a moment to place her, because she was wearing a lovely floral dress instead of coveralls. It was Scar's wife.

"Sarah, nice to see you out and about," she said. She held out her hand. "I don't know if you remember me from earlier. Jin Scarborough, Mark's wife."

"Yeah, yes, hello!" I said. We shook hands.

"May I sit?"

"Of course," I said.

"I'm off tonight, and Mark has some work to do, so I thought I'd come down and see what was going on. If you like, I can tell you a few things about the place that Mark may not have mentioned. Or, just tell you the hot gossip about all of these people." Her mouth twitched into a wicked smile.

"I'd never remember anything about any of them right now, but I'll definitely take a rain check on the hot gossip."

"You got it," she said. "I know Mark tends to be a little more formal in his tours, and heaven knows what Nathan told you. So please feel free to grill me for the regular person's perspective."

"I'd love to hear more about the place. Would you like to show me around a bit?"

Her expression lit up. "It would be my pleasure." We got up, and I cleared my tray.

We walked slowly back the way I'd come in, past the service elevator. Jin took me in all the shops, so I could see the selection of goods available. Then we went to the women's clothing store, after Jin asked me what clothes I had, and I told her that it was just a few things Scar had picked out. She insisted that I choose a few of my own outfits.

"But you don't pay for anything?" I asked.

"No, but we don't get paychecks either. So it all evens out."

"What's to stop someone from taking, I don't know, way more stuff than they need?"

"Peer pressure? Goodwill? We haven't really had a problem with it. I guess most of the people here are so into supporting the cause, and the work we do here, that they know they'd be idiots to screw that up. And we do track things; you'll see when you find things you like."

"Have people screwed it up?"

"Oh, sure," she said. "We've had to kick a couple of people out. But not as many as you'd think. The background checks are pretty thorough, and there are interviews and tests before most people come out here."

"I didn't take the tests or have the interviews, though."

"No, but you're a special exception. Besides which, I hear you made it outside of the administration building less than fifteen minutes after waking up in the hospital wing, so that was kind of an interesting combination of audition and test already."

She picked out a few dresses for me to try and sent me to the fitting room. We were the only ones back there, and I could see her over the very top of the door.

"So, Jin, what do you do here?"

"I'm the head of the mechanicals department, which includes vehicles," she said. "Repairs, new builds, all sorts of stuff."

"How did you get into that?"

"My father was a mechanic, so I grew up tinkering with car parts. By the time I was twelve, I could take an engine apart and put it back together again. I've always had a knack for machines and motors."

I stepped out in one of the dresses, a knee-length yellow number with cap sleeves. "I wish I had some lifelong skill or passion like that," I said.

"I like this dress on you," she said. "As for a skill, not everyone knows what their big talents are. I was just lucky that I found mine early. Even if you don't think you have one, I bet you do. You may just not have found it yet."

"Maybe," I said, not all that certain she was right. I changed into another dress, this one longer, darker, and tighter.

"I don't know about this one," she said. "I think knee-length suits you. And it'd be better for the weather here."

"I agree," I said. I went back in to change again. "So you're in charge of mechanical stuff. What other departments are there?"

"We technically have both large mechanicals and small mechanicals, but the small mech folks like to call themselves the gadgets-and-doodads department. I'm the head over both of those. We also have computer techs, and a lot of different areas under the umbrella of lab sciences, like chemistry and biology. The departments are all in separate areas, but the great thing is how everyone loves to cross-pollinate on projects."

"Cross-pollinate?"

"Sure. A perfect example is a tranquilizer gun we use. One of the gadget guys built the gun, silenced and really accurate. Another of the gadget guys created darts that go into it. And a couple of people on the bio-chem team came up with an entirely new sedative—fast-acting, no side effects, not even a hangover when you wake up. I believe the story is that the four of them came up with the idea while playing Dungeons and Dragons."

"Okay, that kind of freedom sounds pretty awesome." I came out in the last dress, similar to the first but in a rich, saturated blue. "I'm definitely getting this one."

"Get the yellow, too," she said. "I'll show you how to cash out, so to speak."

At a counter near the front, she showed me how to scan my cool orange ChatterBox in front of a screen; then she had me just put both dresses on a pad on the counter. The screen immediately listed both items, and below them a message was displayed: "Thank you, Sarah! Enjoy your items."

"What's the crazy high-tech system behind this?"

"RFID chips," she said. "Not even our tech, although like a lot of things, we've tinkered with it a bit. It also links these dresses to you, so if you got lost on the island somewhere, we could scan for the chip and find you."

"Whoa, wait. You could track me by the clothes I'm wearing?"

"Well, we could already track you by your ChatterBox."

"Isn't that invading people's privacy?" I asked.

"Some could see it that way, I guess. But it's not like you're being actively tracked all the time. We don't have a map with little dots for every person on the island to see where they all are, like that Marauder's Map in *Harry Potter*. It's just a side effect of everything being tied into the same system. Besides, you don't think you could be tracked back home? The GPS in your cell phone, cameras on most corners, your credit cards, your work ID card—everything is designed to keep an eye on where you are and what you're doing."

I shuddered. "Now I feel like I'll always be watched no matter where I go. But not just here—everywhere."

"At least here we have more serious things to do than keep tabs on where you are. I can't really say the same for the rest of the world."

"I'll take your word for it," I said. I didn't like the idea of being tracked, but her argument about cell phones and ID cards made a lot of horrifying sense.

"I'm sorry, I didn't mean to freak you out," she said. "I'm just so used to everything here. It's hard to remember back when everything was new and weird."

"How long have you been here?" I wanted to change the subject. We strolled out of the shop and down toward the grand lobby of the residential area.

"I came to the island about seven years ago," she said.

"Did you move here with Scar?"

"Oh, no. I met him here. We got married just about four years ago."

We continued through the lobby and out the other side, where I hadn't explored yet. There were a number of other shops, some smaller boutiques with luxury items.

"I've noticed that you call him Mark, but Nate calls him Scar. And he said to call him either one."

"He actually loves that nickname," she said. "I know that Nate has called him Scar for years and years; I think it was to separate Mark from his dad, who's also a Mark. And especially here, I think he sees the nickname as the perfect name for a henchman of Doctor Oracle. He says it's kind of menacing, which I think is adorable."

"Henchman? Is that really his job? I thought he was a concierge."

"We all like to call ourselves henchmen now and then. *Minion* is a good one, too. A lot of the sports league teams do plays on those words for their team names."

"Sports leagues? Seriously?"

"Yeah. I know there are softball and bowling leagues for sure. I think there's a football club, but I don't pay much attention to that one. There are probably a couple of others, and Mark would be able to tell you about all of them."

"Does he play in all of them?"

"No, he's just really good at his job. I'm pretty sure he knows everyone on the island by name, and what they do. His job is basically to make sure that everyone is happy and has what they need to be successful."

"I can't imagine remembering all of that information."

"Neither can I. But it's nice to know that my husband will never forget our anniversary."

We finished the tour of the area, which included the library, a small four-lane bowling alley, a gym, two actual bars, and a theater with both a movie screen and a stage. If the other side was about dining and shopping, this end was more about entertainment.

"So do you have to buy drinks at the bar?"

"Nope, still included," she said. "Though since alcohol is a luxury, it's more of a drink-ticket system. You get ten credits every week but can't use more than three in a twenty-four-hour period. That way, nobody gets grossly drunk and we don't have to stock or bring in huge amounts of alcohol."

"And people don't have a problem with limits like that?"

"Not that we've heard so far. After all, how often do you have a drink at home?"

"Maybe a glass of wine at night? Two, if it was a particularly crappy day at work."

"Well, there you go. You could still have a glass of wine at night, and the upside here is, most people don't have crappy days at work. They're doing work that they love, with the freedom to try out whatever crazy ideas pop into their heads."

We strolled back toward the grand lobby. It was getting late, and I was pretty tired.

"Look," Jin said, "I know Nathan wants to take you around tomorrow, but if you get tired of him and want to hang around with me, I'm off work and don't have anything on my schedule. I was just going to tinker with a couple of new ideas."

"I'd love that," I said. And it was true: she was so friendly and easy to talk to. It didn't hurt that she was a huge source of information about the island.

"You can give me a call anytime."

We got into the elevator, and she hit the button for the fourth floor. "You know where I'm staying?"

"Married to Mark, I know way more about where things are than I probably should," she said. "But also, you're right down the hall from us. We're in 401, on the corner."

We walked to my door, and she showed me how to tap the face of my orange ChatterBox against hers so our information was exchanged.

"Thanks for taking me around, Jin. And for the shopping help."

"Anytime, Sarah." She smiled and hugged me, which I didn't expect but didn't mind. I put my thumb up to the panel next to my door, and it slid open for me.

I kicked off my flip-flops, brushed my teeth, realized that I needed to find some pajamas somewhere, then threw on the tank top and exercise pants I'd worn out of the hospital. I opened up the patio door and stepped out. The moon was high, nearly full, and throwing a huge reflection on the ocean. The air was the perfect temperature—not too hot, but delightfully warm. And not terribly humid. I closed the screen door but left the sliding door open so I could hear the waves and the rustling of wind in the palm trees.

I climbed into the bed, which had the same ultrasoft sheets as the hospital bed. It was incredibly comfortable, which meant it probably cost a lot of money.

I thought about my day. It was an awful lot of information to absorb, and I'd met a lot of interesting people. But my experience has always been that the impressions you get on the first day of a new job are likely the ones you'll still have years later; if you like the people, and the atmosphere, and the general feel of the place on day one, it's probably going to be a decent fit. This wasn't a new job (at least not yet, but it certainly had the possibility to become one), but I felt much the same. I liked the people I'd met, I liked the place, and I could get behind their philosophy.

Despite all the information, and my brain not wanting to shut itself down, fatigue eventually took over and I drifted off.

ELEVEN

I had another episode of where-am-I shock when I woke up the next morning. But things clicked quickly into place when I looked out the window at the clear blue water and the even bluer sky. It was so lovely it made me want to get up and do things.

I showered, put on my new yellow dress, and had a bowl of cereal and a banana for breakfast. Scar was right about the milk: it was more flavorful than any I'd ever had before. Likewise, the banana was the perfect ripeness, without a single bruise. I'd never had food straight from the source before; maybe all food was just as delicious when there weren't several days and several handlers between the food and your mouth.

I put on my orange CB and noticed a flashing button on the side. *What the hell*, I figured, and pressed it. The screen showed the words "Message Playing," but I didn't hear anything. After a minute or so, the screen flashed and showed two buttons: "Repeat" and "Delete."

There was something I was missing, and in a moment I figured it out. I popped the earpiece out of the side and put it in my ear, then tapped the screen where it said "Repeat."

The message played again, and I heard it this time. "Hey, Sarah, this is Nate. It's about six thirty, so I'm sure you aren't up yet. I'd love to give you a tour of the operations side of things, if you're up for it. Call me whenever you like. Okay. Um . . . thanks." He paused. "It's great to see you." Then the message ended.

I tapped "Delete" and the screen changed to "Next Message". I pressed that.

"Sarah, hello, this is Dr. Adina Adams. I'm just calling to remind you to report any adverse effects you may feel, no matter how small. Dizziness, headache, blurred vision, anything like that. Otherwise, if you're feeling up to it, I'm happy to clear you for light exercise, but please don't overdo it. I've sent you my number if you need anything."

I really had no plans to overdo anything, but it was nice to have doctor's orders for it.

I tapped the screen to delete the doctor's message, then scrolled through the very brief list of contact numbers, which had grown to include "Adina—Medic" and "Jin—Mech." I found "Nathan—Admin" and tapped on his name. A green button appeared, which seemed like the way to make a call. I tapped on that and waited. A sound that was somewhat similar to, yet almost completely unlike, the ringing of a phone sounded in my ear. Then a click.

"Hi, Sarah. Good morning."

"Good morning," I said.

"So . . . um . . ." He paused, and I waited. "Good morning."

"You already said that," I said.

"Yes. Yeah. Okay. So how about that operations tour?"

"Sounds good."

"Okay. I'll be there in about ten minutes." We signed off. I went to the closet and found a pair of flats with grippy bottoms, a little more substantial than flip-flops for a walking tour, and slipped them on. Despite being fully clothed, I felt vaguely naked leaving without a purse and cell phone and a handful of keys.

The door made its soft chime, and I tapped the panel next to it to let Nate in.

"Hey," he said.

"Hey," I said. I stepped aside so he could come in.

"So, what do you think of the room? I definitely figured you'd want the ocean side, not that the other side is terrible. It has a great view of the jungle, and the mountains, and the pool. Did you see the pool yesterday? I know it isn't on Scar's usual tour, but I figured you might have found it on your own." He paused and looked at me.

"Nate, why are you acting so nervous?"

He took a deep breath and let it out. "I still don't know how pissed off you are at me."

I put my hand on his arm. "Somewhere between zero and five on the ten-point scale."

His expression brightened. "Really? That's great!"

"It could still be a five."

"Doesn't matter. Anything under a seven, I can handle."

"Oh, nothing cocky about that at all," I grumbled.

He grinned. "Just a fact. I have some things to show you today that will definitely chip a couple of those numbers away."

"Then let's get to it," I said. We left, and my door closed silently behind us.

The first stop was the pool, since it was one of the few parts of the residential side of the facility that I hadn't seen yet. And sure enough, it was gorgeous. More a series of pools, connected by waterfalls and streams, than one big pool. It was still pretty early, so nobody was swimming yet. I knelt down and dipped in my hand and wasn't surprised that the temperature was just right. Cool enough for a hot day but not so cold that you couldn't use it in the evening.

"Pool hours are seven in the morning until eleven at night," he said. "We generally have quiet hours from eleven onward, even though the insulation is so good that there could be a party going on outside your room at three in the morning and you wouldn't hear it. And there are a few areas that are exempt: the food court, which always has something available, twenty-four hours a day; also, the bars are open until two in the morning."

"It's all so civil. Practically like a retirement community."

"Well, we've tried to make it comfortable and sensible for everyone and are always open to suggestions from the people who live here."

"And that actually works for you?"

"So far, it works fine," he said. "We're going to head over to the operations side, but we'll take the long way around."

He led me back on a trail beyond the pool, toward the back end of the building that housed the hospital wing. "Administrative offices here, lots of paperwork being pushed. And the hospital, which you've already met. But behind here is an area that really helps keep the island running smoothly."

We took a long, winding path to a clearing that had a few people hustling and bustling around. There were a couple of large greenhouses in the clearing, and beyond them I could see some tidy rows of greenery growing.

"Part one of our on-site food supply is the farm. There are a ton of things we can grow here, and the weather allows us to grow them year-round."

We went down a lane between the two greenhouses and emerged on the other side. The sliver of greenery I could see before turned into a number of large fields, and beyond those fields was a valley with a great number of evenly laid out trees.

"Veggies in the fields, and a great variety of fruit and nut trees out there in the orchard," he said.

"Wow, when Scar called this the garden, he was seriously underplaying what you have here."

"He was probably trying to go easy on you," Nate said.

"Is there anything you *can't* grow here?" I asked.

"Some of the colder-weather crops. Apples don't do well, though we've tried. A number of leafy greens, like kale and cabbage, tend to like it cooler, though one of those greenhouses actually cools the air instead of heats it, so we can grow smaller things in there. If you have a salad for lunch, every vegetable in it is grown here."

"Seems like it isn't a lot of land, for so many people," I said.

"We have a couple of other areas on the island where we grow things, depending on what kind of sun exposure or rainfall those crops like. The wheat fields don't need much attention this time of year, so they're left to their own devices—the spring planting won't happen for a few weeks. One of our computer techs is even experimenting with a small area of wine grapes; she planted them six or seven years ago and has been bottling for a couple of years now. This year's batch is way better than last year's, and last year's was pretty tasty."

"I'd like to see that," I said.

"Evie loves to show people her work," he said. "I'll make sure you meet her on today's tour."

We continued on past the fields, on a path that seemed to lead into more jungle. But the trees were neatly trimmed on both sides of the path, so I didn't feel like I was being taken out to the middle of nowhere. We emerged into another clearing, this one with barns on the far side and fenced grassy fields beyond.

"Let me guess, here's where the meat comes from."

"And milk, and cheese, and eggs," he said. "The livestock make fertilizer, which helps our team over at the farm. We're mostly all about beef, pork, and chicken, although there are a few goats too. We have a couple of people who are allergic to cows' milk."

"And instead of them just not having milk or cheese, you brought in goats?"

"Of course," Nate said. "We have the space, we have people who can take care of the animals, we have a cheese maker who loves variety in his work. And we have people who have dietary issues. Why wouldn't we?"

I shook my head. "I'm starting to see why everyone around here seems so happy."

"I hope so," he said. "The happier they are, the more productive and creative they are. Which means better things for the entire organization."

I met the cheese maker and a couple of the people tending to the livestock, and just like when meeting the people at the fields, Nate introduced me as "new to the organization" without mentioning specifics.

As we took the path that would loop us back around to the operations building, I said, "They're all going to think I work here, when I don't."

"Well, perhaps you should," Nate said.

"As your in-house graphic designer, yeah, you already said. I'm thinking about it."

"Good!" he said. "You may not be aware of the fact, but we had to outsource our very logo design, because we didn't have someone in-house to do it." He gave me a wide grin as we walked.

I whacked him on the arm. "That's different, and you know it. Did Scar tell you that was me?"

"I knew it already," he said.

"How on earth?"

"Sarah, you haven't changed your email address since we got in touch to send you that gift card."

"Oh," I said, feeling like an idiot.

"Fine, no, don't feel bad. I had to look up our records, after Scar reported in that you'd told him you were the designer. But it's true, your email address is still the same."

I whacked him on the arm again, which made him smile even more.

We made it to the operations building, and Nate promised we would take the short way back after he gave me the tour. As opposed to all the fascinating areas of the residential building, the operations building was full of a lot of large work spaces and laboratories with things going on that I didn't understand. One lab seemed vaguely different from the next, but I couldn't tell what made the difference between a biology lab and a physiology lab.

The garages were cool, however. Nate pointed out Jin's office in the corner, then told me about some of the vehicles that were all in partially assembled condition. I figured out some of the parts of transport balls, but I never would have guessed that the silver lump in the corner would be a helicopter someday. There were massive shelves holding a variety of parts for boats, cars, trucks, tanks, even a porthole or two for a submarine. They were ready to fix anything and everything.

"Do you really have a submarine?"

"Two," he said. "But they're pretty small, and don't have much range."

"So there are boats, too, and the chopper. But what about airplanes? How do you get people and supplies out here?"

"There's an airfield on the far side of the island," he said. "Built before us, by the people who built the resort. Takeoff and landing patterns keep us from hearing most of the air traffic over on this side."

We went on to the computer labs, which were unsurprisingly filled with all shapes and sizes of computers. Nate took me in to specifically meet Evelyn, head of the computer division and the amateur winemaker. I was surprised that she was at least ten years older than me, probably closer to fifteen. Working in video games, I'd always thought of computer people as being younger. She was a short spitfire with beautiful gray hair, had a lilting British accent, and insisted that I call her Evie. She also extracted a promise from me to come down to one of the bars the following Monday for a wine tasting. Evie didn't get the stock line about who I was or what I was doing on the island, which I found interesting.

She tapped her ChatterBox against mine so that she could have my number. Instead of wearing the wristwatch version, she had a style that looked similar to a stopwatch, slung around her neck on a lanyard. I liked that the place was full of options, even for something as necessary as the communication device that everyone carried.

Our rambling tour ended up at the front of the operations building, where we went back out into the sunshine. The way back was certainly much shorter—a footpath along the beach that was pretty much a straight shot between the operations and residential buildings. It only took us five minutes or so before we were back in the lobby.

"So no death ray anywhere, then?" I asked.

"Sadly, it's not at the top of our list of things to build," he said. "But there's a team that thinks a shrinking ray is less than three years away."

Nate checked the time on his CB, and I felt my stomach rumble. Both things told us it was lunchtime.

"May I take you to lunch?" Nate asked.

"Only if you're picking up the check," I said.

"Always."

I opted to visit the burger window, and really thought about the beef, the bun, and the french fries I walked away with. It was probably all from right here on the island. I didn't even want to try to get my brain around the idea that the mustard and ketchup might be made here.

Nate led me over to a table with two men seated at it. They were an amazing contrast: One was tall, thin, bald, about my age, with dark brown skin. The other was short, chubby, pink as a deli ham, probably in his sixties, and had an impressive mess of white hair and a tidy white goatee. They were laughing with each other like they were best friends, and it turned out that they were. Nate introduced me to Elliot, the thin one who turned out to be the head of the science labs, and Rupert, the plump one; he made me think of southern gentlemen and mint juleps. Or a hipster Santa Claus. Rupert bowed, kissed the back of my hand, and introduced himself as the head of the department of mysteries.

"Like in *Harry Potter*?" I asked. "I hope it's something less freaky here."

"Disguises, darling," he said. "Special effects. Makeup, prosthetics, costuming. All of the essentials."

Neither of them got the stock introduction. Interesting.

"So, Sarah, how are you liking it here so far?" Elliot asked.

"It's certainly different," I said. "Everything's lovely, and everyone has been great."

"I'm so glad," Rupert said. "Dear, we were so worried about you when you were brought in."

The lack of introductions made sense. They already knew who I was and how I got to the island.

"Dr. Adams says I'm fine," I said. "I'm supposed to get some exercise, although Nate's tour this morning was probably more than enough for the day."

"What does Oscar say?" Rupert asked.

"Who's Oscar?"

"Ah, you haven't met him yet. Amazing boy, he'll get you shipshape in no time. He's almost always in the gym."

I decided to meet him later. Maybe *much* later. The gym didn't exactly sound like the most interesting part of the facility.

Over lunch, I learned about Rupert's past work in the movie business, until computer special effects started taking away his livelihood. He'd joined the organization over ten years ago.

Elliot tried to explain some of his biochemical work in easy terms, but it was still over my head. Then he told me about his failed rock band, Superbang, which was much more interesting. Their one hit song sounded vaguely familiar.

"I still play," he said. "We have a band here on the island called Pink Flood. We play a little bit of everything but seem to have a heavier than usual rotation of Pink Floyd and They Might Be Giants."

"They aren't allowed to participate in the talent shows anymore," Nate said. "After winning three in a row."

"Yeah, but we do regular gigs down at the bar, which is way better," Elliot said. "Everyone buys us beers."

"Except that the beers are always free," Rupert pointed out.

"Well, they use their credits," Elliot said. "That means something to me."

After lunch, I exchanged a hearty handshake with Elliot and got my hand kissed again by Rupert.

"I do hope you decide to stay with us, Sarah," Rupert said. "You can only raise the level of delightfulness here."

"Thank you," I said. "I'm thinking about it."

The men left, and Nate and I strolled out to the beach, taking off our shoes and finding our way to a pair of chairs under an umbrella, just like the day before.

"You've said you're thinking about taking the job twice today," he asked.

"So I have."

"Three times is like Beetlejuice. Or the Candyman. So be careful."

"I'm thinking about it," I said.

Nate grinned. "Good."

"But just in case, just so I know all of my options . . ."

"Yes?"

"What happens when someone wants to leave?"

He leaned back again. "Well, we've had a few people quit. Maybe they didn't like the isolation of the island. There have been a few couples who wanted to leave to get married and start a family."

"They can't start a family here?"

"Kids are a distraction," he said. "It's in everyone's contract when they come here that they can't have them on the island. And most people are vigilant about making sure that kids don't happen, because they know they'd have to leave."

"Most people? Not everyone?"

"Things happen. Life happens. It is what it is. But they're still our people, even when they leave, so we take care of them. Everyone who leaves gets a payout, based on the work they've done here, the projects they've been involved with. And if they choose to go find a job in the civilian sector, they get a glowing reference that's guaranteed to open any door they want."

"A reference from Doctor Oracle? I imagine that would open some doors and slam others shut."

"The reference doesn't come from Doctor Oracle, though. It comes from the TORAC Corporation, which is another one of our companies that can't be traced here in any way. It's hugely known in tech circles, because it's the company that gets the patents for the inventions we opt to send out into the world. Everything from microchips in your cell phone to a more efficient motor in your microwave."

"How much stuff do you put out there?"

"Quite a lot of it, actually. People develop stuff all the time that's handy for us, but it wouldn't hurt us if the rest of the world got hold of it. Like the sliding doors. They even come up with stuff that we have no use for but would make a ton of money out in the open market. But there are other things that the rest of the world is probably not ready to have; a lot of heavy thought goes into some projects, whether things are safe to send out there."

I thought about that. It made sense, in a way. And they certainly didn't owe the world everything they made.

"How did you come up with the Doctor Oracle name?" I asked.

"You know the transport balls?" he asked.

"Yeah."

"We had about a dozen good names on that ballot and put it to a vote. Sadly, I was rooting for Orb-o-Tron. Well, for the name Doctor Oracle, at the time the four department heads and I came up with around a hundred possibilities."

"Only four heads? It feels like I've met more than that already."

"Four plus me, at the time. Now there are seven of us total. Jin and Oscar joined the organization later on."

"So, a hundred possible names. And you voted for Doctor Oracle."

"It was a challenge coming up with even a hundred names, since if you look at all of the comic books, novels, TV shows, movies, and actual superheroes, villains, and in-betweeners, almost every good name feels like it's already been taken. A lot of things on the list were just plain terrible."

"I guess there are only so many ways you can call yourself Mr. Awesome," I said.

"Exactly! Funny you would pick that, since there are actually three Mr. Awesomes out there. So we ended up going with one of the most absurd names on the list. It makes no sense, combining science and medicine with myth and prophecy. And yet, it kind of makes a weird sense, since we're all about scientific developments, and we're trying to predict what the future will need while we're doing it."

"And nobody else was using the name," I said.

"And nobody else was using the name."

I sat back and thought about that for a while. "So Elliot and Rupert are department heads. They were part of that original group?"

"Yeah, plus Evie in computers, and Scar, of course."

"They all know who I am, too?"

"They do. Actually, Oscar was the one who found you at WonderPop. We carried you out together."

"Why did you choose them, specifically?"

"The original group were handpicked by me and Scar, and they were all doing some covert side work against the supers already. We vetted Jin and Oscar in much the same way, and they've made great additions to the team. They're the people I trust the most and whose opinions I trust the most. They all have such widely different backgrounds and interests that between all of us, we can usually come up with a unique angle on any problem." He dug his toes into the sand. "By now, we've been together long enough that we all can predict what the others will do in a situation, which is a huge help when you do some of the things we do."

"Like break into WonderPop."

"Exactly."

"And do their minions in their departments know that they go out gallivanting around with Doctor Oracle on the weekends, breaking into places and stealing things?"

"Nope," he said. "We try to keep everything separate. Five points for calling them minions, by the way. They know that we all head up departments, and most of them think we're at least aware of Doctor Oracle's plans. But for the most part, we try to throw around the idea that Doctor Oracle is usually off-site, and when he needs a team, they're found somewhere off-island. For all intents and purposes, we here just do his gruntwork."

"But don't they wonder when their department heads disappear for a couple of days at a time?"

"Conferences," Nate said. "Training seminars. Despite the fact that we're on a private island owned by a criminal enterprise, it's still easier to fool people with things they know. In their old lives, their bosses had to go on boring business trips all the time. We just perpetuate that belief, that things are similar for the department heads here."

"Huh," I said, soaking that in. It was probably true; even though the jobs here were cooler than most, people probably still thought there were a lot of standard sucky job-related duties for their bosses. That got me to thinking about the job I'd left behind and the day it happened. "What were you guys there for that day? At WonderPop?"

"Computer server," he said. "Remember the day the building was on fire?"

"That was the day I first met you."

He looked over at me, pleased. "Yes, it was."

"Go on," I said.

"The fire set off all of the alarms in the building, so we were able to get into a secured server room to install some code without triggering any of that room's specific warnings."

"You were using your phone. I thought you were texting someone."

"Actually, I was. A two-person team inside the building. Evie did the code installation, while Oscar went in to cover her back. The code took a couple of weeks to do everything it needed to do, which Evie assured me was important. Compile something, move some files. You know. Computery stuff."

"Glad you know the details of your own plan," I said.

"Well, that's the nice thing about having a bunch of genius experts around you," he said. "I don't have to know the various parts, just that things need to happen, and how we can bring all of those parts together into one big plan. Then I throw money at it."

"So you went back into the building for what?"

"We went in to download the code, but Alpha was tipped off that we were there, so we made things quicker and easier by just taking the whole server with us. Saved enough time to get out of the building before it crumbled, and to get you out of there."

"I can't believe he punched the building down," I said.

"You want to see it? We have footage."

Was he kidding? "Are you kidding? Of course!"

"Let's go to my office," Nate said, brushing the sand off his toes.

TWELVE

Nate's office, since he was the head of administration and finance, was in the same building as the hospital wing. He had an impressively large desk, with a cushy leather chair behind it and two guest chairs in front. On the wall behind the desk were a dozen flat-screen monitors, tightly packed into a square shape.

"Wait, now I *know* I've seen this place before," I said.

"Yeah, we do filming here when we need to. You can't tell anything about our location, and the wall of monitors looks pretty cool."

"And still, you say that nobody here suspects that you're Doctor Oracle? Even though you sit in front of his signature big wall of screens?"

"Well, he's been known to borrow my office now and then. But bear in mind, I'm administrator Nate here. I don't wear a white coat or have a big forehead scar. Smart though our people are, the easy thing to believe is that he's someone else. And most people will always go for the easy explanation."

"Still," I said. "Someone is bound to figure it out."

"It helps that I'm often seen out and about while the office is being borrowed by the doctor," he said. "I planned the place, so of course I have secret passages that can get me out of here in a flash."

He settled me into the cushy leather chair. Nate tapped on the surface of the desk in a specific pattern, and it came to life as a huge touch-screen computer. I blinked and smiled—now the way the doctor and nurses tapped on their desk in the hospital made perfect sense.

He tapped around various menus. "Got it," he said, and jumped up to sit on the corner of the desk that wasn't lit up like a computer screen. "I'll put it up on the wall." Suddenly all the screens turned on, and instead of showing the same image twelve times, they served as one gigantic screen.

"Handy," I said.

"It works both ways. I figured you'd want to see this big, not twelve times." He double-tapped on the desk, and a news story started playing. "This was when the news was breaking."

There were aerial helicopter shots of the WonderPop campus, and you could just see Commander Alpha's little white and blue form at the base of my building. The camera zoomed in to get a closer view of him punching the concrete walls. The anchors covering the news blathered about the possibility of evildoers inside the building, excusing Alpha's assault on the poor building in the name of catching the bad guys. The picture cut back to the anchors at their desk, and the playback paused.

"How long did he punch the building?" I asked.

"It wasn't more than ten minutes," Nate said.

"So how did the news crew get there fast enough to be able to film this?"

Nate sighed. "Well, my guess is because he called them."

"He what?"

"Yeah, he does that. We've found records of anonymous tipsters letting the news stations know that Commander Alpha would be taking down some baddies at certain times, in certain places. We're pretty sure it's him; if not, it would have to be someone else in the Ultimate Faction. Who else but they know where they're going?"

"That's gross," I said. But it made total sense, considering how they were all publicity hounds.

"If you think that's gross, you're probably ready to see what we found in the follow-up story."

"Is it worse?"

"Much," Nate said. He leaned around and typed on his desk more, then turned back to the screens. Another news clip came up and started playing.

"In a threat received earlier today," the anchorwoman said, "Doctor Oracle has taken responsibility for the destruction at the WonderPop building and has confessed to kidnapping Sarah Valentine, a WonderPop employee who was in the building at the time. Commander Alpha was on the scene to try to stop Oracle but was unsuccessful in capturing the internationally wanted criminal."

As the lady blathered on, they showed more of the footage of Alpha punching the building. Nate shifted uncomfortably next to me. There was Alpha, punching the building. Then, in a clip that hadn't aired in the other story, he turned aside and grabbed his electronic bullhorn. He pointed it upward to do some shouting, and the camera tracked upward to show the side of the building.

There in one of the third-floor windows, you could barely make out the shape of a person. Thanks to the treatment on the glass, and the distance from the news helicopter, you could only see the broad strokes but no details. The person was just blobs of color—brown hair, pale face, bright pink top, black pants.

It was me, when I'd gone to the window to look down to see what was happening.

The camera tilted back down to Alpha, who put his bullhorn down and went back to pounding the wall. The shot widened to show more of the building, and the figure up in the window was gone. I'd stepped back to my desk by then, to grab my things and get the hell out. You could see pieces on the outside of the building start to fall away, and at the same time inside, I knew that pieces of the building were falling on me.

The news anchor talked about how the figure in the window may have been kidnapping victim Sarah Valentine, or it might have been a member of Doctor Oracle's organization. Either way, Alpha was unable to capture or rescue whoever it was. The story ended, and the screen paused again.

I looked up at the screens for a few minutes. Eventually, I realized I was gripping the nice leather armrests of Nate's chair way too hard. I eased up my grip and turned to him.

"He knew that wasn't a member of your team," I said. There was no chance that anyone robbing a building would do it with their face and head uncovered, wearing bright pink.

"Yeah," Nate said quietly.

"And if it wasn't a member of your team, it had to have been a civilian."

"Yeah."

"And he didn't care, did he?"

"No, he didn't." Nate hopped down off his desk. "He was trying to catch the bad guys. Sometimes there are casualties."

"But why doesn't the news even mention the fact that if it was me, kidnap-victim Sarah Valentine, that Alpha might have injured or killed me?"

Nate sighed again, went around the desk, and sat in one of his guest chairs. "What I came to learn a long time ago is that the whole world is just like high school," he said. "And the supers are the kids who rule the school. The captain of the football team, the head cheerleader, whoever. And the government is pretty much the principal, who will crack down hard on most of the student body for any infraction but who will give their star players a pass so they can keep winning games and getting trophies."

"And the news just plays along?"

"Sure they do. Because if they suck up to the cool kids, then they'll keep on getting those anonymous tipster calls when the juicy stories are going to happen. They'll gladly cover up little bits of the story if it means they get the inside scoop on taking down the next evil genius or mad scientist."

"That sucks," I said.

"Indeed it does," he said. "But it's the world we live in. Can you blame us for trying to change it?"

"The fact that you are the evil genius, the mad scientist, while they're the heroes. It's so disgusting."

"You don't even have to be evil or mad," he said. "Your goals for using your genius or your science simply might not align with what the supers think is the right move. Boom, you're branded. Is it any wonder we have so many brilliant people working here? We let them do what they're good at instead of telling them that they're monsters for being good at it."

"Ugh," I said. "After watching that, I feel like punching something."

"Perfect," Nate said. "I know just the guy."

THIRTEEN

Nate took me over to the gym in the residential building and introduced me to the Oscar I'd heard about. Oscar Halleck was a little shorter than Nate, probably about twenty-five, and fit in a slim, wiry way. His black hair was cut short, his skin was either naturally brown or deeply tanned, and he moved around like he had too much energy and nowhere to put it. He went around the corner from handsome into territory that you could almost call beautiful, but it was spoiled a little bit by the feeling that he knew all too well how good-looking he was. He shook my hand, told Nate he'd take good care of me, then shoved Nate out the door.

I didn't think Nate minded too much. He'd expressed his dislike of the gym to me in another life, and that was one of the things he'd told me that had a ring of truth to it.

"All right, *chica*," Oscar said. "Let's see what you can do."

"I've been taking kickboxing classes for three years," I said.

"Show me." He took me over to a heavy bag and got me a pair of gloves. I kicked my shoes off in the corner and took out some of my aggression on the bag while he watched. He grabbed a pair of arm pads from an equipment locker, and I spent some time kicking at him instead of at the bag. It was pretty therapeutic.

After enough kicking to get the anger out of my system, Oscar tossed the pads aside and asked me to hop up on a balance beam. It was a weird request, but I obliged. I walked across from one end to the other, then turned back to him.

"Run this time," he said. I did. He had me do a few laps back and forth on the balance beam. He said, "You have great balance. How have you trained for that?"

"I don't know," I said. "I roller skate, and referee for roller derby?"

"Ah," he said, and clapped his hands together. "Yes, that makes sense. Balance, speed, and I bet you know how to fall."

"Yeah, I had to learn that fast. I certainly did it enough in the beginning."

"There's a certain fearlessness in derby, even on the outskirts," he said. "Which can be a help, but also a hindrance. Fear can hold you back, but it can also make you sensibly cautious."

"Oh, don't worry. I have caution down to an art form."

"Nate told me that you play video games," he said.

"I do," I said, puzzled by the turn of the conversation.

"Let's try something," he said, and led me toward a closed door at the back of the gym. He pressed his thumb against the lock panel, the door opened, and we stepped through. Inside, there was another room twice the size of the gym we'd just left. There were all sorts of obstacles in the middle of the room, from small boxes to pillars ranging in height from two to at least ten feet. Around the outside of the walls were platforms and ledges.

I looked around for a second, then snorted. It was like a puzzle room in a video game, brought to life.

Oscar smiled at me. "You see what this room is," he said. "We call it the escape room. There's the goal." He pointed toward a hatch high up in the corner of the room, with a small ledge underneath it. None of the other ledges or pillars seemed to be close enough to get to it.

"There's no way I could get up there," I said.

"You don't have to," he said.

"Good."

"You're going to tell me how to get up there."

"Oh, great."

"Yes," he said. "You can't climb on anything, although you can move around the room to see things from different angles. Stay on the floor, and tell me where to go."

I cracked my knuckles and blew out a breath. It was a challenge. I just had to pretend that this was *Secret Ninja II* and Oscar was my assassin. His target was on the other side of that hatch.

I started by having him leap up to grab a couple of different platforms and ledges, to see how high he could jump. Then I had him stand on one of the short pillars and jump to a couple of other short pillars. He made two of the jumps but fell to the padded floor with the third, not quite making the distance.

"Why are you having me do these things?" he asked. I had a feeling he already knew the answer but was testing me as I tested him.

"No sense in finding out your limits when you're up high," I said. "Down here I can learn how far I can send you in any direction without you getting hurt."

"Sensible," he said. "Very sensible. Shall we begin?"

I walked a lap of the room, then had him start on one of the shorter padded pillars. From there, I told him to jump to a higher pillar, and from there to a platform along the wall. From that platform to a slightly lower one, then a higher ledge straight above. On my direction he hung on the ledge with his fingertips and scooted along, then swung his body to leap to the next platform.

He obviously had a ton of parkour experience; it was amazing to watch him gracefully leap from place to place. I bet it would be really cool to see him free running in an open space.

He came to a dead end, and I couldn't see how to get him to the goal, so I had him come down and try another way. That was also a dead end. We tried a few different paths, but none of them could get him to the final platform and the hatch. It was just too far from any of the nearest other platforms.

I knew there had to be something I was missing, so I walked another lap of the room while Oscar sat patiently on a platform high above my head, near enough to the goal to be frustrating but not close enough to make the jump without suffering serious injury.

As I walked, I took closer notice of the obstacles on the floor. Some were just padded cubes, but others looked like they could be boxes. I grabbed the top of one, and it came off smoothly. Inside were a number of dodgeballs.

I looked up at Oscar, who was smiling and watching me closely.

I went around the room and opened up all the other boxes I could find. Finally, inside one in a dark corner of the room, tucked away underneath a low platform, I found a rope. I pulled it out and laid it out straight on the floor to check its length. Then I went and stood underneath Oscar and paced off the distance to the platform under the window.

"Okay," I said. "Would you please come down?"

Oscar hopped from platform to platform like a mountain goat, then executed a backflip off the lowest one to the padded floor. Show-off.

I tied an adjustable loop on one end of the rope, scanned the walls, then sent Oscar back up one of the earlier routes we'd tried with the rope coiled over his shoulder. When he made it to one of the platforms that was just a little bit too far from the final goal, I asked him to try to lasso the platform itself with the rope.

He nailed the platform on the second try. The loop rested firmly around the final platform.

"Now stretch the rope across the gap, loop it around the platform you're on, and tie it off," I told him.

"Any particular knot?"

"Anything stronger than a shoelace bow should be fine," I said.

He tied off the rope, and I had him drop down from the platform so that he was dangling from the edge by his hands. He worked his way around the side of the platform, grabbed the rope, then made his way hand over hand until he reached the far platform. He hoisted himself up on top of the platform and opened the hatch.

I couldn't help myself: I applauded. He grinned and took a bow, then reached into the hatch and pulled out a rope ladder.

It rolled over the edge of the platform and dropped down to the floor. He quickly scampered down.

We went back out to the main gym, where he mopped the sweat off his head with a towel. He grabbed a couple of water bottles from a cooler and handed me one. We sipped our water and sat on a pile of gym mats.

"You knew how to get up to the hatch," I said.

"Actually, I didn't," he said. "Hadn't been in there yet today, and a couple of my team members love to move things around on a regular basis. That's an order of platforms and pillars that will probably never be seen again."

"Huh," I said.

"Sarah, I rarely *ever* get up to the hatch with someone directing me," he said. "And never on someone's first try."

"Really?"

"Really. A few things you did really stood out to me. First, you tested my limits on the ground first. Not a lot of people do that, and if they want me to make a dangerous jump, I'll call off the test. Secondly, you didn't get frustrated and give up, or tell me that the task was impossible. I've had that happen a number of times."

"Well, I figured it was possible, or else why do the test?"

"Also, you didn't just take what was in the room at face value; you looked around and found things hidden away. That's the mark of a video gamer. And I don't mean to sound sexist here, but it's something that female gamers are much better at than men. A lot of guys will just charge ahead in games, guns blazing, while a lot of women tend to look around, open containers, and see what's there."

"I always figure it stretches the game out. Lets me savor it more. Plus, I'll admit, I'm curious. I want to know what's inside every box."

"That's the key to the escape room," he said. "Yes, it's good exercise and fun to climb around, but its real purpose is to help people to open up their eyes to see every possible object around them and to figure out how to use those objects to their advantage."

"Combining the mental and the physical," I said.

"Exactly," he said. "You have physical potential, for sure, but I'm more excited to see what kind of mental leaps you can make with the options you're given."

I snorted. "You're talking like I'm going to be here for a while."

"Are you?"

"I'll give you the answer I'm giving everyone else, since it seems to be the question of the century. I'm thinking about it."

"Cool," he said. He jumped up from the mats with a surprising amount of energy, as if he hadn't just spent all that time exerting himself. He offered me a hand to pull me up, and I took it.

We shook hands, and I went to find myself some dinner. It had been another long, interesting, tiring day.

FOURTEEN

The next few days passed with a lot of the same. Getting to know people, learning about the island and its operations. Meals with Nate's select group, all of whom I liked quite a bit. Jin seemed delighted to have a woman her own age in the inner circle, although we did plenty of things with Evie too. Evie gave me a tour of her vineyard and winery, and I went to her wine-tasting event. It was surprisingly good.

I worked out some with Oscar, and he had me guide him around the rearranged escape room a few times. There wasn't always a rope, but there was always something in the room that could be used to bridge the gap so he could get to the hatch, hidden among dozens of containers of useless stuff. One day it was a plank of wood; the next it was a small ladder that he was able to lay flat across the higher-up platforms and cross like monkey bars.

Elliot invited me to his lab and showed me around, though I have to confess, I didn't understand most of what he was working on. He told me about the variety of tranquilizers they used out in the field, most of them fast-acting and free of side effects. Then he apologized that they'd used some of the same compounds on me when I'd first come in, to keep me asleep while they watched to see if I had any brain swelling. I forgave him.

Jin took me out for a ride in one of her vehicles, a six-wheeled thing with controls that were more like an Xbox controller than a steering wheel, and let me drive around a bit. When we got back to the garage, she showed me a few easy techniques to pick locks. Not that the knowledge would help at all on the island, what with the automatic doors, but it was pretty cool stuff to learn. She had a wall with dozens of small doors installed, each one just large enough for a hinge on one side and a doorknob or deadbolt on the other. I finally managed to pop one of the locks myself, which delighted Jin.

"Wait until I can show you some tricks with safety pins and bobby pins," she said. "Really, every girl should be able to pop a lock with a bobby pin. It's up there with changing a tire and fixing things with duct tape, as essentials for a girl's education."

"I don't think we all got the education you did, Jin. Although I can totally change a tire."

"I'm just glad to have the skill set I have," she said. "I'm totally useless in a fight. Oscar has tried training me in various hand-to-hand techniques, but I'm just bad enough to be a danger to myself."

Nate took me around a bit and spent as much time as he could hanging out with me. I tried my hardest to keep some sort of anger at him, but his easy charm and open honesty chiseled away at me. Plus, there was always something new and wonderful to see and explore.

Then a day came when he let me know that he and Oscar were going off the island for a bit, so he wouldn't be available.

"You probably can't tell me where you're going," I said.

"Not right now, no."

"Fine, but you should be careful, whatever it is."

"I'm always careful," he said.

I put my hand on his arm. "I'm serious."

He looked at me for a long moment, then gently touched my face. "I'll be careful."

I thought for sure he was going to kiss me. Then he didn't. And then he was away on whatever mission he was away on. I didn't want to admit it to myself, but I was jealous. I bet he was having adventures and excitement.

Rupert invited me to his work space, and I found that much more fascinating than my time in Elliot's lab. He had an incredible array of wigs, facial hair, and prosthetics, as well as a huge room dedicated to manufacturing and repairing clothing. He showed me the sleek black suits the team usually wore when out in the field, made out of an ultrastrong material that was resistant to bullets, knives, dog bites, and any other kind of sharp injury.

His area was much more secure than others on the island, with most of the costuming team working in a large space separate from his studio. He explained that only he worked in the studio so that the rest of his staff could remain in the dark about the identities of the people going out on missions. They made the clothes and disguises but didn't know who wore them.

For fun, Rupert put me in his chair and gave me a fake nose and chin, put me in a long blond wig and blue contact lenses, and gave me a cool pair of cat-eye glasses. The look was amazing; I was unrecognizable from my usual self. I looked in the mirror and tried to figure out who the strange woman in the mirror was. I tried out a few voices from my long-ago college drama days and settled on a southern belle.

"Ah do declare," I said. "Ah would be most obliged for you to bring me a mint julep, my good man."

Rupert beamed with delight. "Fantastic, my dear! I don't even see you anymore!"

"I love this look, Rupert," I told him.

"I'll hold on to it for you, darling." We carefully peeled everything off, and he stacked it all neatly in a box. He went to a large, securely locked cabinet. He typed in an intricate code and put his hand on a panel to be scanned, then opened the double doors; inside were at least fifty similar boxes, each neatly labeled. I saw "Oscar Nerd," "Jin Sexy," and "Nathan Oracle" among them.

"Can I see the 'Nathan Oracle' stuff?"

"Of course, my dear!" He pulled the box out and placed all the contents on the counter. A nose, padded cheekbones, a tidy little chin beard, and a container of liquid latex in the color of the famous scar were in a smaller box, on top of a cool vintage-style white lab coat and black mask. There were also reference photos inside the box, showing Oracle fully made up, so Rupert would know exactly where to put the scar. The photos looked nothing like Nathan.

"It's amazing, you'd never know they're the same person."

"That's the point," Rupert said. "We took quite a bit of time crafting just the right parts to distract the eye."

I looked over the boxes again and found another in the corner labeled "Nathan Hart."

"What's this one? There's no indication of a disguise," I said.

"On the contrary," Rupert said as he pulled the box out. He put all the Oracle items back into their proper places, then took the items out of the Nathan Hart box for me to see. There was another nose, a number of pieces of chin and neck, and a pair of wire-rimmed glasses very different from the thick black frames Nate wore around the island. There was also a full wig, the same color as Nate's own hair but much more sparse and thinning.

"What are these for?"

"When Nate has to go be *himself*," Rupert said. "That is to say, when he has to go to Hart Corporation meetings or make some sort of appearance. He can present himself as a reclusive owner all he wants, but he does have to be seen sometimes. Otherwise people get nervous. He also has a number of padded suits for when the occasion demands them."

"So nobody here could recognize him as himself," I said.

"Exactly."

"But . . . oh, it makes perfect sense," I said. "I was going to ask why not go as himself to the board meetings and be in disguise here, but he's here far more of the time, isn't he?"

"That's exactly right. As far as plain old Nate goes, this is his home, and by a weird extension, the three hundred people here are his family. It's the one place where he can really, truly be himself." Rupert packed up the box again and put it away on the shelf.

With Nate and Oscar away, I spent part of the day with Jin and Scar and part kicking around by myself. I visited the library and picked up a couple of books. I browsed through the TV shows and movies available on my room's TV; they were all surprisingly recent and available on demand. That was one of the perks of living on the secret island lair of a supervillain, I supposed—no commercials.

I went out to the beach in the afternoon with one of the books and a tall glass of iced tea from the food court. I arranged a lounge chair and an umbrella so that I could lean various body parts out into the sun for short periods of time, to avoid burning myself to a crisp. I'd made my way through both arms and my right leg, and had my left leg sticking out in the sun when I saw the top of a transport ball pass quickly from the vicinity of the operations building over to the hospital wing. It wasn't speedy, but I was surprised at how fast they could actually go.

I tried to get back into my book, but something about the speed of travel bothered me. I felt a weird uneasiness in my gut. So I packed up my things, took them back up to my room, then made my way over to the hospital.

The administrative hallway was deserted, but most of the admin staff worked a fairly regular eight-to-five shift, and it was nearing six o'clock at that point. I stopped at the hospital door, which didn't open automatically. I pressed the green button on the panel next to the door and was happy that the door opened for me.

Louise, the day nurse, was at the desk. She looked up and smiled as I entered. "Sarah, what brings you here? Are you feeling all right?"

"I'm fine, but I had a weird feeling . . ." I looked around the room. It was mostly empty, but I could see Dr. Adams leaning over someone in one of the beds. The uneasiness in my gut grew, and I took a tentative step forward.

Then the bathroom door off to the side opened, and Nate stepped out, holding a wet towel to his arm. Dr. Adams turned to look at him, and I could see Oscar sitting on the bed behind her, holding a towel to his own chin. Both men were dressed in the all-black suits they wore for covert operations.

"I cleaned most of the grit out, Doc, but you might still find something in there," Nate said.

"You couldn't have the courtesy to get cut cleanly?"

"And make things easier for you? Nah," he said. He turned and caught sight of me. "Sarah! Are you okay?"

"I'm fine," I said, putting my hand on the nurse's desk to steady myself. "But I didn't think you were."

"Hey," he said, coming over. He reached out the hand of his injured arm and took my hand with it, as he was still holding a towel to that arm with the other hand. "I'm fine."

Dr. Adams led us both to the bed next to Oscar's; I took a chair next to the bed, and Nate hopped up on it. I watched Oscar pull the towel away from his chin and check the amount of blood on it. His chin was certainly a big red mess, but I couldn't tell how much damage had been done.

"How did you know we were here?" Nate asked.

"I saw the transport ball haul ass in here," I said. "And I just . . . had a feeling."

Oscar laughed. "See, Nate? I told you. Great powers of observation, great instincts."

"You guys were talking about me?"

"Nothing big," Nate said. "He was just telling me about how good you are in the escape room."

Dr. Adams came around to Nate's bedside with a surgical sewing kit and a few bottles and towels. I'd never seen a wound stitched up, as I'd never required stitches myself.

"You may want to look away," said Dr. Adams.

"No, I'm good," I said. "I've always wanted to see stitches."

Dr. Adams took Nate's towel away and started cleaning the cut on his arm. Whatever she used must have stung a little bit. Nate cringed and sucked in a breath. "I don't know, Valentine. My stitches are my own private business."

"Oh, come on," I said.

"Hmm," he said. "All right, I'll let you watch on one condition."

I pursed my lips. "What's that?"

"You have to forgive me for lying to you before."

"Done," I said. "Bring on the pain."

Turns out, there wasn't all that much pain. Adams swabbed some numbing agent on his arm before she started her stitching, so Nate barely even flinched. Still, it was really cool to watch. I held his free hand the entire time, but my attention was completely on the doctor's work. She put eleven neat stitches in the wound, then slathered a nasty-looking gray goo over the top of everything. After that, she wrapped his arm in bandages and taped everything securely.

"The nanogel will do its thing, so come see me in two days and we'll check your progress," she said.

"Nanogel? Is that the gray stuff?" I asked.

Dr. Adams moved over to Oscar and started cleaning the cut on his chin. "It is," she said. "The bio-chem team and gadgets guys came up with it, and it's a huge help for us here. It cuts healing time by two-thirds and results in minimal scarring. It's a combination of a new antibiotic, anti-inflammatory, antiseptic, probably a few more anti- things that I'm forgetting, and the nanobots."

"Nanobots?" That sounded more like science fiction than medicine.

"Exactly what you think they are. Microscopic robots that do a single task. These guys clean out the dead skin and any infected cells and carry them out to the surface."

"That's . . . kind of cool?" I thought about it. "But kind of gross."

"Science is a majestic thing," Oscar said, sweeping his arm through the air. Adams poked him.

"Keep your head still, Oscar," she said. "Or I won't be able to keep you so pretty."

"Yes ma'am," he said, and let her work on his chin. He only needed three stitches; then he got a helping of the nanogel and some bandages, too.

I heard the door open, and turned to see who it was. Scar stepped into the hospital wing with a bag under his arm. He saw me there and smiled.

"Sarah, what a surprise. Nate didn't say that you were here."

"She wasn't when I called you," Nate said. Scar tossed the bag on Nate's bed, and Nate dumped the contents out onto his legs. Two shirts and two pairs of shorts fell out, along with four flip-flops. Nate separated the items into two full outfits, got up, and set a stack of clothing on the foot of Oscar's bed. Oscar lifted his hand in a thumbs-up as Adams was just finishing up his bandages.

Nate headed into the bathroom to put on his fresh clothes, since the supposedly cut-proof sleeve of his outfit was sliced open.

"So what brings you around here?" Scar asked.

"I saw them come in," I said.

"Not entirely true," Oscar said as he took off his jacket, which was still intact but had quite a bit of his own blood on the front. "You said you had a feeling."

"That, too," I said.

Nate came out of the bathroom dressed in the clothes Scar had brought: a pair of board shorts and a lightweight long-sleeved T-shirt. He kept the sleeves down, and the bandage on his arm was completely covered.

"Lucky," Oscar said, pointing at his bandaged chin. "I'll have people asking me about this for *days*."

"You mean you'll have women fawning all over poor, injured you," Nate said.

"Yep," Oscar said. "Now I just have to figure out what kind of amazing story to tell about it." He stood up from his bed and threw his jacket down on it, showing his smooth, muscular chest to everyone in the room.

"Please," said Louise from the corner, "there are ladies here."

"That's why I figured I'd change out here," Oscar said.

"Oscar Halleck, if you take off your pants over there, I'll assume you want a vaccine," she said.

Oscar grabbed his clean clothes and went into the bathroom, sticking his tongue out at Louise on his way. Nate wadded up his suit with the ripped arm and handed it to Scar.

"What the heck cut you?" Scar asked. "These things are normally much tougher."

"One of the Ultimate kids," Nate said. He saw my puzzled look and explained. "There are the established members of the Ultimate Faction, the old ones like Alpha and Firewolf. But they're always on the hunt for new blood, so they have a bunch of provisional members who get the grunt work, in order to prove themselves." He turned back to scar. "This one had claws, maybe artificial or augmented. Purple outfit. Not anyone we've seen before. Have Rupert's team take a peek and see if they left anything behind in that cut on the jacket; maybe he can make some improvements to the fabric."

"You got it," Scar said. "And we'll try to figure out who this new member of their team is."

"I would expect no less, my friend," Nate said.

"You must have bled all over, wherever you were," I said.

"Maybe not *all over*, but yeah, she got us both good," Nate said.

"Aren't you afraid they're going to find out who you are from the DNA in the blood?"

"Not to worry," Nate said. "The blood they'll mop up isn't a DNA match to anyone they have on file from anywhere. Those of us who go out into the field have our records permanently altered in all of the government systems. Although for medical reasons, we keep our own records safe and sound here on the island."

Scar piled Oscar's bloodstained jacket on top of Nate's torn one. Oscar came out of the bathroom dressed in his T-shirt and shorts. He threw his black pants at Scar, who deftly caught them and put them on top of the jackets.

Nate looked at his watch. "After all that excitement, it's about dinnertime." He held out his uninjured arm to me. "Buy me dinner, and I'll tell you about our little field trip," he said.

Since the food was all free, it was the easiest choice in the world. I looped my arm through his. "You have yourself a deal."

FIFTEEN

Nate and I strolled back to the residential wing, arm in arm. We made it to the lobby, and he paused in front of the elevators. "We could do the food court, or I could show you the more formal dining room," he said.

"It's my treat, so I say we go fancy," I said.

We went upstairs, and Nate exited the elevator behind me on the fourth floor. "I'm down this way," he said, pointing the opposite direction of my room. "I'll come pick you up in, what, ten minutes?"

"That works for me," I said. I went down to room 404 and let myself in. I didn't have much in the way of clothes overall, though Jin and I had gone for another shopping expedition after our first one, so at least I had a good assortment of underwear, pajamas, a new bathing suit, and a few other things.

I decided to put on the blue dress we bought on our first trip out; I hadn't worn it yet, and it fit perfectly. I threw on a pair of wedge sandals and hoped I was fancy enough for the formal dining room.

Nate rang the doorbell and I let him in. He'd swapped the shorts for slacks, changed from the more casual long-sleeved T-shirt into a button-down that had a little more starch to it, and traded his flip-flops for leather shoes. No tie, no jacket, so I didn't feel underdressed at all.

"I called down to the dining room," he said. "They can squeeze us in in a few minutes."

"What, do you need reservations for this place?"

"Usually, yes. But there are *some* perks to being in charge of the whole place. Or at least being a part of the group that's in charge. I could have gotten us in immediately, but I asked for one of the more private rooms. Some of the things we do here, even though we're as transparent as we're able to be, aren't quite fit for public discussion."

"So we have a few minutes to kill," I said.

He took a step closer to me and ran his hand down my bare arm. He lowered his voice. "What should we do with ourselves?"

I poked him in the chest. "You, sir, are still on my list."

"Hey, I let you watch me get stitched up. I thought I was forgiven."

"Forgiven, yes. But not forgotten."

"Where am I at on the anger scale now? Down from five, I hope."

"Even if you're just a one, you're still not quite down to zero," I said. "Besides which, do you really think we could go back to where we were before? Not only before you abruptly left me in the lurch, but before I learned about this place, and everything here, and *you*?"

Nate leaned against the counter in the little kitchen. "Do you want to go back to where we were? Or, more to the point, do you want to go back to where *you* were?"

"Not necessarily, no. But I'm not sure where the way forward lies."

"Do you need to know? Do you need a map or a plan? Or can you just trust yourself and go?"

I slumped against the kitchen counter myself. "I just don't know."

He stepped toward me again and touched my chin. I raised my head up to look at him.

"That's the beauty of being here," he said. "Stay as long as you need and figure things out. Whether you want to take this job with us or not, you can have all the time you need. Decide on what you want, not what you're willing to settle for, not what you're willing to tolerate. Figure out what will make you happy, and we'll find a way to get it."

He moved even closer, and then his ChatterBox beeped.

He looked down at the face and tapped once. "They're ready for us downstairs."

I was glad for the distraction, and felt like fanning myself. We went back out into the hall and down to the elevators, and I thought about what I really wanted. Well, to be fair, right then I was mostly thinking about *who* I really wanted. It wasn't the money or the power; I'd been attracted to Nate when I thought he was a scruffy mailroom clerk. And I thought I had a pretty good handle on who he was inside; most of what he'd told me back home had a ring of truth to it, and nothing he'd done or said since I'd arrived on the island had a different tone. All of his staff thought he was fantastic, and they'd been around him years longer than I had.

We rode down to the first floor standing side by side, each thinking our own thoughts. Once we reached the lobby, he led me along the same corridor that went to the food court, but turned early down a hallway on the left. It curved around to a small hostess stand, where an attentive young woman stood.

"Hey, Janelle," Nate said. "I just got a ping that the blue room is ready for us."

"Absolutely," she said. "If you'll follow me."

Despite the fact that Nate probably knew where the blue room was (since he'd had at least a hand in laying out the entire complex), he dutifully followed Janelle as she led us through the small restaurant to a back hallway. The main area had a dozen or so tables, spaced far enough apart to offer some privacy, all with couples chatting with each other. It seemed like the best place on the island to take someone on a date, or for a special occasion. I could also see, from how few tables there were, why reservations were a necessity even in this small community.

Down the back hallway were a number of ornate doors, all amazingly old-school with doorknobs. Janelle led us to the one at the very end and opened it for us. Inside was a lovely dining room, with a table that could seat at least six but was only set for two. The wall lighting was soft, augmented by candles on the table. The walls, tablecloth, and upholstery were all complementary shades of blue.

Janelle pulled out a chair for each of us on opposite sides of the table and let us know that a server would be around in a moment to tell us about the specials for the night. She excused herself and closed the door behind her.

"I actually had no idea you'd be wearing blue when I asked for the room," Nate said. "I just asked for one of the back rooms, and this was the one they had open."

"Maybe it's a sign," I said.

"I don't believe in signs."

"Says the guy who named himself after an oracle," I laughed.

"That wasn't entirely my choice," he said. "I voted for Mr. Mishap but lost out."

"Thank goodness," I said. "Doctor Oracle has a nicer ring to it. Plus, it doesn't have destruction right there in the name."

A server knocked politely on the door, waited a moment, then came in. As he poured us glasses of ice water, Nate smiled at him. "Tom, good to see you."

"Nate, a pleasure as always." Tom looked at me, but it clearly wasn't in his job description to be nosy.

"Tom, this is Sarah. She joined us fairly recently, so she's still getting the lay of the land."

"A pleasure to meet you," Tom said. He then told us about the specials the chef had prepared for the night. Since price was no object, I opted for the lobster bisque and filet mignon, medium rare. Nate requested the same and asked for a specific bottle of wine. Tom nodded, never writing anything down, and left the room.

"So," I said, "you had a bit of an adventure today."

"That I did," Nate said. "But to explain where I was today, I should first explain what I was doing at WonderPop."

That delighted me. "I thought you'd never fill me in on that," I said. "You told me you stole a computer server, and something about some code, but that's all."

He looked serious for a moment. "I'll tell you anything you want to know, Sarah."

I reached out my hand toward him. "I know."

He took my hand in his. "Good. Okay, so, WonderPop. Did you know anything about what they did up on the sixth floor, on the end of the building that burned?"

"Not really, no. After the fire, I went up there to try and check things out. I had no idea it was so extra secure up there; I thought we all just did office software, games, that sort of stuff."

"Mostly that's what the company does. But up in that corner of the sixth floor, that special secure area is where they develop various things for the government. Top-secret, hush-hush kind of stuff. Programs for spying, or running military systems. That's the reason the company had more security than usual; very few gaming-software companies have twenty-four-hour security."

"I'd never really thought about that. It was my first software-job, so I figured that's how most of them were."

Tom knocked on the door again, so we paused our conversation. He came in, popped the cork on a bottle of wine, poured a small amount for each of us, and waited for us to taste. We both swirled our glasses and took a sip. It was an amazing wine, just the right balance of body and flavor. I grinned at Nate, who motioned for Tom to pour away.

After Tom left again, Nate sipped his wine. "This is a 2001 cabernet from the Napa Valley. It's just about the perfect time to drink it, and the year is regarded to be one of the best vintages in the last forty years."

"Must have cost a pretty penny," I said.

"Not so bad," he said. "The winery gave us a few cases in trade for specialty upgrades to their irrigation systems, which allowed them to almost double their yield."

I laughed. "So you really are doing good for the world."

"We try." He put down his wine and continued his story. "So, WonderPop. The software we wanted was a new system for satellite navigation. We figured we could make better use of it here. So I went in first and checked out the area, since my mailroom job got me easy access to a lot of secured areas."

"Then you started a fire."

"Yeah, I started a fire. A small one in a trash can, with some files full of paperwork stacked around it. Underneath a wooden desk. Which was a shame, because the desk kind of looked like an antique."

Tom came back and swiftly delivered our bowls of soup. He topped off our wineglasses and left just as swiftly.

"This guy is good," I said.

"I would hope so," Nate said. "We got him from one of the best restaurants in New York."

"And he's happy here?"

"He lives for fine food and wine, and loves to make people happy. A bunch of the so-called superheroes based out of New York loved to eat at his restaurant, and they were apparently the most whiny, demanding, biggest pains in the ass he'd ever met. And they'd always stiff him on tips, because it was supposed to just be an honor to serve them."

"Aw, jeez," I said. "That's terrible."

"Here, he runs our wine program, gets to eat gourmet food every night prepared by our chef, who earned Michelin stars for two different restaurants, and he doesn't have to worry about tips at all. Everyone is great to him, and in turn, he's great to everyone."

The lobster bisque was just as amazing as the wine. In between spoonfuls, Nate continued his story.

"The fire burned on the front side of the building, setting off all the alarms. All of the attention was out on that side. My team, which was Oscar and Evie, went in to the back side of the building and planted a virus in the system while all the alarms were going off so their intrusion wouldn't be noticed.

"The big problem was that the secure servers with the software we wanted weren't connected to the outside world, so we couldn't access the code that way. And as soon as the alarm went off, that special sixth-floor server room locked up tight as a drum. But the handy thing was, those secure servers *were* connected to part of the building's internal network."

"Your virus did something with *other* computers?"

"Exactly. Evie and Oscar got into a less secure server room and planted Evie's virus, which communicated with the secure servers. It then downloaded the programs we wanted from the more secure systems to the less secure systems. Which were still pretty damned secure, I assure you."

"Then you came back a couple of weeks later, to get the server."

"We didn't plan on taking the whole thing, but yeah. We were just going to download all of the code from the server we'd stashed it on. Unfortunately, alarms got tripped, blah blah blah, we ended up just grabbing the whole server and hauling it out of there."

"And grabbing me along the way," I said.

"Well, of course," he said. "I couldn't very well let a building fall on top of you, especially after I'd disappeared so rudely."

"Why did you leave so suddenly?"

"It's the damnedest thing," he said. "That week before, we found out that the Ultimate Faction knew that something was going to go down at WonderPop. So I got out of there right away, in case they made a surprise visit. Sorry again about that." I nodded. "We moved the heist itself up to Sunday during the day; it was originally planned for the next Tuesday night. We figured nobody would expect us to steal anything in broad daylight."

"And yet, Commander Alpha was there waiting for you."

"We talked about it afterward, and figured they must have been watching the building, since they knew something was going to go down."

I set down my spoon. "So if they were watching, then they saw me go in."

"Maybe," Nate said quietly. "Probably." We sat in silence for a moment. I took a sip of the delicious wine.

"Bastards," I said.

"Yep."

Tom knocked on the door, startling me. After his usual polite pause, he came in with a pair of beautiful steaks, accompanied by lumpy garlic mashed potatoes and asparagus. Everything was drizzled in a butter sauce. He cleared away the soup bowls, made sure our water and wineglasses were topped off, and slipped out the door again.

I dug into my steak, which was cooked to a perfect medium. Being accompanied by red meat made the wine taste even better, if that was possible.

"Okay, so. You got the server with a bunch of satellite software from WonderPop. How was that connected to today?"

"We had the software, but not the satellites to use it on. So we popped over to California, to the Griffith Observatory. Funny thing, they keep really good records of all satellite traffic, no matter how secure or secret those satellites are supposed to be."

"What, they just keep a list of what satellites go overhead?"

"Sort of. They don't know what all of those satellites are, or who owns them. But they track the direction they pass overhead. Really, they keep track of everything in the heavens; satellites just happen to be part of that. From that data, we can figure out which ones are the ones we'd like to ping with new software."

"And you couldn't just tap into their records over the Internet? Have Evie hack their systems or something?"

"Astronomers are creatures of habit," he said. "And some of those habits are old and outdated, like keeping records in ledgers."

I laughed. "You're kidding me! You went to steal some books, like it's the last century?"

"That we did." He topped off our glasses of wine. "Unfortunately, someone was waiting there for us, just like at WonderPop. A newbie, not all that well trained, so we were able to get away mostly unscathed. But she got me with a claw, or whatever it was. And punched Oscar in the face, which just shows how unexpected she was. He rarely ever gets caught by surprise."

"So that's two places where they knew you would be?"

"Yeah, which raises the question of how they knew. There are only a couple of options that I can see. One of the seven members of our group is leaking information, which I find nearly impossible to believe. There could be a mole among the minions, getting information in some secret way. Or the Ultimates may have acquired someone new with some sort of psychic or predictive powers we've never seen before."

"Or there's some other option you haven't thought of."

"Exactly. We'll have to have a team meeting to figure this thing out, before we schedule any more excursions. So we need to roll fast, because other projects are in the works already."

Our conversation turned to lighter topics as we finished our dinner and polished off the bottle of wine. Nate told me about the black eye he got the first time he trained with Oscar, and also how he met and recruited a couple of the other members of his inner circle. I told him details of my much more mundane life. It was almost like a real date in the real world.

Tom came back in after a knock and a pause, cleared our plates away, and offered dessert. We were both far too full, but Tom offered to have a slice of blackberry-almond tart sent up to each of our rooms later. We both accepted the offer. Nate shook Tom's hand on the way out, and we made our way through the now half-empty restaurant. It was later than I thought; we'd spent over two hours with dinner and conversation.

Nate offered me his uninjured arm again, and we went back through the lobby and up to the fourth floor. He walked me to 404, where I pressed my thumb to the locking panel. The door opened silently behind me, and I took a step through. I turned back to Nate.

"Do you want to come in?"

I could see him seriously think about it. "It's been a pretty long day, and I'm a little bit short on blood," he said.

"Oh, right, okay. No, fine," I said. I felt my face flush hot. I was confused in general about what I wanted in life, but I was pretty sure that he was what I wanted right then. It was awkward to be turned down.

He stepped up to me where I stood in the doorway and kissed me hard. It was just as fantastic as when he'd kissed me back in Seattle, but infinitely nicer without the scruffy beard.

Finally, we broke apart, and he rested his forehead against mine. "If I'm going to come in there with you, I'd like it to be when I'm not this tired, with my arm wrapped in gauze and gray slime."

"Oh." My face got even hotter, and I'm sure I was a bright red in contrast to my blue dress. ·

"But I'd like a rain check."

"Um . . . I think something can be arranged."

He grabbed my hand in his and tangled our fingers together. "Things really aren't all that less complicated, are they?"

"Then I guess we have made it back to where we were," I said.

He lifted our hands up and kissed the back of mine. "Good night, Sarah Valentine."

"Good night." He let go of my hand and stepped back. I took a step backward into the apartment, and the door did its job by shutting between us.

I changed for bed, brushed my teeth, and tried to get into one of the books I'd borrowed from the library. I figured my brain would be going a hundred miles an hour, refusing to allow me to sleep. But after an afternoon of fretting, a hearty dinner, lots of information, and one of the best kisses I'd ever had, I guess my brain was happy. I conked out before finishing two pages, with the sound of the ocean outside my bedroom window and a smile on my face.

SIXTEEN

The next morning, I had a message waiting from Nate. He let me know that the core team would be meeting that afternoon to discuss the possible leak in their organization. I wasn't invited to that, but they were going to have dinner afterward and were thinking about turning it into poker night after that, and they'd love it if I came to eat and play.

Everyone was busy checking their departments for moles during the day, so I had to entertain myself. Which was probably a good thing: I had a number of topics to think about. I took a cup of tea out on my deck and watched a few morning sunbathers out on the beach. The water was so clear I could see a pair of people snorkeling way out by the reef that kept the beach free of big waves. It really was a magical place.

The question was, did I want to stay there and take the job they were offering? There were a ton of things in the pro column, from the great people to the great food. I could easily get behind their cause, to make the world a better place without any kind of oversight.

And there was also Nate, who was definitely a positive. Attractive, smart, funny, and even though I was into him when I thought he worked in the mailroom, it didn't hurt that he turned out to be much more interesting.

But Nate was kind of a negative, too. Yes, I wanted to get involved with him. But he was the boss, and getting involved with the boss is never, *ever* a good idea. At least the job offer meant

I wouldn't be moving somewhere just for a man, something I'd always sworn to myself I'd never do.

But whether it was this new job or my old job, I needed to get busy with some sort of work. I was already starting to get twitchy from the lack of having something to do. It helped to train with Oscar and learn about the labs from Evie and Elliot, but I really did yearn to get back to creating things.

Here I'd thought I was lazy and complacent, and I was itching for work. Crazy.

I passed the rest of the morning by trying my new swimsuit, both in the swimming pool back behind the residential complex and in the ocean out front. I liked the ocean better; it was easier to just float on my back in the salt water, looking at the blue sky and thinking about my future.

After lunch, I went back to my room and read a book. I'd found it in the library in the "Island Authors" section, which was pretty cool. The book itself was from one of the usual publishing houses and didn't hint about the author's occupation or location; it just had a photo of a smiling woman and brief biography on the back flap: "The author, Janine Wells, has worked in computers and IT for the last fifteen years. This is her first novel."

There was an additional piece of paper inserted by the librarian, noting that Janine was part of the computers and technology team, played on the Marauding Minions softball team, and had participated in the 1,000 Gold Bars project. I wondered what that was.

The afternoon crawled along. I spent some time on the couch, flipping through channels of TV shows and movies. Nothing could really hold my attention, and I couldn't stop wondering about what I would find out at the postmeeting poker party.

I really wanted to know what was going on. With everyone. I wanted to know if there was a mole on the island, sending secret information off to an unknown source. I wanted to know what their next heist would be.

And, I realized, I didn't just want to know. I wanted to help. I wanted to be part of the planning, and maybe even part of the execution of the plans. Which I chalked up as an item in the con column; I figured that even if I took the job, and stayed on the island, and got over either my hots for Nate or my concerns about dating the boss, I'd probably have to settle in to a nine-to-five schedule and wouldn't have access to all the plans the core group of seven discussed.

I was a little mopey by the time Nate pinged me on my CB that they were done with their meeting and that I was welcome to come on down to his apartment. I put on my shoes and made my way down to the door marked "465." It was at the very end of the hall, almost as far as possible away from my own room.

My grumpy brain took that as a sign. He wanted me as far away as possible. Ugh, stupid brain.

I moved to press the button on the panel next to the door, but before I could, the door opened automatically for me. Nate was standing in the kitchen, as handsome as ever. He had his sleeves rolled up, showing his bandaged arm. I glanced around—a couple of the others were sitting in the living room area, chatting. Looking at his apartment, the layout was almost exactly the same as my place, though there were a couple of additional doors. Nate came around the small kitchen island to greet me.

"I hope you don't mind; I set the door to just let you in."

"I don't mind at all," I said. Hell no, I didn't mind. Chalk that up in the pro column. Evie, Jin, Rupert, and Elliot all called out greetings from the living room. Evie and Rupert both blew me dramatic kisses.

"Scar and Oscar went downstairs to get takeout," Nate said. "Want to help me set the table?"

"Sure," I said. He handed me a stack of plates, with bundles of silverware wrapped in napkins, and somehow managed to arrange the stems of eight wineglasses between his fingers so that he could carry them all in one trip. He led me out of the kitchen and through one of the doorways I didn't have in my apartment.

It turned out to be a second bedroom, but instead of bedroom furniture, the room was made up like a conference room. There was a round wooden table in the middle of the room that could probably seat a dozen people, and we started setting up places.

"So . . . did you guys figure things out?" I asked as I put out the plates and silverware.

"We might have some ideas," he said.

We went back out to the kitchen for water glasses and bottles of wine, and Nate didn't offer any more details. So that was it. I'd been shown a glimpse of the inner workings, but now I was starting to be shut out. It made sense; I wasn't a part of their core team, so of course they couldn't share *everything* with me. But I'd seen so much and learned so much about the operation already, to be blocked in any way hurt a little bit.

Oh, who am I kidding. It hurt more than a little bit.

We finished setting the table and went back out to the living room. The others all looked at Nate, then at me, then back at Nate. Which was weird.

"Um," Nate said. He led me back to the kitchen, which was still within view of the now silent people in the living room. "Uh, Sarah, can we speak privately?"

"Sure," I said, feeling like a chill had just passed over my body. My brain went into overdrive. I'd done something wrong. They were rescinding the job offer. I'd waited too long to give them an answer. Thanks but no thanks; we're kicking you off the island.

Nate led me through his main bedroom and out the sliding door. His apartment was on the back side of the complex, with great views of the pool and jungle and mountains beyond. Since it was a corner unit, the balcony wrapped around the side; from up there, I could see the top of one of the greenhouses, a barn roof, and a number of green fields full of vegetables. I could also see the administrative building, the huge operations building, and a sliver of the ocean. It was the perfect balcony. I was glad I got to see it before I left.

Nate made sure the door was securely closed behind us; then we leaned on the railing next to each other, looking out over his empire.

"So, we didn't just talk about our mole problem, Sarah. We talked about you."

"Okay," I said.

"You've only been here a week or so, which isn't very long."

I nodded, ready for the axe to fall. *We think that's more than enough time hanging around, especially since you refuse to give us an answer. Which means you're not really interested. We've decided there really isn't a place for you here.*

"But it was unanimous: we all want you to stay, if that's what you want."

Okay, not what I expected. "So you want an answer."

"If you're ready to give it," he said. "No rush. But we finalized the logistics of what the graphic design job would be. You could be in the administrative building, or there's plenty of good space available in the operations building, too. We thought you might work well near Evie, since she's all computer stuff, and a lot of what you do is with computers. Rupert also made a good case for bringing you into his area, because of the artistic nature of both of your work."

So there it was. At least Nate wouldn't be my boss; he wanted to stash me away under Evie or Rupert. Yes, I could stay and be a part of something bigger than myself, doing work that supported a cause I could get behind. But also, I'd go back to being an underling, trying to be happy being out of the loop while watching them go off to supersecret meetings to discuss . . . I don't know, the fate of the world or whatever.

I remembered what Nate had told me before: *Decide on what you want, not what you're willing to settle for, not what you're willing to tolerate. Figure out what will make you happy.*

I couldn't help it: I started to cry. I'd been shown a whole new world, wide open and full of possibilities. But I didn't think I could sit in a corner of that bigger world and do my little corner's worth of work now that I'd seen a brief glimpse of the whole thing. I didn't want to settle for minion status.

"What's the matter?" Nate asked. He pulled a handkerchief out of his pocket and dabbed at my cheeks. "I'm so sorry, I really thought you were liking it here. What can I do?"

"Nothing," I said. "It's a great offer—it always was—but I don't think I can do it."

He looked surprised. "Why not?"

"Nate, it's like being shown a huge cake, then being told I can only have one tiny slice."

"What?"

"I've probably seen way too much already. I know about things that none of the minions should know. And if I hadn't seen and learned all of those things, I'd probably be happy to take your offer. But you know that I wanted adventure and excitement. This place is amazing, but I couldn't just sit at a desk for forty hours a week while watching you guys from the sidelines. I'd rather go back to my boring job and boring life than know that so much was going on near me but I couldn't be a part of it." I took a deep breath and let it out in a sigh. "So that's why I'm going to have to say no."

Nate grimaced and pinched the bridge of his nose. "Oh. Okay, I see."

"It's a great offer, Nate, and you're doing great work here. It's just . . . you asked what I wanted, and I want more than you can offer."

"No, no, I'm sorry, I totally screwed this up. We all just assumed we were being clear about the details, and that's totally our fault." He put his hand on my arm. "Sarah, we don't want you to be a cog in a machine, or a minion, or a henchman. We want you to join the team. This team. *Our* team."

"I . . . Wait, what?" I said. It was what I wanted but what I never figured I'd get.

"The graphic designer job is there, sure, but the more important job would be expanding this core group from seven to eight. And really, you'd be a department head like the rest of us; we just don't have an art and marketing department yet. That would be yours to develop."

"Seriously? For real?"

"Seriously. Look, all this time you haven't been running Oscar's escape room or picking locks or playing with wigs and characters just for fun. You've basically been auditioning for the team every minute since you got here. We were just idiots who failed to *tell* you that, because we all assumed you already knew."

"Chalk it up to coming onto the island in such an unorthodox way, I guess," I said.

"Yeah, but we were still remiss, and I'm sorry about that. Heck, we even counted your escape attempt as part of your audition. There was a six-nothing vote that you should become a part of the team, because we all see that you bring a great set of skills to the table. And more importantly, we all like you and get along with you, which is maybe even more important with this group."

I wiped my eyes. "Six-nothing? Who didn't vote?"

"I didn't vote," he said. "We all figured my vote would be biased anyway; I want you to stay because of the work you could do here, but I also want you to stay because I like having you here, and I want to see where this thing between us could go. Plus, our dates back in Seattle were enough audition for me. You were game to try anything, whether it was rock climbing or laser tag or fake skydiving. So please, please stay."

"Nate." I took a deep breath. "Okay, this is more than I was expecting. It's a lot to take in."

"And?"

"And I'd be an idiot to say no. As long as you're not my boss."

"I'm not anyone's boss in this group. Sure, Hart money started the whole thing, but those loans were quietly paid back long ago. As far as I'm concerned, Doctor Oracle is seven people, each with an equal voice and equal footing. Eight people, if you say yes. So no, I'm not your boss. We'd be equal coworkers."

"Good," I said. I grabbed the front of his shirt and kissed him. "I just couldn't date the boss."

"Is that a yes, then?"

"Yes, it's a yes."

He grabbed my hand and kissed it. "Fantastic! Wonderful, thank you. Really, thank you. Let's tell the others; then we can go over tonight's meeting."

We went past the bedroom sliding door to the one that led to the living room. Scar and Oscar had returned, and bags of food were stacked on the kitchen island. The six of them were all in the living room, waiting.

They all looked at me as we came in, silent as a funeral.

I smiled and said, "My answer is yes."

Everyone made noise at once, some laughing, some blowing out a held breath. Evie jumped up from the couch and hugged me. That turned into a reception line of hugging.

"I'm so glad, darling," Rupert said. "I can't wait to get you into a couple of new wigs I've been working on."

"Let's take it slow at first," I laughed. "I'm still getting used to all of this."

"You'll be a natural," he said.

We all went into the spare bedroom that served as a boardroom, which tonight served as a dining room. Food was dished out, wine was opened, and they told me that they would all be combing through their teams to try to find the mole in the organization, paying especially close attention to the few people who'd arrived on the island in the last few months, since the leaks only started recently.

Elliot was fairly sure there wasn't a psychic working for the Ultimate Faction; he went into an explanation about how mental superpowers were only just starting to develop, and DNA analysis predicted that there wouldn't be a full psychic for another seven to ten years. As with most of the hard science, he lost me pretty quick.

After dinner was cleared away and the dishwasher was loaded, Nate brought a felt tablecloth and stainless steel case out of the spare-bedroom closet. The case held poker chips and cards, and we played and talked and laughed for a few hours. We all stayed up too late, and had a little too much wine, with no drink credits in sight—one of the perks of sitting at the big kids' table.

And now that I'd said yes, I was ready. Ready to start the graphics work, sure—it was what I went to school for and was still something I enjoyed doing. But I was even more ready to stretch my legs, find out what I could really do, and launch into a new life of adventure.

SEVENTEEN

The next couple of weeks were incredibly busy. If I'd been living in a movie out of the 1980s, it would have passed in a five-minute training montage, backed by an inspirational song about achieving goals and believing in myself.

First off, there was an impressive stack of paperwork to fill out, including tax forms, contracts, and another more detailed nondisclosure agreement that went on for a *lot* of pages. I was, after all, a new hire. On the plus side, part of the paperwork was to have the rent on my apartment paid through an untraceable series of transactions. I didn't have to worry about my meager possessions getting sold at an auction. And I really did love that creaky old loft.

I was still technically kidnapped by Doctor Oracle, and we had to figure out a way to resolve that. In the meantime, I got to record a video assuring the world that I was fine and that I was being well taken care of. Nate wore his Doctor Oracle disguise, and we had to start filming over again a number of times, because the overblown speech and deep voice he put on were hilarious to me. But watching it after it was edited, before it was sent to the news stations, it was effective. The lighting was dramatic, I managed to cringe and cower appropriately, and Nate looked genuinely threatening in his disguise.

They had this thing down to an art form, that's for sure. And nobody would have ever guessed in a million years how different it actually was.

We made ransom demands, but nobody thought that payment would be made. I was, after all, just one ordinary person, without parents or a trust fund or even very many friends. Small potatoes. Which made me sad, but also made me even more determined to fit in and do a good job for this group of people who saw value in me.

I got an education from almost everyone in the group, and they passed me back and forth so I could get a nice, even variety of new information. Learning became my full-time job, but it was way more entertaining than college had ever been.

Jin taught me more about picking locks and gave me both access to her wall of doorknobs and a lock-picking kit of my own, wrapped in a buttery soft leather case. I was finally taught the thing every girl should know: how to pick a lock with bobby pins. She had me unlock a few common doorknobs in a variety of situations—upside down, in the dark, with only one hand. Turned out I had a bit of a knack.

Jin also showed me a few simple ways to disable cars, from the brutal (but fast) screwdriver-through-the-tire technique to the much more technically savvy removal of the fuse box or starter relay. I got a few lessons on hot-wiring a car, something I'd always wondered about from the movies. It's actually pretty close; you just have to be willing to smash open the starter column, and you have to connect wires in a very specific order.

I also talked with Jin about her experience in dating someone on the team, since she and Scar had met on the island and ended up married after three years. Her main piece of advice was to take it slow and figure out if we could build the kind of relationship where we could still be friends and work together if the romance part didn't pan out. At least I didn't have to worry about breaking new ground by seeing Nate, since they'd already proven that interteam dating could work.

Oscar ran me ragged in the gym, using a combination of resistance training and cardio to build my core strength and stamina. He also had me start making my own way through the escape room, starting with all the platforms nice and low, with thick mats underneath, so I could improve my jumping and dangling abilities without injury. He taught me how to climb a rope and how to slide down one safely, skills I might have known way back in grade school but had long forgotten.

He also sat with me and talked about his own experience as the new member to the team, since he'd been the last to join the inner circle around five years ago. It helped to have someone who had gone through the same intense learning curve that I was working on.

He'd been recruited based on a series of online videos, where he did free-running stunts and mocked his local supers for not being as flexible. Just like me, they found someone they liked, and they acted fast to get that someone on their team.

Oscar gave me an idea of what to expect with everyone's crash courses and let me know that it wasn't a big deal if there were things I wasn't good at. He admitted that he was terrible at picking locks and other "little teensy stuff," and he only went undercover if he absolutely had to.

My clothes started to fit a little looser, and I lost most of the annoying five-to-ten pounds I'd always fretted about. It probably also helped that I walked everywhere, though I did learn how to operate the transport balls.

Rupert worked with me on a variety of accents and characters and taught me a few improvisation tricks to help get out of sticky situations. He tested a variety of wigs and prosthetics on me, and together we came up with a few good characters, should they be needed. I started getting my own set of boxes in his disguise cabinet.

Evie tried to teach me some simple computer-hacking tricks, but I was a terrible student for her. We finally decided that I just wasn't skilled with back end computer code and that I'd do better to learn a few other ways to defeat technology. She opened up the cases of old computers and showed me the easiest ways to remove all the various components, and how to quickly and neatly remove a server from a rack. After all, that's exactly what they'd ended up doing at WonderPop.

Elliot turned out to have a hidden wealth of knowledge. I wasn't about to learn how to brew up complex chemicals or go through a crash course on biology; fortunately, Elliot was part of the team that had developed their silenced tranquilizer guns, and he was an ace shot himself. He took me out to the firing range on the far side of the island with a variety of weapons, from pistols to shotguns to an AR-15. Thanks to my video-gaming experience, I was able to hit a target. Maybe not in the bull's-eye, but after a few sessions I was able to get bullets to go in the general vicinity I wanted them to go, and I stopped flinching so much when the guns kicked in my hands.

Elliot explained that they didn't take any weapons aside from the tranquilizer guns out in the field with them, but of course, guards were frequently armed, and we all needed to know how to handle their firearms if we ended up in possession of them. I was never going to be a sharpshooter, but I was good enough in an emergency.

Even Scar had some things to teach me. He actually had a background in psychology, and taught me some techniques to keep calm if a situation ever got crazy. He also expanded on Rupert's work by giving me a number of tried-and-true ways to talk with people that would get them to open up and tell me information.

The minions had seen me around the island for a couple of weeks at that point, but the team started passing around that I was the head of the new art and marketing department. Everyone looked at me with less curiosity and more respect, which was nice. I also got a number of résumés in my new inbox.

As for Nate, per Jin's advice and since I'd be buried under my unique education, we decided to back off and take things slow. That was on a personal level—as far as learning the operation, he taught me just as much as everyone else. Plus, I got to go back to the hospital wing with him for his two-day follow-up. Dr. Adams unwrapped Nate's arm from the bandages, and there was a shiny pink scar where there had been an open wound two days before.

She put on more nanogel, wrapped him back up, and told me that Nate's arm would be scar-free in another week.

Nate took me around to show me how the entire island was organized into the various tiers of employees. We went out to the airfield on the far side of the island and he showed me their fleet, which consisted of helicopters, a hot-air balloon, and planes with both propellers and jets. There were plenty of hangars for everything, to keep the aircraft safe and clean and to keep them out of sight of any prying eyes.

There was also a marina on that side of the island, with a variety of watercraft, from a bunch of Jet Skis to what looked like a small yacht. The more mechanically complicated boats were under cover in boathouses; Nate pointed out the very tops of his pair of small submarines. Only pleasure craft were out in the open for the world to see, to keep the outward appearance of being a vacation resort.

"You certainly are prepared," I told him.

"One never knows what one is going to need," he said.

There was another resort-like residential building on that side of the island, even though it was only a fifteen-minute drive around to the main building, where I lived. Most of the pilots and mechanics preferred to stay near their planes and boats in case they were needed on short notice, and because they loved the machines so much.

Nate took me for a more extensive tour of the farms and ranches around the island so I could see the entire scope of the on-site food production. It was an impressive enterprise. There was also another small residential building out between the fields and the main livestock barn, even though they were very close to the main building. Again people were given the choice to live near their passion, and many of them took it.

"The farms aren't a giveaway that this isn't really a resort?" I asked.

"Not really, no. A number of island resorts grow some of their own food, to reduce dependence on shipments and to have on hand in case of emergencies. We've done a ton of studies on what we can get away with out in the open."

All in all, it was an impressive job of finding out what made their people happy, and giving it to them. Of course, not everyone could have everything they wanted, but everyone had enough.

On another day, back in his office, Nate showed me how Doctor Oracle, TORAC, Perceptive Solutions, and the Hart Corporation all fed into each other without any obvious or traceable links. I don't think I could explain it to someone else, which was probably a good thing, but it kind of made sense when he explained it to me.

"I'll never remember how this all works," I told him.

"You don't need to," he said. "After all, you don't know exactly how a car works besides the fact that you turn the key and press the gas pedal, right? There are hundreds of other things going on in there, but you take it on faith that someone figured out how to make it all work. You don't need to know every single little detail."

"Jin knows, I bet."

"Of course she does, but that's her specialty. If she needed to pick five colors that go together, in a . . . What do you call that?"

"A color story?"

"Yes, that. Ask her to do that, or ask me to do it, we'd be lost. That's something you can do that she can't. But she can enjoy the end result, just like you can enjoy being able to drive that car."

"Yeah, but her skills are a bit more important."

"Are they? Think about wartime. What do people pay more attention to—the machines around them, or the propaganda posters? Your work is a lot more visible, and it's something that people can connect to in a way that they never could with the fiddly bits of an engine."

"I guess you're right," I said. "Didn't you tell me once that you follow that same theory, of not needing to know how everything works?"

"Heck, yeah! I have the best of the best working here. If they tell me that something will work, and show us a proof of concept, we'll totally roll with it. I have no idea how the desalinization plant works, except that somehow it takes the salt out of seawater and makes it drinkable. All I need to know is that it works, which I can tell by the water I drink and the sea-salt by-product that we can package up, label as exotic, and sell at a huge markup."

The next day, I got to learn about the location of our tropical island; it was the perfect spot, not too far away from the rest of the world but far enough away to avoid most boat traffic. We also weren't on any airline flight paths or shipping lanes, so we didn't have to worry about being spotted. And even if someone did come near, all they would really see was the outward appearance—an exclusive resort hotel and a beach dotted with lounge chairs and umbrellas. Everything was hidden in plain sight, which made the perfect disguise.

"We thought about a skull-shaped mountain," Nate said, "but that seemed like overkill."

"Seems a little cliché, too," I said.

"You'd be surprised," he said. "I know a guy who went with the whole skull-cave thing up in Canada."

Another day in the office, Nate showed me what was probably the most valuable thing they owned. It was a computer database, and it was kept on a system all its own, connected to none of the other computer systems, on the island or off-site. Even the terminal he used to access the database was in a small secret room off the main office, behind a hidden door.

"Only the eight of us have access to this room," he told me. "We've added your thumbprint and a set of access codes in. Evie set up a doozy of a system here—there are way more layers of security than you can see. There's no way to hack into it from the outside, and anyone trying to get unauthorized access would be in for a number of nasty surprises. This system has ten redundant backups," he told me. "We've only ever had one layer fail so far, but better safe than sorry. It's some of the most important information you could have in this line of business."

It was a database of everyone in this crazy industry, amateur and professional, on both sides. Nate scrolled through thousands of entries for superheroes, supervillains, evil geniuses, mad scientists, and even world government officials. For the supers, they had a wealth of information—a surprising number of their entries contained secret identities, histories, and origin stories.

"Anyone you want to look up?" Nate asked.

"Yeah, the guy who almost killed me. Commander Alpha."

"Ah, yes, one of my favorites," Nate said. "Sometimes I wonder if I'm one of his favorites, too." He ran a search for "Alpha" and selected the commander from a list of results. I had no idea there was also a Major Alpha, Alphaman, Alpha Squadron, or someone going by the name of Alphabet Soup.

"That's more Alphas than expected," I said.

"Well this is worldwide, not just our little corner of the globe. The Alpha Squadron works out of northern England, just like we have the Ultimate Faction in the northwest United States. I'm always delighted by Alphabet Soup. He's a baddie, pretty small-time capers mostly, but he leaves behind some pretty funny gloat notes."

I looked at Commander Alpha's entry. It had his real identity: Tyler Royce, age thirty-eight. I knew that his power was superstrength, but I had no idea he'd acquired it in his midtwenties after an accident at a nuclear plant. There was a copy of his photo ID from the nuclear plant in the file, so I could see a picture of him from before the accident. He was skinny to the point of being scrawny, with thick-framed glasses from a time before they were worn by hipsters everywhere. The glasses didn't do a good job of hiding the bags under his eyes.

"His power is a weird mix of improvements and problems," Nate said. "The accident gave him all that strength, but it affected his speed. He can't run anymore, just this sort of speed-walking thing."

"That must suck," I said.

"The island is perfect to deter him," Nate said. "The guy can't stand water."

"Why?"

"Because he sinks like a stone. He discovered that by accident back when he was new, when he was in a fight on a pier. It broke, he sank, and he was fortunate enough to be close enough to shore to walk to the shallows so he could breathe again. I think it's related to how he can't run; he somehow got way more dense, much heavier than a normal person. The guy doesn't ever leave his own continent, because if he was in a plane going over the ocean and it crashed, he'd be toast."

"But wait . . . isn't commander a naval rank?"

"It sure is," Nate said with a grin. "The question is, did he choose the name for irony? Or is he just that dumb?"

"He's never seemed to have much of a sense of humor, let alone humorous irony."

"That's what I've always thought. If you go back before the accident, you can see that he was a janitor at that nuclear plant. We have his high school transcripts, and it's average all across the board. He was a scrawny, geeky kid. Not that there's anything wrong with that; I was one, and we have plenty of scrawny geeks here now."

"Yeah, but your scrawny geeks are doing amazing things in fields they love."

"True. His school records show he reported being bullied more than once. Once he got that superstrength, I'm not surprised that he turned into one of the biggest bullies of all. It's how he'd always been treated."

"But a bully that the world adores," I said. "That's so not right."

"It is what it is," he said. "It's what we have to work with, or work around, as the case may be."

I understood why the database had to be kept secret, but I worried about what it could be used for. "This thing is really, really dangerous. You could take down the supers with it."

"Well, sort of. First, we'd have to analyze their powers to expose a weakness. Then we'd have to develop a manner of attacking that weakness. Multiply that by the tens of thousands of people in the database, and you've got way more work than I'd ever want to do. Besides which, we don't want to take them down. In a perfect-world scenario, all I want is for them to leave us alone."

"Which, of course, they'll never do."

"So we have to be prepared for them. What is that sports metaphor? The best defense is a good offense? Or maybe it's the other way around. Either way, we keep this information not to attack them but to protect ourselves against them."

I learned a few facts about some of the other major players in the Ultimate Faction, as well as some of the other American groups.

Nate also showed me some of his favorite entries out of the tens of thousands in the database, including ROFL, a guy based out of New York who called himself a villain but mostly just threw cream pies in the faces of all the supers he could.

"Doesn't ROFL stand for 'rolling on floor, laughing'?" I asked.

"He pronounces it 'roffle,' and his whole point is to make laughingstocks of the supers."

"Whatever floats your boat, I guess."

"There are weirder ones in here, believe me."

"Do they have a database like this?" I asked. "The Ultimate Faction, or any of the other super groups? Do you think they know just as much about you as you do about them?"

"I don't think so," Nate said. "If they knew about me, wouldn't they have moved against the Hart Corporation? Maybe they've tried to find out, but we've been very cautious since the beginning. Probably overly cautious, but it's what keeps us safe. Layers of shell companies, false fronts, and a stack of lawyers behind that."

I was passed off to others in the afternoon for more education, but after going back to my apartment for a shower, I met up with Nate for dinner in the food court. Evie joined us, telling us bawdy jokes in her charming English accent. There was time for leisure, too—after dinner we went down to the small bowling alley. Halfway through our second game, I saw Elliot come in—his tall, thin frame and bald head were hard to miss. He looked around, spotted us, and made a beeline to our lane.

As he got closer, I saw that his forehead was crinkled with worry. He came around between me and Nate and leaned down between us. His voice low, he said, "I'm pretty sure I have an answer about our mole problem."

EIGHTEEN

Nate pinged everyone else to meet in his apartment in fifteen minutes. He and Evie and I changed our shoes quickly, then went upstairs with Elliot in tow. Scar and Jin showed up quickly, followed by Rupert and Oscar. The eight of us went into Nate's spare bedroom and sat around the table.

Nate cut right to the chase. "Elliot says he's figured out our mole." We all turned to Elliot.

"It's all my fault," Elliot said, his chin almost quivering. "I'm so sorry, everyone."

Rupert put his hand on Elliot's shoulder. "My friend, whatever it is, we'll deal with it. Together."

"As long as *you're* not the mole, you're not to blame," Nate said.

"Still," Elliot said. He pulled out a handkerchief and wiped his face. "Okay. So I figured I'd check into my team but that I should also check into who's closest to me. Besides all of you."

"Makes sense," Rupert said.

"I was over at Tammy Archer's apartment. Evie, you know her; she's part of your team."

"That she is," Evie said, starting to frown. "Go on."

"I sat down on her couch and felt something fall out of my pocket. It was an empty vial; I'd put a few in my pocket earlier when I was working on a project. I waited until Tammy went into the bathroom before I went digging around under her sofa cushions. And underneath, I found a tape recorder and a bunch of tapes."

Elliot pulled a microcassette recorder out of his pocket and set it down on the table.

"What was she recording?" Rupert asked.

"Me," Elliot said. "While I slept."

"She got into your apartment somehow?" Jin asked.

"No, I've slept over there," Elliot said, his brown skin flushing with pink.

Evie picked up the recorder and turned it over in her hands. "Brilliant," she said. "None of our regular sweeps for bugs or transmitters or digital devices would have found this; it's so perfectly clunky and archaic."

"I thought you were seeing Cathy, from Jin's team," Rupert said to Elliot.

"I am," Elliot said. "We're not exclusive, though."

"So what's on the tape?" Nate asked. Evie hit the play button, and we heard mostly silence, punctuated with the occasional snort and sniffle. Then a single muttered word: *Griffith.*

Elliot put his head down on the table.

The soundtrack of Elliot sleeping continued on with some heavy breathing. "Is that it?" Nate asked.

"Isn't that enough?" Elliot wailed. "I've been talking in my sleep! Giving up secrets to the enemy!"

"It's *one word*, you big lummox," Evie said, pressing the stop button on the recorder. "Anyone could slip up with that, even while awake."

Rupert handed Elliot a fresh handkerchief. "You'd think I'd be the dramatic one in this friendship," he said.

"Did you get the rest of the tapes?" Nate asked.

Elliot sniffed. "I got a couple of them, but I could feel more under the cushion."

Nate looked at Scar. "Take Oscar, go down, and see what you can find. If Tammy is there, take her to 463."

Scar and Oscar got up and left the apartment.

"What's 463?" I asked. It was probably a secret torture room. Or a cell in the supersecret prison I hadn't been shown yet. Or some weird experiment. Whatever it was, I hoped it wouldn't make me regret the choice to join the team.

"The room next door," Nate said.

Right. His apartment was 465.

Jin turned to me. "The room next to this one is used mostly for storage, mainly so that we could have a little extra buffer of privacy for our meetings here."

Okay, that was good. "What are you going to do with her?"

"Ask her some questions," Jin said. "Maybe make a few threats."

"And then?"

"We'll probably kick her off the island."

"That's it?" I asked. "That's all?"

"What, you want us to torture her?" Nate asked. "Besides the fact that torture is notoriously unreliable, we don't operate that way."

"Kicking her out is worse than torture anyway," Evie said. "We'll blindfold her for transport out, the same way everyone comes in. That keeps her from knowing our location. I'll scrub her records with various government agencies, but not completely. She'll technically still exist, but in a fairly poor state. No credit cards, no work history, no place to live."

"And don't forget the threat of being watched for the rest of her life, because a team of bloodthirsty lawyers will always be prepared to storm down on her if she ever says anything about anything to anybody," Nate added.

"Okay," I said. "You're right; that's pretty harsh."

Nate turned to Evie. "How long ago did she join your team? Four or five months?"

"Around that," Evie said. "Passed all her background checks, so either this opportunity was presented to her after she arrived or she was well prepared by someone who at least knows something about our organization."

"I'd hate to think it's the first, but we have to keep an eye out for it. For now, let's pursue the second. Former employee? An enemy who knows too much?" Nate looked around at the five rest of us. Elliot had dried his eyes and blown his nose, but his face was still blotchy. Evie and Jin both had scowls on their faces. Rupert just looked concerned for his best friend, rubbing Elliot's back.

Scar and Oscar came back into Nate's apartment. "She's next door," Scar said. "Well secured."

Oscar pulled a stack of microcassettes out of his pocket and spilled them on the table. There were at least a dozen, all labeled the same way: the letter *E* and a date.

Evie stacked up the cassettes. "I'd like to run the audio on these through some of my systems, to see if there's anything else on them besides the occasional word. We can get an idea of how much she's been able to figure out."

"Good," Nate said. Evie scooped up the stack of tapes, grabbed the recorder, and left for her computer lab.

"We're going to my apartment," Rupert told Elliot, "and you're going to have some whiskey." Elliot nodded. They left together, Rupert with his arm around his friend.

"Will he be okay?" I asked.

"He'll be crushed with guilt for a while, I bet," Oscar said. "I can't wait to rub it in."

"Ladies and gentlemen," Nate said, "I believe we have a date with Tammy."

* * *

Scar and Oscar went into room 463 first. They turned Tammy's chair around to face the back wall, and in doing so turned Tammy, since she was tied firmly to the chair. Then, for good measure, they put a blindfold on her. Nate, Jin, and I went into the room and stood behind Tammy.

"Sensory deprivation," whispered Nate. "Makes people panic, say things they shouldn't."

Tammy, a petite blonde who vaguely reminded me of Amy at WonderPop, twisted her head around. "Who's there?" she asked.

"A number of interested parties," Scar said. "We know about the tape recorder, and that you've been passing information about this organization off the island."

"I don't know what you're talking about," Tammy Said.

"Don't you? I don't think that's quite true," Scar said. He reached forward and pinched her upper arm.

"*Ow!* What was that?" Tammy shouted.

"A combination of scopolamine, sodium thiopental, and three-quinuclidinyl benzilate," Scar said, the complicated words rolling off his tongue. "You're familiar with our biology and chemistry labs, I'm sure. They've worked up a doozy of a truth serum."

I looked at Nate, who looked amused. What the hell?

"It'll take hold in just a couple of minutes," Scar said. "So why not relax and just tell us what we want to know?"

Tammy struggled against her restraints, clearly eager to get out of the chair, the room, and our company.

Nate pulled me back toward the door. "All of those ingredients are real things," he whispered, "and have been tried in truth serums before. Sadly, we've yet to actually develop one that works worth a damn. On the plus side, the placebo effect *is* real, and we've found it to be quite effective."

"So just because she *thinks* she's been given a truth serum, she'll tell the truth?" I whispered back.

"That, and a couple of other techniques," Nate said.

Tammy twisted more in her chair, moving her blindfolded face back and forth. "I can hear you whispering back there! I know someone is back there!"

"Don't worry about them," Oscar said in a strangely soft voice as he leaned down and stroked Tammy's forearm with one finger. "Just concentrate on the feeling of the drugs in your system. They're making you feel heavy all over. Very heavy." He kept running his finger down her forearm. "Even heavier now.

You can barely keep your head up it's so heavy. Your entire body is full of a great weight, pulling you down into your chair."

"Hypnosis technique," whispered Nate. "I love this part."

"Heavy," Tammy said, ceasing to struggle and sinking down into her chair.

"That's right," Oscar said. "You're so very heavy right now. Do you know what's weighing you down?"

"What?" Tammy asked, sounding as if she herself was talking in her sleep.

"Lies," Oscar said softly. "But if you tell the truth, you'll get lighter and lighter."

"Lies," echoed Tammy. "Lighter."

"You want to be lighter, don't you?"

"Yes," she said. "Feel so heavy."

"All right," Oscar said. "Why do you have the tape recorder?"

"Find out information," Tammy muttered. "Bring down Doctor Oracle."

"What do you do with the information when you have it?"

"I tell it to *her*," Tammy said. She shuddered. Clearly, she wasn't a fan of the 'her' she was giving the information to.

"How do you tell her?"

"Helicopter radio," Tammy said. "Late at night. One two five, six five zero."

"What are those numbers, Tammy?" Oscar asked, still gently stroking her arm.

"Radio frequency," she said. "Call at three thirty on Thursdays. Pass along all information, even just overheard words. Said she could figure it out."

"Does she know who you were recording? How you found out information?"

"Never told her," Tammy said. "Didn't want her to know about Elliot. He's too nice."

Nate, Scar, and Oscar all exchanged glances over the top of Tammy's blindfolded head. Everyone looked serious.

Scar knelt down in front of Tammy. "Tammy, do you know who she is?"

Tammy cringed even farther down into her chair. "No," she said. "Don't want to know. Didn't see her face. Mean. Freesia. Said she'd hurt Momma."

Oscar scowled. "She threatened your mother?"

"Can't let her hurt Momma. Said she'd find me anywhere. Said she'd be watching Momma."

The guys exchanged another series of glances, and all ended up nodding. Oscar stroked Tammy's arm some more. "Tammy, you've told us a lot of good things. A lot of truth. Can you feel the lies leaving you? Can you feel the heaviness leaving?"

"Less heavy," Tammy said. "Good."

"You're so much lighter now," Oscar said. "So much lighter you could just float off to sleep. A wonderful sleep, full of wonderful dreams."

"Dreams," Tammy sighed. She wasn't as squashed down into the chair now. Her head nodded off to the side. In a few moments, her breathing evened out. We all tiptoed out of the room, locked the door, and went back to Nate's apartment.

"Well, I don't know about you guys, but I don't feel especially good about scrubbing her records and dumping her off in the middle of nowhere," Nate said.

"No," Oscar said. "Whoever she's reporting to is clearly a nasty piece of work. Threatening someone's mother," he said, shaking his head with a frown.

"So we know it's a she, and whoever she is, she's not afraid to go after someone's mom," Jin said. "And something about freesia."

"What the heck is a freesia?" Oscar asked.

"It's a flower," I said. "Or a family of flowers." Everyone looked at me. "What? It was my mother's favorite perfume. I didn't care for it myself, but I smelled it all throughout my childhood."

"So maybe that's a perfume our mystery woman wears," Jin said. "Would you know it if you smelled it again?"

"I'm pretty sure," I said. "It's been a lot of years, but I bet it would come back to me if I smelled it."

"Scar," Nate said, "hop down to the office and get all of Tammy's background information you can, will you? I want to find her mother. Her weekly call back to this mystery woman isn't until Thursday, which gives us a couple of days."

"Got it," Scar said. He hustled out of the apartment.

"Oscar, Jin, please conduct a thorough search of Tammy's apartment; then take her back there and lock it down. She'll be on house arrest until we can get her out of here. If we can find her mother, we'll relocate them both with new identities. I'm sure Tammy will prefer that to having her ID scrubbed and being dumped. We'll discuss all that with her when she wakes up."

Oscar and Jin left the apartment, and it was down to just me and Nate.

"How did Oscar know all that hypnosis stuff?" I asked.

"He also does close-up magic," Nate said. "His grandfather was one of the greats, I guess. Wrote the book on marking cards."

"Wow."

"Yeah, he's taught me a couple of card tricks, but I don't really have the knack. Or the willingness to put in all of the practice hours, to be honest."

"So what happens now?" I asked.

"If we find her mother, we relocate them both, just like I said. Clearly there's someone here who isn't playing by the rules."

"There are rules?" I asked, incredulous.

"Well, more guidelines than anything else. An unwritten code. Even with the Ultimate Faction, and all of the other squadrons and corps and groups. You don't mess with someone's family."

"Maybe it isn't any of the supers, then," I said.

Nate ran his hands through his hair. "Maybe not, and that doubles our suspects to search. But at least since it's a woman, that cuts things down a lot."

"Unless the woman is just a middleman."

"It's possible, but I don't think so. Tammy had such a negative reaction to just mentioning the woman. I can't imagine a hired hand inspiring that kind of revulsion."

I sighed. "This is kind of more intense than I was thinking it would be."

Nate shook his head. "This will work itself out. It's not that big a deal in the grand scheme of things. And if she hasn't passed on too much information, we can carry on with the plans we have on the drawing board."

"Something big?" I asked.

"Big, beautiful, and more powerful than you can imagine."

NINETEEN

Nate worked on putting together the details of the next big job over a couple of days, while I continued learning everything I could from the team. I was kept in the loop on everything; I found out that Tammy's mother was found in New Mexico, Tammy was shipped off the island, and both of them were relocated across the country with new identities, histories, and small but sufficient bank accounts. I heard that Tammy wept with joy when they told her that she wasn't going to be given the scrub-and-dump treatment.

Everyone put out feelers to try and find the mystery woman Tammy was feeding the information to, but everyone came up empty. All we had to go on was that she was a mean woman with questionable taste in perfume. There were at least a hundred women in the database of supers who were tagged with *anger*, *cruelty*, or *hate*.

Two nights after the emergency meeting, we reassembled in Nate's apartment. The furniture had been rearranged so that everything faced the television on the wall, and a couple of extra chairs had been brought out from the conference room. Rupert brought up pizzas from the food court; armed with slices and glasses of wine, we settled in for the presentation. I'm not going to lie: I was pretty excited to be participating in my first planning session.

Nate plugged a portable USB drive into the side of his TV and used the remote control to flip through the material on the drive, like a slide show.

"So, here's the latest thing," Nate said. He looked at me, and I figured there was probably going to be a good deal of recap for the others. I was glad he explained everything from the beginning for my sake. "About a half dozen team members from small mechanicals—the tech and gadgets guys—along with some computer techs have been working together on a new source of energy."

He hit the button on the remote control, and what looked like a golf ball appeared. He clicked through a couple more pictures, one showing that the golf-ball-looking thing was actually larger than a beach ball, the next with the top half of the ball removed.

"The team has been working with diamonds and lasers, which I'm sure is oversimplifying to the extreme."

"Simple but true," Jin said, whose mechanical team was involved.

"Allow me to give Sarah my layman's understanding of the project," Nate said. "They're shooting a laser beam, which emits a certain amount of energy, into a diamond. The carbon structure of the diamond, as well as the particular way it's been cut, causes the beam to refract out into multiple beams. Each of those resulting beams is less powerful than the original, but when you add all of them up together, they're outputting ten times more energy than the original beam is using. Right so far?"

"Exactly," Jin said. "The sphere on the outside is a collector, which channels the resulting energy into our power system. We're already lighting a portion of our offices with the small diamond we've been working with. An even larger diamond would create even more energy. Given a large enough diamond, we could power the entire island. No more generators, so no more need to ship in all that fuel. We'd be far more self-sufficient than we are now. We'd have an endless store of energy."

I tentatively raised my hand.

Nate grinned. "Sarah, you have a question?"

"Yeah. Um . . . what about solar power? Or wind power? Aren't those options?"

"Good questions," Nate said. "Wind power is out, though we've tried it. It's just not windy enough here. We get the tropical breezes, but not the rip-roaring constant wind like you see in the valleys where they use turbines. As for solar, we do use some here, and it helps keep our fuel costs down. There are a couple of problems with solar power, though. First, we'd need way more panels than we have now, and we already have a number of them on the roofs of our buildings. We're trying to keep a low profile, so it'd be odd to have huge fields of solar panels where any satellite or airplane flying overhead could see them. Second, solar panels are manufactured with mercury and lead, toxic chemicals we don't necessarily want a lot of here on the island. Third, we have a *lot* of people who prefer to work at night. Which would mean that we'd have to get a huge pile of batteries to store power so we could run whatever we needed to without worrying about running out of juice."

"Imagine ten thousand solar panels," Jin said. "Now imagine that you could make more power with one sphere, small enough to be carried by one person."

"Okay," I said. "Makes sense."

"Good thoughts, though," Jin said. "We've tried a bunch of different things, and this is definitely the best thing we've ever come up with. I'm just tickled with the whole project, for more than one reason."

Nate hit the button on the remote, and a picture of a black, shiny gemstone popped up on the screen. He motioned to Jin to continue.

"Here's the diamond that we've had the best luck with so far," Jin said. "Carbonado, commonly known as the black diamond. We've tried clear diamonds, as well as other colors, but the black diamond won out over all the rest. It's the toughest form of natural diamond, so it holds up exponentially longer. You'd think that the dark color would create less laser light, but that was offset by the unusual clarity of black diamonds. With fewer flaws, less power is lost, and the end result was an overall gain."

Another picture flashed on the screen, of a black diamond on a red velvet stand. It looked like it had about a thousand facets.

"This," Nate said, "is the Midnight Star. She's a hundred-and-seventy-three-carat black diamond, cut from the Espantoso Diamond, which was found in Brazil in 1958. This is the largest stone that came from Espantoso. They used the Princess one forty-four cut, one of the modified brilliant cuts, which means there are a hundred and forty-four facets. The more facets, the more energy can be refracted out."

"How big is a hundred and seventy-three carats?" I asked.

"About the size of a baseball," Nate said. "It would fit in the palm of your hand, but I'd probably carry it with two."

"Although if you dropped it on your foot, I'd be more worried about your foot than the diamond," Jin said.

"So where is this Midnight Star?" Oscar asked. "How do we get it?"

"That's the best part," Nate said. He hit the button on the remote, and a picture of a building came up. It was like a castle and a house had a baby, and that baby was *huge*. Upon seeing it, several members of the team started laughing.

"This," Nate said, "is Sedgewick Manor. Home of one Melinda Sedgewick, owner of the Midnight Star."

Scar noticed my puzzled expression as I watched everyone else giggle. He put his hand on my arm. "Melinda Sedgewick is the Green Lady."

Of all people, we were going to go after a member of the Ultimate Faction.

The Green Lady, whom I now knew was Melinda Sedgewick when she was at home, was one of the oldest members of the Faction. I'd have to look her up on the database after the meeting for more details, but from what I could recall, she was probably midfifties or so, elegant as hell, and just green enough to let you know that she probably wasn't human. I recalled that her powers were related to plants. Or something like that.

"She keeps the diamond at Sedgewick Manor, in a trophy room," Nate said. "There are apparently a lot of other beautiful works of art there, too. The woman is rich, even richer than we are."

"She's bound to have a good security system," Evie said. "I'll start researching."

Oscar chimed in. "I bet there are plans and blueprints for the house somewhere. I'll try to find out what we're looking at having to climb."

"We'll be able to check the place out from the inside," Nate said.

"That'll be a neat trick," Oscar said. "How do you plan on doing that?"

"Easy. She's hosting a charity ball in two weeks. I can get an alter ego on that guest list, in order to case the place."

Rupert said, "Patron of the arts? Benevolent giver to charity? I've been working on just the thing."

"Perfect," Nate said. He turned to me. "How about it, Sarah? Want to go to a fancy party?"

"Who, me?" I asked. "I . . . Not only am I probably not ready, wouldn't you rather take Jin? I bet she has way more experience."

"I'll be the driver," Jin said, grinning at me. "I can't stand crowds, and that goes double for snooty crowds. Not to mention, they always serve lobster and shrimp at these kind of things, and I have a shellfish allergy."

"Nate," I said, feeling my heart rate speed up, "seriously. I'm not ready." I felt a little clammy and sweaty.

"You'll be fine," he said. "Don't worry. We'll go out for a practice run beforehand."

"Practicing what?"

"Being someone else," he said. "I know just who to bother for a ticket to that party."

* * *

The next week passed far too fast. Rupert fit me in a number of wigs, and tried out some interesting fake noses and chins. We worked on various accents and came up with a persona for my practice run. Though I didn't know what exactly that run would entail.

I continued training with everyone, while they all also did their research on the Green Lady's house. Evie came up with some details about the security system but wanted us to get eyes on certain things to make sure that any plan she came up with was accurate. Oscar found blueprints of the house in the city planning office but was also suspicious that there might have been unexpected changes during construction.

They were all overly cautious, which should have made me less nervous. It didn't, though.

A week before Melinda's party, it was time for the test run. Nate pinged me to meet him in Rupert's studio at five in the afternoon so I could get in disguise.

I walked in to find Nate already in Rupert's makeup chair, the famous scar halfway done on his forehead. There was a second chair waiting for me next to him.

"We'll need about two hours here," Nate said. "We'll meet Jin at the plane. The flight is a little over two hours, so we'll be showing up around nine thirty."

"Showing up where?" I asked.

Nate grinned. "The most wretched hive of scum and villainy."

TWENTY

Jin dropped us off in front of Chalmun's nightclub, then drove off to find parking a few blocks away. We were in an industrial area in the outskirts of Los Angeles, full of worn-down brick buildings and equally worn-down warehouses.

Nate and I stood on the otherwise deserted street, looking up at the neon sign over the front door. He was wearing his full Doctor Oracle costume, complete with nose, chin, scar on his forehead, and the neat little chin beard pasted under his mouth. It added to the slightly sinister air. He wore his own hair, but rumpled and spiked with various hair gels and mousses. His white lab coat, black gloves, and black mask completed the look.

I was wearing a new costume Rupert had come up with just for the occasion. A long blond wig, pinned to my head tightly enough that it was more than a little itchy, with a blue mask. My outfit was a matching blue and silver. "I thought about a red theme but figured with a name like Valentine, that might be a bit too on the nose," he'd told me.

At least the outfit had a skirt over leggings instead of being skintight over my whole body. I was uncomfortable enough as it was. I wore a pair of surprisingly cushy silver knee-high boots, and had silver gloves on. My orange ChatterBox was back home, since it clashed with the outfit; I'd been given a new blue one, which was only connected to the ones Nate and Jin were currently wearing. I was used to the stupid thing already; the familiar weight on my wrist was comforting.

We both wore full-length black hooded cloaks over our outfits, which was apparently one of the requirements in order to visit the club. That way, even if someone was keeping an eye on the door, they wouldn't know who exactly was on their way in.

Nate nodded at the doorman and pulled his hood back just far enough to show his mask and fake scar. The doorman practically bowed and ran to open the door for us. I worked on making sure I stood up straight and proud, because anyone who walked anywhere openly with the great Doctor Oracle was probably a pretty big deal.

The absurdity of the situation relaxed me a little. I had Nate with me, so how bad could it be?

We dropped off our cloaks at a little coatroom just inside the front door. We were each given a claim check, but looking at the collection of plain black hooded cloaks hanging up behind the counter, I figured they probably could have just heaped them all in a pile, then given everyone a random one on the way out. The last step was a trip through some sort of metal detector to check for weapons, then we were in.

The main room was large and open. It wasn't overcrowded, which was a blessing. There was a huge first floor, then a balcony running around three of the interior walls. People were mingling everywhere, and a number of them were shaking their booties out on the dance floor. Almost everyone in the room was wearing a costume with a mask, which helped boost my confidence a little more. We weren't the only ones hiding our identities, so we didn't stand out at all.

Nate got a variety of reactions from other people as we passed—mostly nods and handshakes, but there were a couple of glares here and there. He led me straight out onto the dance floor, in front of a four-piece band doing surprisingly good renditions of hits from the '80s. He pulled me close as we danced.

"It's all baddies here," he said. "Villains, madmen, or people just angry at the world. This club has moved around a number of times, but it's been at this location for a couple of years. I guess since the supers never quite know who will be here on a given night, it's not worth staking out or raiding the place. As you've seen from the database, the vast majority of the bad guys are harmless small potatoes."

"Charming," I said. "Seems like the folks here either love you or hate you."

"Weeeeell, I've stolen things out from under a couple of people's noses. Some guys get a little bent out of shape."

The song changed, and we started dancing even slower.

"How many exits do you see?" Nate asked. We danced a full turn so I could scope out the room.

"At least three on this floor," I said. "The front door where we came in. The kitchen, which is bound to have access to the outside so that things can get delivered without bringing them through the main room. And there's an emergency-exit sign over the restrooms, so there must be a way out back there. I see a couple of other doors, but I'm not sure about them."

"Good," Nate said. "Anything upstairs?"

"There are a bunch of windows up there, which are likely. If there's furniture to climb on, we could escape that way, too."

He spun me around so I was facing a red door next to the stage. "The red door leads to the owner's office, and there's a secret passageway out through there. You twist the model of the *Millennium Falcon* on its base to get the door to open."

I chuckled. "No wonder you called this place a wretched hive of scum and villainy. Is Chalmun the owner? Sounds like he's a fan of *Star Wars*."

"More than you think," he said. "The owner's name is Jimmy. Chalmun's is actually the name of the Mos Eisley cantina where Luke and Obi-Wan meet Han Solo for the first time."

"And I thought I was a geek. I've never heard that one before."

The song finished, and Nate led me to the bar. He ordered a club soda with lime for each of us. It looked like we were drinking, but we stayed sober and alert. We wandered over to a corner, Nate getting more handshakes, fist bumps, and a couple of additional glares along the way. Nobody dared to ask him who I was, which was nice.

"Keep your eyes peeled. Our guy will be wearing purple with lightning bolts," he said. We stood in our corner, sipping club soda and watching the room.

"Sounds hard to miss," I said. He'd laid out the plan on our plane ride out. It seemed simple enough: meet up with his contact, exchange the invitation for a small envelope containing a medium number of large-denomination bills, then meet up with Jin, who was parked a few blocks away.

Nate suddenly turned around so that his back faced the room. Which I thought was a terrible move, considering the fact that several people in the room probably wanted to injure him. One of the first things Oscar taught me was to never turn my back on an enemy.

"What the hell is wrong with you?" I whispered.

"There's a woman in red over by the bathrooms," he said.

I saw her immediately, because it was hard not to. She had long, curly red hair and wore a skintight metallic-red bodysuit. Which, of course, showed off a nearly perfect body. She had an equally red phone in her hands and was tapping away on the screen with both thumbs.

"I see her. What's up?"

He glanced over at me. "We . . . uh . . . went out a couple of times."

I snorted. "So you don't want the ex to see you here with someone else?"

"I don't want her to see me here, full stop. She's both crazy and evil, probably about a fifty-fifty split."

"Just your type, then."

"Sarah, it was just a couple of dates. Years ago. As soon as I figured out how nuts she was, I was out of there. But every time I see her, she acts like we're still together. It adds creepy into the crazy-evil mix."

"Perfect," I said. I looked around the room. "Just your luck, our guy just came in the front door."

Nate looked over and breathed out a sigh of relief. "Stay here; I'll go get this done." He stuck to the outside of the room, trying to keep as many people as possible between him and the woman in red. I watched him greet the man in purple, and they walked together to the opposite corner of the room. I tried to see what they were doing, but there were too many people in between.

I turned back toward the bar and let out a squeak, because the woman in red was standing in front of me. She just looked at me silently, her head cocked slightly to the side.

"Um . . . hi there," I said.

She continued to look at me, openly checking me out from head to toe. With nothing better to do, I checked her out right back. She had a perfect face of makeup, from the black-lined eyes to smooth, flawless skin, to bright red lipstick; she was one of the few people in the club not wearing a mask, but maybe the makeup was all the mask she needed. She was utterly beautiful but looked mean as a snake. She had what Amy at WonderPop always referred to as "bitch face," a permanent sneering look that made her appear as if nothing in the world could ever make her happy.

"Nice night, huh?" I asked.

She looked me in the eye, and her face got even meaner looking. I didn't think it was possible.

"So," she said.

"Yeah?" I said.

"New girl."

"Um . . . yeah, pretty new." Best to stick with the truth as much as possible.

"Who do you think you are?"

"I beg your pardon?"

"Waltzing in here on Doctor Oracle's arm, nose in the air like you own the place. And nobody here has ever seen you before. So what I want to know is, who the *hell* do you think you are?"

"Um . . ." I certainly didn't want to give this woman my name. "Amy?"

"Well, *Amy*," she hissed, "I don't like you."

Somehow, I doubted that she realized she'd made a *Star Wars* reference.

"That's a shame," I said. I'd knuckled under to enough mean girls in school; I didn't need to do it here.

She stepped forward and got right up in my face. Her perfume was so strong, my nose tickled with an oncoming sneeze. I sniffed it back and got another strong whiff of her perfume.

"What's a shame," she said, "is how your ugly little face is going to get even uglier when I'm done with you."

"I think what's really ugly here is your attitude, Cat," Nate said. We both turned to find him standing next to us.

She stepped back away from me, and I was able to breathe again. She ran her hand up Nate's arm. "Jeremy," she purred, "I was just letting your new little friend here know that you and I were an item."

He looked at me, and I raised one eyebrow at him. *Jeremy?*

"Cat, we're not an item. I haven't even seen you for six months."

"Absence makes the heart grow fonder," she said.

"Highly doubtful," he said. "I'd advise you to walk away, Cat. You don't want to mess with us."

Her face twisted into a sneer. "I'll do what I want, when I want. And if what I want is to mess with little *Amy* here, then that's just what I'll do."

"So should I go get Jimmy? And tell him you're threatening *my* friend, in *his* club?"

She stepped back again. "Fine, you bastard. Have it your way." She turned back to me and jabbed a finger at me. "We're not through, you and me." She stalked away to the bar, hopefully to find someone else to beat up.

"Wow. What was that?" I asked.

"So, that's Catalyst. Charming, isn't she?"

"Does she have an actual name?"

"Catherine, which makes Cat a good all-purpose nickname."

"Are you sure that's her real name, *Jeremy*?" I asked.

"Come on, *Amy*. Like I'm going to give out my real identity to anyone here, dating or not."

I linked my arm through his. "I feel special, then. I'm the only one here who knows who you really are."

"Too true," he said.

I felt a tickle in my nose and turned away to finally let out the sneeze that I'd bottled up before.

"Bless you," Nate said.

"Thanks," I said. "Her perfume was . . ." Now that my brain was no longer tied up in the potential fight-or-flight situation of someone in my face threatening to beat me black and blue, it was able to take that cloying, sweet perfume and run it through my mental database of scents. I sucked in a breath.

"What?"

"Freesia," I whispered. I turned to him and grabbed his arm tighter. "Nate, she was wearing freesia, I'd swear it."

Nate started looking around, checking out the room again. Everything looked normal. Well, at least as normal as a room full of people in full costume can look. It was like a perfectly ordinary sci-fi convention but with far fewer duplicate outfits.

"We better get out of here," he said. "The deal is done; I have the invitation."

"Good call," I said. We turned toward the front door, just as it was torn off its hinges.

TWENTY-ONE

We didn't wait around to see who was coming through the front door. Nate grabbed my hand and pulled me around the outside of the room toward the red office door next to the stage. People were screaming and panicking all around, which was a helpful distraction. I saw a few people head into the kitchen and a few more going down the hallway to the bathroom. But it appeared that most of the guests at Chalmun's that night hadn't bothered to look around to spot all their exits.

It was a nice reminder that I was working with a real professional.

We made it to the red door, and Nate pushed it open. He ushered me through, closed the door, and turned the flimsy lock on the doorknob.

The owner's office was an amazing homage to sci-fi. A variety of memorabilia spanning decades sat on shelves, hung from the ceiling, was framed on the walls, and there were a number of tchotchkes on the big desk in the corner. A man with a huge red beard was getting up from behind that desk. He wore a light blue shirt, black pants, and wore a blue cape lined with a color that could be generously referred to as mustard. I guessed that this was Jimmy, the owner of the club, honoring his love of *Star Wars* by dressing like Lando Calrissian.

"Doc? What the hell is going on out there?" Jimmy asked.

"Well, you no longer have a front door," Nate said. "Looks like unwanted visitors have arrived."

"Damn it," Jimmy said. "Just when we got comfortable here, we'll have to move again."

"I'd recommend giving Catalyst a permanent ban from the new place."

Jimmy rolled his eyes. "What did she do now?"

"Called in the Ultimate Faction," Nate said. Jimmy's expression went from exasperation to fear.

"Are you kidding? Ultimate Faction is here? We're way out of their jurisdiction!"

"I'm pretty sure," Nate said. "My guess is Commander Alpha is the one doing the remodeling on your front door."

"Aw, crap," Jimmy said. He fetched an empty box with liquor brand logos on the sides and started placing his collectibles in it.

"Mind if we use the back way?" Nate asked.

"Be my guest. I'll be behind you shortly. Most of this stuff is replaceable, but I do have a few pretty rare items."

Nate walked over to a set of deep bookshelves and reached for a small model of the *Millennium Falcon*, mounted on a heavy black base. He gave it a gentle twist to the right, then turned it back again. The bookcase next to the one with the *Falcon* popped open.

"That reminds me," Nate said, "I was on a job and happened upon a mint-in-box Jawa with the vinyl cape."

"Are you kidding?" Jimmy said. "That's one of the rarest action figures around!"

"I know. It's yours. I'll bring it by when you relocate, because I totally owe you one."

Jimmy spared a moment of packing time to vigorously shake Nate's hand; then we slid through the passageway behind the bookcase. Nate hit a switch on the opposite side, and the bookcase closed behind us.

There wasn't much to see behind the bookcase—it was a tunnel made of concrete and lined with pipes and cables. Murky lights strung along the ceiling made things visible, but they were either too dark or too bright to make things attractive. We walked quickly through the tunnel, keeping silent because it seemed like the sensible thing. The whole experience was a little dirty and a lot sweaty, since we'd left the air-conditioning of the club behind.

The tunnel ended in a ladder, which led up about eight feet to a metal hatch. Nate went up first, unbolted the hatch, pushed it up a tiny bit, and peeked through. I couldn't see anything but darkness through the crack.

He looked from side to side, then gently closed the hatch, threw the bolt again, and came back down the ladder.

"Would you like the good news or the bad news?" he asked.

"Let's start with the good," I said.

"This hatch opens up in a pretty dark alley. We're at the far end. So we can get out and probably not be seen."

"That's it for the good news?"

"Yeah," he said. "As far as the bad news, there are two police cars at the open end of the alley. Besides them, I'm pretty sure I saw a super strutting around down there, but they passed by pretty quick."

"So we're trapped at the end of the alley."

"Looks like. Want to take a peek, see what you can see?"

"Hell yes," I said. I climbed the ladder, unlocked the hatch, and opened it just enough to get the lay of the land. It was exactly as Nate had described—we were at the closed end of an alley, and the police cars blocked the open end. The alley was a good fifty feet long, at least, and pitch dark on our end. At least nobody would see us coming out the hatch unless they were shining a light down the alley.

I looked to the left and right. There was a rickety fire escape on one of the buildings, but it looked solid enough to climb. Unfortunately, it was probably also rusty and would make a racket if we jumped up and pulled down the ladder leading to the first landing. There were a couple of garbage cans near the mouth of the alley, but neither was large enough to hide in.

I re-locked the hatch and went back down. "This is kind of grim," I said.

"Damn it, this was supposed to be an easy job," he said. "Okay. There's the fire escape, but I figure it'll make noise."

"Can you jump high enough to pull down the ladder?" I asked.

"Yeah," he said. "What are you thinking?"

"You're going out that way," I said.

He looked at me intently in the murky light of the tunnel. "And what way are you going out?"

"The front of the alley," I said.

"No."

"Nate."

"No, Sarah. We don't leave team members behind. We don't let team members get captured."

"Nate, think about it," I said. "They don't know I'm on the team, remember? They still think I was kidnapped."

He sat silently for a moment. "So you'd go out and . . . what, get rescued?"

"Exactly," I said. "I'll make some noise with the garbage cans so you can get the ladder down and climb out."

He thought about it for a while. Then thought about it for a while more. "Crap," he said. "I can't think of anything better. But this sucks. It's your first time out."

"I'll be fine," I said. "I'll probably be back in my apartment in a day or two. Then I can leave properly and formally, and you guys can come get me. Nobody will be the wiser."

He sighed and looked back up at the hatch. "Okay, hold on a minute." He went up the ladder, opened the hatch just wide enough to get his arm through, and pulled back a garbage bag. He brought it back down, backtracked a bit down the tunnel, and emptied out the trash.

He handed me the bag, and I held it as he pulled off his white jacket, revealing a black T-shirt underneath. Smart—it'd be much harder to see him without the bright white. He also pulled off his mask, prosthetic cheeks and chin, little beard, and he peeled the fake scar off his forehead. All of it went into the bag. If he got caught, nobody would know who he was.

I passed him the bag to hold and removed my wig. It was a shame to throw it in a garbage bag; it was truly beautiful. I tugged off the cap underneath that kept my own hair in check, and shook my head back and forth. There wasn't much that could be done about the outfit, but I thought I had a good plan to explain that. I took off my own mask and prosthetics and dumped them all in the garbage bag.

The last thing was my ChatterBox. I took it off and handed it to Nate, who put it in his pocket. I was sad to see the little guy go, but I certainly didn't want a direct line to Nate or Jin getting into the wrong hands.

I reached down to the floor of the tunnel, which was a little wet from seepage and a lot dirty, and picked up some mud. I smeared it in a couple of places on my face and put some in my hair for good measure. I artfully put some on the beautiful costume Rupert had made me, and with Nate's help, ripped a couple of holes in the outfit.

Nate went back up the ladder and opened the hatch, this time slipping through. He held it open just enough for me to crawl through. He quietly lowered the hatch back down, and we crouched in the dark corner of the alley, looking at the police cars.

"This is crazier than jobs usually are," he whispered.

"If only we hadn't run into your ex-girlfriend," I whispered back. "They're always a pain in the ass."

"You're telling me," he muttered. "And seriously, she wasn't my girlfriend."

"Semantics."

He got a serious look on his face. "Be careful. Don't trust anybody."

"I won't," I said. "Be safe. Get ready to pull that ladder down when I knock over the garbage cans."

"I will," he said.

His hair was a mess, he looked a little tired and a lot sweaty, and I was pretty sure right then that I was falling in love with him. I grabbed the front of his T-shirt, pulled him toward me, and kissed him.

I let him go and grabbed the garbage bag full of costumes, then crept toward the mouth of the alley. I didn't look back to see what he was doing; I knew he could take care of himself without my supervision. I got near the front of the alley, my back pressed hard against the brick wall. No streetlights were shining where I was, so the only light was the occasional blue and red flashing of the police lights. I quietly lifted the lid off the garbage can closest to me and buried the costumes deep down under whatever unseen and unmentionable things were in there.

I put the lid back on and crept past that garbage can. I plotted my trajectory so that I would push the garbage cans nearest to the mouth of the alley outward, so even if they turned on spotlights, the light would shine in a way that would still shield the fire escape at the far end of the alley.

I took a deep breath and made my move.

I stumbled into the cans, shoving them in front of me. The cans and their lids made a huge clattering noise when they hit the pavement. I staggered out into the street, taking the corner so that I was fully out of the alley and drawing all possible attention. Three police officers quickly drew their weapons and pointed them at me.

"Help me, please!" I said, throwing my hands up in the air. "Oh, thank goodness! I'm Sarah Valentine. I was kidnapped by Doctor Oracle—please help!"

The officers all holstered their weapons. Two of them ran to me, while another grabbed the radio in his patrol car. I looked around the street as I let my knees buckle, and allowed the men to catch me as I fell to the ground.

"I think he ran off down the street," I sobbed. "That way." I pointed in the direction away from the building that Nate was hopefully in the middle of climbing. One of my rescuing officers ran off down that way, while the other held on to me. The third finished on the radio and came over.

"You're safe now, miss," he said. Suddenly there was another person there with us, a younger man wearing a gold bodysuit. I recognized him as Action Alex, one of the members of the Ultimate Faction. I also knew, thanks to the database, that he was a junior member of the team and often ended up with the crap jobs.

"Miss Valentine," he said, "we're so glad you're all right. Commander Alpha will be here in a moment, but rest assured, you're safe with us."

"I'm sure I am," I said, my voice shuddering. "Anywhere away from that horrible Doctor Oracle has to be safe."

I felt the ground shake a little as Commander Alpha turned the corner down the block and slowly ran up to us. Yeesh, the guy really was surprisingly dense if he made the earth quake a little bit when he ran. And Nate had been right: it was really more of a fast duckwalk than a run. Poor guy.

"Miss Valentine," he said, "you're safe with us."

Did these guys have a script? I played along. "Thank you so much! It was horrible!"

"We're on the lookout for Oracle now," Alpha said. "He won't be able to get far."

One of the police officers went down the alleyway with a flashlight, then came back quickly. "Nobody down there," he said. I breathed a sigh of relief and disguised it as another sob.

"Take care of her," Alpha told the police officer who was already cradling me in his arms while kneeling on the hard pavement. "Alex, a moment?" They stepped off to the side.

I wept a little bit, and wiped the mud around on my face while I tried to listen in to their conversation. I heard "questions," then "safe." Alex said something, but I couldn't catch it. Alpha talked some more, and I heard something that sounded like "opportunity."

They both came back over. "We'll take care of you, Miss Valentine. We'll keep you safe." Alpha nodded at the kind police officer who was cradling me. The man got up off the pavement, and I saw that the knees of his uniform were a little shredded from the rough roadway.

He gently helped me up, and another of the officers brought a rough brown blanket from the trunk of one of their patrol cars and draped it over my shoulders, even though it wasn't cold out. I guess it was to help me with the chills from shock.

A van pulled up alongside the police cars. It was sleek and white, and it had a huge Ultimate Faction logo on the side, which was so obvious that it went around the horn to become arrogant. If you didn't think anyone could take you down, I guess there was no reason to operate in stealth.

I looked closer at the logo and realized that it wasn't painted on; it was on a big magnet. It wasn't even their own van; it was probably a rental, and they just slapped the logo on the side. But it still seemed nice, and fairly expensive.

The police officer helped me into the van; at least its seats were soft and smooth. For all I knew, they were upholstered with baby-seal pelts. After all I'd learned about the Ultimates, it wouldn't have really surprised me.

Action Alex leaned in. "We'll take care of you. You've had a hard night, Miss Valentine."

"I certainly have," I said.

"We'd love to have you talk to us about your experience, if you'd be willing. It might give us precious insight into Doctor Oracle's operation."

I was pretty sure they'd ask me about it even if I wasn't willing. I didn't want to make things easy for them, but I wanted to make things easy for *me*. Besides which, I still had the kidnap-victim role to play.

"I don't think I saw all that much," I said. "But I'm happy to help in any way I can."

"Wonderful," Alex said. "You must be thirsty after your ordeal."

"I guess so," I said. He handed me a small bottle of water. I opened it and took a drink. It tasted a little funny, like it was stale. Immediately after swallowing, I knew it was a mistake.

"We'll get you out of here to somewhere safe," said two guys in unison. They were both a little blurry, and they both looked like Action Alex. I blinked, and they morphed back into one, then split into two again. Everything got fuzzy; then everything got more blurry; then everything went dark.

TWENTY-TWO

I woke up slowly with a huge feeling of déjà vu, real thoughts slowly taking over from hazy and easily forgotten dream images. I stretched and lay in bed for a moment, my eyes still closed, knowing that something was strange and trying to figure out what it was

There was no sunlight coming into the room, for one thing. I couldn't smell the sea. And the sheets on the bed were decidedly cheap and coarse.

I opened my eyes and looked around. The room was definitely not my apartment with the beautiful beach view. But at least this time, I didn't have a headache from having been knocked unconscious by part of a building, and this time I knew exactly who my captors were. I also had a vague hungover feeling from whatever they'd put in that water.

I sat up in the bed and analyzed my surroundings. It was one of the most boring bedrooms I'd ever seen, and I've stayed at a number of cheap hotels on various vacations. White walls, white sheets and comforter on the narrow bed, and for variety, a boring brown dresser with matching nightstand. Unlike a cheap hotel, there were no thrift-shop paintings on the walls; they were completely blank. Everything felt cheap, but at least it was all clean. There was a single lamp on the dresser, casting its bland yellowish light over the room.

I pushed the covers aside and swung my legs over the side of the bed. Clearly someone had changed my clothes while I was unconscious—my mud-spattered costume was gone, and I was wearing a set of blue medical scrubs, so fresh out of the packaging that they still had wrinkles in a square pattern all over them. I started to wonder why everyone felt it necessary to drug me and change my clothes.

I pulled the elastic waistband out and checked. At least I was still wearing my own underwear.

There was one non-hotel thing in the room—a small camera up in one of the corners. Most of the camera was painted white, but I could still see the tiny black aperture. I hadn't been with the Oracle organization long, but even I knew that wasn't a good sign.

There was a pair of cheap hospital slippers on the floor, so I slid my feet into them. I shuffled out of the tiny bedroom and found a half bathroom next door—just a toilet and a sink. At least I couldn't see any cameras.

I looked at myself in the mirror. My face had been wiped fairly clean, but there was still mud dried in my hair. Once business in there was taken care of, I went to see the rest of my new (hopefully temporary) accommodations.

A short hall led from the bedroom and bathroom to a very small living area, just large enough for a couch, a TV, and a small table and chair. No kitchen, no fridge. It really was like an ultracheap motel room, just with a separate bedroom. Two tiny cameras were up in opposite corners, to get a full view of the room. There was one more door, which I assumed led outside. It had a small mirror in the middle, at just about eye height. I'd never seen a more obvious one-way window.

I tried the doorknob, knowing it would be locked. Then I pressed my face up to the mirrored glass and tried to shield my eyes from the light of the room. I thought I could maybe make out another door on the other side, which was strange. It was reassuring that I could see anything at all; clearly they'd cheaped out on their one-way glass the same way they'd taken the cheap road on everything else in the room.

Figuring *what the hell*, I knocked on the door. "Hello? Anyone there?" I called.

A few minutes later, I heard the sound of a door being unlocked, then opened. My door didn't budge. Then I heard the sound of a door closing and being locked again. A few heavy footsteps; then the doorknob on my door rattled as someone unlocked it from the outside. It opened, and I caught a fast glimpse of what lay beyond the door: a tiny room and another door, making a kind of airlock. I caught that glimpse around the bulky side of Commander Alpha, who swiftly shut the door behind him. It was unlocked, but I wouldn't get too far rushing it, since the outer door had been re-locked.

"Miss Valentine," he said, smiling in a way that was probably supposed to be charming and calming but totally wasn't. At least not to me. "You've had a very hard few weeks. Please, sit down."

"Where am I?" I asked.

"You're safe with us," he said. "The last thing we want is for Doctor Oracle to be able to get at you again."

"Oh," I said. I had to play the part here. "Good. He was a horrible, horrible man."

"I know," he said. He swept his hand toward the small sofa, and I took that as my cue to sit. He pulled the small chair out from the small table and turned it around so he could sit and face me. It creaked dangerously under his weight.

"But surely he wouldn't come back after me. I'm a nobody."

"Oh, on the contrary, Miss Valentine. It's entirely possible you saw things during your time in his captivity that could help us find him. Perhaps even something so small you didn't even really realize what you were looking at. That's why we'd like to ask you some questions while you're here."

"Of course," I said. "I'll help in any way I can to bring that monster to justice."

"So why don't we start at the beginning," he said. "When you were at—"

"Um," I interrupted. He jumped a little bit, and I realized that he was a man utterly unused to being interrupted. "I'd love to answer your questions, but I don't suppose we could actually start with something to eat? I'm starving. And I'd love a shower so I could wash this mud out of my hair." I held up a curl that was frozen in a perfect crusty brown circle. "I feel kind of gross, and there's no shower in this room."

I saw him clench his giant jaw, trying to swallow back his irritation, but it didn't work all that well. Clearly, this was a guy who got his own way all the time, but he realized that I could be a valuable resource.

"Yes, of course," he said. "I'll step out and get someone to take you to a shower, and have some food delivered here when you're done. Then we'll have quite a few questions to ask you."

"Great, thank you so much," I said. "I know I'll be treated well here." I gave him what I hoped was a grateful smile.

He got up off the small chair, and in my mind I heard it give a sigh of relief. He left, locked my door behind him; then I heard him unlock, open, close, and re-lock the far door. I wondered how long I'd have to wait.

Not very long, it turned out. A sullen-looking teenage girl came in next, after the whole locking/unlocking/relocking cycle. She had purple-dyed hair that was badly faded, wore a bright purple costume and a matching purple mask, and had a sneer on her face that could melt butter. She held open the door, waved her hand impatiently, and muttered, "After you, ma'am."

I opted to kill her with kindness. "Thank you so much," I said. "You're very kind. My name is Sarah; what's your name?"

Her sneer turned into an expression of confusion, as if she didn't know what to do with civility aimed at her. "Bethany," she said. Either she didn't have a made-up super name, or didn't care if I knew her real name. Or, she'd chosen Bethany as her super name, which struck me as both hilarious and sad.

"It's a pleasure to meet you, Bethany," I said. "I love your outfit; purple is the color of royalty, did you know?"

She looked even more confused. "No, I didn't," she said. She opened up the outer door.

I hesitated in the airlock, looking around it. "Are you sure it's safe to go out there?"

"No problem," Bethany said. "We're locked down pretty tight here."

Okay, so escape might not be all that easy. "Good," I said. "I'd hate for Doctor Oracle to try to grab me again." She led me out the door, and we walked down a long, straight hallway. Concrete walls, concrete floors, fluorescent panels in an industrial ceiling. A real cheery place. There were more doors along the hall, ones that looked like the outside of my airlock door. Was this a prison?

"He's not getting by me again," she said.

"You've fought with him before?" I asked. "No kidding! That's so brave!"

Bethany's confusion was slowly turning into boastful pride. "Almost had him, too. Him and some other guy."

"Did you see what he looked like? I never did get to see his face while I was his hostage."

"Ugh, no," she said. "Stupid mask. But I took a good slice out of him."

"A good slice?"

"Yeah," Bethany said. She stopped in the hall and turned toward me. She quickly flicked her hand, and her fingernails, which had been a normal length, shot out to be about a foot long.

"Holy crap," I said.

"Right? Pretty awesome," she said. She flicked her hand again, and the nails went right back to normal. At least now I knew how Nate's arm had been sliced right through his protective clothing.

"That's . . . amazing," I said. She turned and continued walking down the long hallway. "I bet you're one of the top heroes here, with a power like that."

She snorted. "You'd think, right? But no, they don't care how cool your powers are. All they care about is seniority. I could be able to fly and they'd still put me down here in the crappy dorms."

I didn't want to seem like I was asking too many questions, but it certainly sounded like this was the dormitory for the younger members of the Ultimate Faction. But why would there be extra security on the rooms? And why would there be cameras?

We turned the corner, then another corner, and went through a door into a big communal bathroom. Bethany flopped down into a cheap-looking folding chair in the corner and waved her hand toward some curtained areas. I peeked behind one of the curtains and found a private stall with a bench near the curtain and a showerhead on the far wall. A towel was folded on the bench, and I wasn't surprised that it was clean and white but not particularly fluffy or soft .

I went in, shucked my clothes and threw them on the bench, then turned on the shower and got scrubbing. There was a dispenser of thick orange liquid on the wall, which was my only source for both soap and shampoo. It did an adequate but not impressive job at both. I soaked my hair, trying to soften some of the harder clumps of mud. My hand ran into something solid, and I slowly pulled out a bobby pin.

Hallelujah. Thank you, Rupert, for overpinning that wig on.

I felt around and found a second one at the nape of my neck. I didn't want to take any chances, so I tucked them both in my mouth, pressing them against my cheek so I wouldn't swallow them. I lathered up my head a couple of times to get all the mud out; even though the soap wasn't great, I felt a hundred times cleaner.

I quickly dried off with the rough towel and put my own undergarments back on. I topped them with the same medical scrubs I'd worn in, since there didn't appear to be any other options. I took the bobby pins out of my mouth and put them in the tiny breast pocket of the scrubs.

I pushed the curtain back and found Bethany still slumped in the same position in her chair. She waved her hand toward the sinks, where I saw a new (cheap) toothbrush and a new (cheap) comb waiting for me. Clearly her talkative time was done. I brushed my teeth, combed my hair, and was ready to go back for whatever cheap, crappy food they had in this cheap, crappy place.

Bethany led me back down the hall and took me into my little room again. Lunch had been delivered while I was away—there was a wrapped sandwich, a bag of potato chips, and a bottle of water sitting on a metal cafeteria tray, waiting for me on the table. She locked me back in without saying anything else.

I unwrapped the sandwich, which was as boring as the rest of the place—ham and swiss on white bread. At least it had a few toppings. I investigated everything, under the guise of pulling the tomatoes off. I didn't like tomatoes much anyway, so it was a useful way to justify picking the sandwich apart. The chips were sealed, and when I squeezed the bag, I could feel that it was still airtight.

I opted not to drink the water. Fool me once, shame on you. I finished the food in record time, not only because I actually wanted to get to the questions but also because I was pretty hungry. I figured the things they asked me would also tell me a lot of information about what they already knew.

I had no idea what time it was, or how much time had passed since I'd been taken away from that street behind Chalmun's, but clearly it had been a number of hours, since I'd slept and was so famished.

As soon as I finished the last potato chip, and wiped my hands on the scrubs because I hadn't been given a napkin, I heard the sound of various door locks. Alpha stepped in, so I smiled up at him as if he were my greatest hero. I held out the plastic sandwich wrap and empty chip bag back to him.

His expression twisted in revulsion, then quickly settled back into what I figured was his calming smile. Bethany came scuttling in after him and collected the waste, hurrying back out and closing doors behind her. She left the full bottle of water behind.

"I hope you're ready to talk now?" Alpha asked.

"Absolutely," I said. "Thank you so much; I feel a thousand times better. I felt so unclean when I was being held captive."

This time he sat on the little sofa, since I was already in the chair. The sofa seemed just as unhappy to hold up his weight as the chair had.

"So, then, let's start at the beginning," he said. "You were in your office at WonderPop."

"I was," I said. I was going to stick with the truth as much as humanly possible; I didn't need training by villains to know that was the sensible move. "I thought I'd get a couple of projects done when it was nice and quiet."

"Did you see anyone inside the building with you?"

"Besides the guard at the front desk, no," I said. "As soon as I felt the building shake, and heard the alarms start going off, I looked out the window. I saw you down there, trying to capture Doctor Oracle." And not caring at all about anyone else who might be inside.

"Then what happened?"

"I went back to my desk to get my purse and keys so I could get out of there," I said. "And something hit me on the back of the head. I think I blacked out."

"And where did you wake up?"

"I'm not sure where it was," I said. "I think I was in a hospital bed? Something like that." All truthful so far. I still didn't know the location of the island well enough to be able to find it on a map. But now I'd have to start making some things up. Best to keep it as simple as I could.

"What did it look like? Did you see anyone that you could describe?"

I wrinkled my nose, as if thinking about it. "It was pretty dark," I said. "And kind of musty. Everyone wore masks, so I didn't get a look at anyone's faces."

"Dark and musty," he said. "Do you have any idea where that could have been?"

"I have no idea," I said, shaking my head. "Maybe underground? I didn't see any windows." Now I was just starting to describe the very place where we sat.

"Did you stay there the entire time?"

"No. I think I was there for a few days, as my head healed up. Then they moved me to a small room, no windows, very limited furnishings."

"Did you see anything when they moved you?"

I shook my head again. "They blindfolded me whenever they moved me around."

"Anything strike you as unusual about the room?" His questions were fast and abrupt, almost cutting me off before I could finish my answers.

"Not really," I said. "It was just a room with a bed, and a small toilet room off to the side. Someone brought me food a couple of times a day."

"Hmm," he said. He got up from the sofa and paced around a little.

"I'm sorry, I really don't think I saw very much."

He walked away, then spun back. He pointed at me. "You filmed a video in Doctor Oracle's office."

"Yes," I said. "I was blindfolded on the way there and back. And tied to a chair when I was there, with those bright lights in my face. I tried to look around, but couldn't see much."

He paced some more. "Then he brought you to that seedy little club. Why?"

"He did," I agreed. "I don't know why. I was blindfolded for the trip. I think we flew for . . . oh, maybe four or five hours? I know there were other people on the plane, but it must have been a large plane. I could hear voices in the distance, but nobody was close enough that I could hear their plans."

"And so how did you escape from him?"

"Just luck, I guess," I said. Now was the time to flesh out the story I'd sketched in my head when we made our escape from Jimmy's secret escape tunnel. "They put me in a back office or something, but didn't bother to tie my feet, or tie me to a chair. I pulled off my blindfold, and managed to find a rough corner on a metal desk to saw through the rope on my hands."

"We found you in a costume," he said. "Were you wearing that when you entered the club?"

"No," I said. "I was wearing plain old yoga pants and a T-shirt, the same thing I was abducted in. As soon as I got myself untied, I knew I'd have to sneak out. I peeked out of the office, and there was a blonde in that outfit, right near the door. I . . ." I swallowed. "I'm afraid I had to be violent," I said.

"You had to do what you needed to do to escape," Alpha said, waving his hand with a dismissive air. "What did you do?"

"I used the cut rope, and looped it around her neck, and pulled her back into the office. I'm pretty sure I just strangled her until she was unconscious. I hope I didn't kill her."

"We didn't find anyone dead at the scene," he said.

I sighed and slumped in my chair. "Oh, thank goodness."

"And then?"

"So I took her clothes and put them on, figuring I could just sneak out the front in that disguise. Just as I peeked back out the office door, the whole place started going crazy out there, people screaming and running. So I looked around for another way out."

"How did you find that way out?" Alpha asked. He seemed really interested in this answer. I decided more truth couldn't hurt. They would have analyzed Jimmy's office thoroughly already.

"I figured, all those bookcases? Some sort of office in a club full of unsavory characters? There had to be a secret passageway, right? So I just started pulling and twisting things. Sure enough, there was some white spaceshippy thing that turned, and a bookcase opened. I hauled ass out of there, down a tunnel. Fell down a few times, got pretty dirty, and found a hatch at the end. I climbed out, and that's when I found the police and you guys."

"So you really didn't see anything," he said.

"I don't think I did," I said. "But I'll certainly think about it, go over everything in my mind."

"You do that," he said. "I'll be back to talk more later. You should get some rest."

"Will I be able to go home soon?" I asked. "People must be worried about me."

"We've let everyone know that you're safe and sound," he said, taking on a tone as if he was explaining things to a child. "But we don't want Oracle coming back after you. We'd like to keep you here until we know it's safe."

Which could be forever. I sure didn't like the sound of it, but then again, I didn't plan on staying as long as he planned on having me stay. "That's great," I said. "Thank you. You've been so kind."

He left my little cell, locking all the doors along the way. I went back into the bathroom and double-checked everywhere for cameras. Finding none, I took the bobby pins out of the pocket of my scrubs and clipped them on the chain in the toilet tank.

I got the bottle of water, took it to the bathroom, dumped it down the sink, then rinsed and refilled it. I wasn't going to trust these guys any farther than I could throw them.

I went back into the living room and turned on the TV. Best to try to appear as normal as possible. It only received five channels, none of which was a live feed of any kind from the outside world. And the programming sucked on every one of the five channels. I was missing the comforts of the island more and more every minute, but I needed to scope the place out in much more detail before I even tried to come up with an escape plan.

TWENTY-THREE

Bethany brought me dinner that night, another sandwich. This time accompanied by an apple. The food arrived again on a metal tray that looked like a relic from the '50s.

"Thank you, Bethany," I said. "I hope it isn't too much trouble to bring this to me."

"Nah," she said, picking at a loose thread on her purple costume. "It's just from the crapeteria."

Ah, so this *was* some sort of dormitory or something. My assumption was right. Which made me wonder if it was attached somehow to Ultimate Faction headquarters, or located elsewhere. If it was a separate facility, escape might be easier.

"Well, it's still kind of you to bring it."

She rolled her eyes. "Whatever. I'll get the tray when I bring breakfast."

"Okay. Thank you."

"You don't have to thank me. I'm just doing my stupid job. Babysitting."

Clearly, she wasn't in the best mood. I didn't think I was going to get any more information out of her that night.

Bethany left and locked me in. I picked apart the sandwich, but there was nothing suspicious or interesting. Under the guise of polishing it, I checked the apple for any puncture marks. Everything looked fine, so I ate it. I took the new bottle of water into the bathroom and dumped and rinsed it like the first one.

Then I kicked around for a while, bored out of my skull. I needed to get out of the room and see more of the facility so I could make a plan to get out. I thought about that for a while, came up with the scenario I figured would work the best, then shut off all the lights and went to bed.

The sheets weren't as comfortable, and the room was so pitch dark I felt like I was in a cave. I missed the moonlight through my curtains, and the sound of the surf breaking on the beach. I missed the food, and the company, and the lessons. I thought about the fact that I didn't really miss my Seattle apartment, and I definitely didn't miss my old job at WonderPop.

I tossed and turned for a while but eventually fell asleep. Without the benefit of sunlight or a clock, I had no idea how long I slept, but I woke up and felt rested enough. I stumbled around and turned the lights back on again. I turned on the TV and found that one of the channels had the time displayed down in the corner. It was just past seven in the morning.

A little after eight, Bethany came by with breakfast. It was just about as glamorous as lunch and dinner had been—a plain bagel, a foil package of cream cheese, a couple of strips of the limpest looking bacon I'd ever seen, and a banana. It wasn't prison food, but it wasn't much better, as far as I could see.

"Good morning, Bethany," I said. "I hope you slept well."

"Eh," she said. She gathered up the dinner tray, with its sandwich wrapper and empty water bottle.

"I hate to be a bother," I said, "but I wonder if I could go for a shower again today?"

She looked at me and wrinkled her nose, as if she was smelling the air. "I guess I could ask."

"Thank you," I said.

She left me alone again, and again I was left for a few hours with nothing but my thoughts and outdated TV shows. If this was dormitory life for the younger initiates, it's a wonder they didn't all go insane from boredom. I tried my best to go over things I'd learned in my head. Picking locks, hot-wiring cars, that sort of thing. I did a few stretching exercises but kept things simple. The last thing I wanted was to be seen on the not-so-hidden cameras practicing any kind of defensive moves.

I also spent a good bit of time worrying that Nate hadn't escaped, but I had to assume my presence in this crappy place meant that they hadn't caught him.

Bethany brought another sandwich with chips for lunch, along with news. "I asked Alpha. He says I can take you for a shower after lunch."

"Wonderful, thank you," I said. "I'll knock on the door when I'm done."

"Yeah, okay." Off she went.

I checked the food over and ate quickly, wanting to get out of the room so I could hopefully check the place out. I knocked on the door, and a couple of minutes later, Bethany was back.

"Ready?"

"Yes, thank you." She led me down the hall again, then around the two corners to the bathroom. I scanned for any avenues of escape—the entire wing I was in seemed to be a dead end. I'd have to see what was beyond the communal bathroom.

Bethany flopped into her chair again, and I went into the same stall I'd used the day before. There was a fresh towel folded on the bench, but it looked like I'd be putting my same old scrubs back on again. I didn't rush through the shower, but I didn't dawdle.

I pushed the curtain aside and went to the sinks, where the same toothbrush and comb from the day before awaited me. It didn't seem like this bathroom got all that much traffic.

"So this is your dormitory?" I asked Bethany after I brushed my teeth.

"Not this part," she said. "We're all over in the east wing."

"Is it nicer than this part?"

She snorted. "Not really, no."

"That's a shame," I said. "I bet the big guys live it up pretty nice."

She pulled on a lock of her faded purple hair and started tying it in a knot. "Probably," she said. "I've never seen their headquarters. We hardly ever see them around here."

So we weren't in the same place as the regular Ultimate Faction members. Good. "It must be pretty cool, then, to have Commander Alpha around right now."

She snorted again. "Right. Cool." Clearly, *cool* was not a word she'd associate with the guy.

"Hey, so," I said, "it's kind of weird down here, without any windows or anything. I don't suppose there's a place with a little sunlight, where I could stretch my legs?"

She kept tying her hair in a knot but looked at the ceiling in thought. "I'm supposed to stay with you."

"That's fine," I said. "You could take me wherever. I'd just love to breathe a little fresh air."

"Um," she said. "I guess the courtyard is open. Everyone's in class right now."

"Okay, sounds great," I said. "Wherever you want to go."

She led me out of the bathroom and into the hall. I kept track of the turns we made, but it wasn't too hard: one left and one right from the bathroom and we were at an industrial pair of double doors. They had tall, narrow windows in them, with crosshatched metal inside the glass. It was like a school building from my childhood.

She pushed one of the doors open, and we went out into a very small courtyard. It was partially brownish grass and partially concrete slabs with picnic tables on them. Getting outside didn't make the place feel any less like a prison. I tried to figure out where I was geographically, but there weren't even any trees or anything to judge from. The temperature and humidity felt pretty close to Seattle, so I guessed that we were back up in the Pacific Northwest somewhere. We may not have been attached to Ultimate Faction headquarters, but I bet we were relatively close.

"Sometimes we eat lunch out here," Bethany said. I breathed in deep and slowly turned around, looking at everything. Four concrete walls, each with identical doors in the middle. I couldn't see any obvious cameras or spotlights in the area; it looked as if it'd be dark and deserted at night, which would be helpful for an escape. The door we'd come through had a big *W* over the top; clearly I was staying in the west wing. Across the way, there was a big *E* over the door.

"So is that the east wing, where you stay?" I asked.

"Yeah," she said. Then she amazed me by pointing at the *N* and *S* doors. "Classrooms are that way, and the crapeteria and some offices are over there."

It was more information than I'd even hoped to get out of her, but I decided to push my luck. "Hey, I gotta admit, I don't really feel all that full after that sandwich. Is there any chance I could go get something else to eat? Or maybe something to take back to my room for later?"

She furrowed her brow. "I don't know," she said. "I'm probably not supposed to."

I decided to go all out. I laughed. "Well, it's not like I'm a prisoner here. Alpha brought me here to help out with his fight against Doctor Oracle, right? So he's probably cool with it."

She thought about it some more. I couldn't figure out whether she wasn't all that smart or just a lazy slacker. Or a combination of the two. Whichever it was, I felt pity for her, being stuck in this weird place.

"Plus," I said, "I bet you have to go back to classes after you're done with me, right?" She nodded. "So the more time you spend with me, the more time you can skip class."

That did it. She led me through the south door. The cafeteria wasn't that far down the hall, just shy of a blind corner, so I couldn't get a look at the offices. Inside, the cafeteria was like another memory of my school days, but less pleasant.

A scowling lunch lady stood behind a small hot-foods counter, but it all looked like brown mush and overboiled veggies. There was a cooler of pre-made sandwiches like the ones I'd been given. A second cooler held a small selection of fruit and a variety of store-brand cans of soda pop. Not even the name-brand stuff for these poor kids.

I grabbed another bag of chips, a banana, and a can of generic diet cola.

Bethany and I started toward the door, then she stopped. "Hey, I gotta use the bathroom. Can you just wait here for a second?"

"Sure," I said, doing a small cartwheel inside my head. "No problem."

"Cool," she said, then went back toward the courtyard; the restrooms were the first door after coming inside. As soon as she went in, I crept down toward the corner in the hallway. Maybe I could get a look at the offices, or whatever was down there. I peeked around the corner, then quickly pulled my head back. There were people down there.

I pressed my back against the wall and listened. In my quick glance I'd seen two guys, one dressed in white and the other in orange, so I was pretty sure who they were before they spoke.

"I can't put my finger on it," I heard Commander Alpha say. "But it feels like there's something she isn't telling me."

"You think she's lying to you?" It was Firewolf.

"I don't think so," Alpha said. "But you never know."

"Well, if she doesn't know anything, she doesn't know anything."

I heard a thump and felt the wall vibrate, and jumped a little. Alpha must have punched the wall. "Damn it, Brady, I'm so close. I thought this would be my way to finally get that guy."

"Didn't Mel have some chick with a mole in his operation?"

"Not anymore, apparently. Melinda said that the mole was gone, and she wouldn't give up who her source was." I remembered that the Green Lady was named Melinda. So she was the person Catalyst was feeding information to!

"Well, you only questioned this girl once. Maybe she'll remember something else. Or maybe we could try out one of those new truth serums that Professor C came up with."

"Maybe," Alpha said. "I'll definitely have to pick her brain some more. I don't care how long we have to keep her here; I'll find out what she knows."

"Did you let the press know that she's back?"

"Yeah. Told 'em we have her in protective custody. The nice thing is, we can always dispose of her when we're done. Just tell the press she was working with Oracle, and another useless civilian disappears."

Suddenly, listening in didn't seem like all that good an idea anymore. Plus, Bethany would be coming out of the bathroom soon. It felt like she'd left a half hour ago, but it was probably only a couple of minutes. I crept the few steps back down to the hallway and ducked back into the cafeteria.

I sat down and ate my banana, trying to calm my shaking hands. If ever I needed a bright flashing sign about who the good guys and bad guys were, I just had to compare giving Tammy the mole and her mother new identities and a small stipend with making a *useless civilian* disappear. From Alpha's tone, I was pretty sure these guys didn't mean relocation.

Bethany came back into the cafeteria. "Ready to go?"

"Sure am," I said. "Thanks again." I threw my banana peel in the trash, grabbed my extra bag of chips and can of cola, and we left the cafeteria. We ran right into Commander Alpha outside.

"Bethany," he said, then turned to me, surprise evident on his face. "Miss Valentine! I didn't expect to see you here!" He plastered a smile on his face, but I could see the glare he shot at Bethany.

"It's my fault," I said. "I was still hungry after lunch, and wanted a breath of fresh air. I didn't think it would be a problem."

"No, no," he said, putting one of his slightly-too-large hands on my shoulder. I fought the urge to shudder. "It's fine, we just want to keep you safe while Doctor Oracle is still out there. You should really go back to your room."

"Of course," I said. I wanted to find out the timeline of his plans. "I've been thinking more about what I might have seen while I was being held captive. Will you be coming by later to talk some more?"

"Unfortunately, Ultimate Faction business calls tonight. But I'll be sure to come by first thing tomorrow."

"Oh, good," I said. My escape attempt would definitely have to be that night.

"Off you go now," Alpha said. "And Bethany?"

She turned toward him, furiously tying some of her hair in a knot, her head down. "Yeah? Um . . . yes, sir?"

"Come see me once you get Miss Valentine settled back in her room."

"Yes, sir," she said.

We walked silently through the courtyard back to the west wing, down the deserted hallway, past the deserted bathroom, to my lonely little cell. I could tell that Bethany was really, really angry. Probably with me. She rattled the locks and slammed the doors open. Once I went inside, she slammed the doors again and locked them up tight.

I did feel genuinely bad that she was going to get in trouble. I hoped it wouldn't be too bad or that she wouldn't somehow "disappear." But I had to look out for myself first and foremost.

My can of cola was getting warm, so I drank it, and thought about my escape plan. It would have to be at night, when everyone was asleep and Alpha was away. I thought about the layout of the courtyard and those picnic tables. Since I'd started training with Oscar, my vertical jump had increased a few inches. If I dragged one of the tables over near a wall, I could probably make the jump from the table and just grab hold of the edge of the roof.

Where I went from the roof would be a mystery, but I'd at least be out in the open, with the freedom to move around.

The afternoon dragged along, until it was finally dinnertime. I heard the doors unlock, and someone new came into the room with a tray of food. He wasn't quite as young as Bethany but still looked to be in his late teens. His outfit was green and blue, with a green mask to match.

He set down the dinner tray (sandwich, chips, and an orange this time) and picked up the lunch tray.

"Thank you so much," I said. "I haven't met you yet. I'm Sarah."

"You're welcome, ma'am," he said. He didn't offer his name. I guess word had already gotten around that being nice to me would get you in trouble with the big guy.

He locked me back in and left me to eat dinner. I then had quite a few hours to kill before I tried to escape. I paced around the room, trying to commit the furniture placement to memory. I planned on leaving the lights off and hoped that I wasn't important enough to merit night-vision cameras.

I visited the bathroom and fished my bobby pins out of the toilet tank. I spent as long as I could in there without being suspicious, while I bent the pins into the shapes Jin had taught me. When they were done, I put them both into the pocket of my scrubs.

I turned on the TV so I could keep track of the time, and also to keep me awake. I figured I'd make my move around two in the morning. I settled in on the couch and did what I could to keep from falling asleep.

TWENTY-FOUR

By the time two o'clock rolled around, I'd recited the Gettysburg Address at least twenty times. (I also recited Samuel L. Jackson's speech from *Pulp Fiction* a few times.) I'd counted holes in the acoustic ceiling tiles until eleven, then shut off the lights but left the TV on. When the clock on the TV read two, I shut it off.

I made my way to the bathroom, both to ensure an empty bladder for whatever lay ahead and to let my eyes get used to the pitch darkness. I dragged my fingertips along the wall as I went, counting the steps I'd measured off earlier. It would have been nice to have gloves on for the whole operation, but they already knew who I was. There was no keeping my fingerprints off of things.

After the bathroom, I paced off my steps through the tiny living room. Six steps to the couch, hand along the back of the couch, then five more steps to the wall. Two steps to the right brought me to the door. I could see a little bit; my eyes were getting used to the dark, and a tiny bit of light came through the mirrored glass in the window. I pressed my face up against the poorly mirrored window and could just barely make out the shape of the door on the opposite side of the airlock. I didn't see anything or anyone else.

I carefully pulled the bobby pins out of my pocket; dropping them would be catastrophic. I held them in one hand while I wiped the other on the pants of my scrubs, then swapped and wiped down the other hand. Slick and sweaty was no way to pick a lock.

I felt around for the doorknob, then put my first bobby pin in, the one I'd bent to a ninety-degree angle. I slotted it into the bottom of the lock and put gentle pressure on it, in the direction the knob would turn. The other pin, which I'd straightened out, went into the top part of the lock. I wiggled and jiggled it around for a minute, pulled it out, and put it back in at a slightly different angle. A few more jiggles and the lock tumbled.

I pulled the pins out carefully, since I still had at least one more door to unlock and didn't want them to break. I put them back in my breast pocket for safekeeping. I listened at the door for a full minute, to make sure nobody was out there and had heard the lock open.

After waiting, I turned the doorknob as quietly as I could and opened the door. The harsh fluorescent light in the airlock felt blinding. I got through the door as fast as possible and shut it behind me, hoping nobody was watching the video feed. I gave myself a minute to get used to the light, then listened at the far door. I couldn't hear anything.

The second door was much easier to unlock, since I could see what I was doing. I left that door closed, carefully put the pins back in my pocket, and quickly went back into the living room. I grabbed the metal cafeteria tray from the table; it wasn't much, but it was the best handheld weapon I had available. I got back in the airlock and shut the door behind me.

I knew I had to get moving; if anyone *was* watching the video feed, they would have seen the door open and me bent down over the knob as it did. I was hoping that nobody would be bothering to watch me while I was supposedly asleep, but you never knew with that group.

I listened again at the door; hearing nothing, I turned the knob and slowly pulled.

The hallway beyond looked like it always did—gray, dull, and deserted. It could have been any time of day or night. I found myself hoping that the wing with the trainee dormitory rooms at least had a coat of paint.

I slipped out the door and closed it behind me. I looked for a key in the outside knob of the door, but no such luck: just an empty keyhole like on the inside.

I started creeping down the hallway, sticking as close to the wall as I could, with my metal tray at the ready. After a few steps, I realized how incredibly loud my flimsy slippers were in that deathly quiet hall, making a crinkling sound like they were made of paper. I slipped them off. I didn't want to carry them, since I wanted both hands free for my tray. I didn't want to leave them behind either, because walking across a roof with bare feet didn't sound all that fun. I finally decided to wedge them down the back of my pants. I braced them under my waistband; then I crammed them into my underwear just to make sure they didn't slip free and slide down the back of my legs.

It was classy as heck, but hopefully nobody would see it.

Barefoot, I continued down the hallway. I knew it was a left turn, then a right in order to get to the bathroom, then another left and right to get outside. I got to the first corner and thought about how I was going to check around it. I looked down at the metal tray in my hands. It seemed shiny enough.

I got down on my hands and knees, figuring that if anyone was looking my way, they'd be looking at eye level. I slid the tray slightly out in the hallway, angled so I could see around the corner. The reflection was muddy and warped, but I could see that the hallway was clear.

Rounding the corner, I breathed a sigh of relief. One corner down, three more to go, then outside. I crept down the hall along the right-hand wall, getting ready for my next corner. I made it down there, got back down on the ground, and pushed the tray at an angle around the corner.

I caught a flash of movement, felt my heart stutter, and pulled the tray back. I closed my eyes for a second and breathed deeply. I pushed the tray back out, just slightly, enough to see a solitary figure all in black at the far end of the long gray hallway. I pulled the tray back and thought about my options.

I could hustle back to my room; both doors were unlocked for me. But that would leave me here for the next morning, when Commander Alpha had promised to visit again for more questioning. And I already suspected that if I stayed, I might learn about what real interrogation techniques they used. Besides which, from what he'd said earlier, I was pretty sure they didn't plan on letting me out for a long, long time. Or possibly ever.

So, flight back to the room was out. Fight appeared to be my only option. If it was just one person, I might be able to take them out. I had the element of surprise on my side, as well as my tray. It wasn't a cast-iron frying pan, but it might be enough to take someone down. I also had my kickboxing to fall back on, and a bunch of moves Oscar had taught me.

I stayed at the corner, my back pressed against the wall, listening as hard as I could. The person was quiet; I could barely make out their footsteps, even in the empty hallway. I tightened my grip on the tray.

A shoe scuffed on the ground, really close. I took a deep breath, then launched myself around the corner with the tray raised at head height. The figure in black was right in front of me, wearing a hood and goggles. I swung the tray around at their head, grunting from the effort. The person managed to jump back just in time, the tray whistling by inches in front of the hooded face.

I pulled back for another swing, and the person held up both hands in a gesture of surrender. I held off for a second, and they reached one gloved hand up to pull off the goggles.

"Hey," Nate said with a grin. "Fancy meeting you here."

I launched myself at him and hugged him.

After I untangled myself, Nate tapped on his ChatterBox. He was already wearing the earpiece. "Found her," he said. "West hallway off the courtyard."

"Who else is here?" I asked.

"Jin and Oscar. They're checking out a couple of the other areas, but I knew I'd find you down here."

"How did you know?"

He pulled a small device out of his pocket; it had a tiny screen with a green arrow on it, pointing straight at me. Jin and Oscar rounded the corner behind Nate and joined us, dressed all in black and still wearing their hoods and goggles.

"What on earth is that?" I asked.

"Remember when we went shopping?" Jin asked. "RFID chips in the clothing. We figured that even if they gave you new clothes, we could track the old ones if they were nearby. Looks like you're still wearing something of your own under those . . . delightful scrubs."

"I've never been happier to have a tracker in my bra," I said.

Oscar shrugged a backpack off his shoulder and held it out to me. "We brought you something a little more black to wear."

We were right near the bathroom with the showers, so I pulled everyone in there with me. I knew there were no cameras in there. Once inside, Oscar and Jin took off their goggles and pulled their hoods back. I took the backpack behind one of the curtains and changed clothes.

"I don't know how much time we have," I said. "There were cameras in my room, so they may have seen me getting out."

"Already taken care of," Oscar said. "We found the control room. There was one poor little guy in there, already pretty much asleep. He's taking a much deeper nap now. And the footage of the last twenty-four hours has mysteriously disappeared."

The clothes felt amazing after my time in the same set of coarse scrubs. Even though it was a protective material, it was still soft and flexible. I found my own gloves and goggles in the bag but didn't put them on yet. I did, however, put on the shoes. I was done skulking around barefoot. I pushed the curtain aside and joined the others.

"How did you get in?" I asked.

"Over the roof, down into the courtyard," Nate said. "Security here is a joke."

"That was the way I was going to head out," I said. "Glad to know the plan would have worked."

"How far did you get on your own?" Jin asked.

"Two locked doors, one of them in the dark," I said. She beamed with pride.

"What is this place, anyway?" Oscar asked.

"This is where the Ultimate trainees and new recruits live," I said. "They have a dormitory and classrooms here. And the big guys don't seem to really give a crap about them."

"Shocking," Jin said, rolling her eyes.

"I met the girl who slashed open your arm," I told Nate. "She's just an angry teenager."

"You can build her entry in the database," he said. "We'll have to think about ways to infiltrate this place; maybe we can stop the next generation of Ultimate Faction before it begins."

"But right now," Oscar said, "we should get moving. Who knows if there's a late-night shift change in the control room."

I grabbed my discarded scrubs and stuffed them in the backpack; no need to leave them behind to raise suspicion earlier than necessary. Plus, I was pretty sure I was going to frame those bobby pins and put them on the wall of my apartment when we got back to the island. I put on the black gloves, even though my fingerprints were probably all over the place and they already knew who I was. It was just a good habit to get into, always wearing gloves with your tactical suit.

I strapped the new black CB on my wrist and put the earpiece in my ear. Nate tapped the face of his against mine, and I was looped into the communication channel they had open. We put our hoods and goggles on, Oscar took the backpack from me and slung it on his back, and I picked up my metal tray.

Even though most of his face was shadowed by the hood or masked by the goggles, I could see Nate look down at the tray, then back up at my face, a smile twitching at his lips.

"What?" I said. "We're not out of here yet."

"Fair enough," he said. We listened at the door, then slipped out into the hallway. I felt a lot more comfortable about the trip now, surrounded by three professionals. We cautiously took the last two corners, then lined up on each side of the courtyard doors.

Oscar adjusted his goggles to night-vision mode and leaned over to look through the slim window in the door.

"Nothing," he said. "All clear."

We made our way out into the courtyard, which was lit only by moonlight. Clearly it wasn't meant to be used at night. I switched on the night-vision button on my own goggles, and the courtyard glowed brilliant green. The team led me over to the corner between the east and south wings, where a pair of ropes were hanging down from the roof.

"Piece of cake," Oscar said. "Just remember what I taught you."

Oscar and Nate went to one rope, and Jin and I went to the other. "After you," Jin said. I tugged on the rope, then paused as I tried to figure out how to take my tray up with me.

The door to the south wing popped open, and a gold flash went straight for Jin, who was standing closest to the door. The person in gold rammed into her, knocking her to the ground. Instinct kicked in, and I turned and slammed the tray down as hard as I could on the person's head.

He fell to his knees, and I could see that it was Action Alex, another one of the junior members. He'd been with Alpha outside the nightclub. He shook his head and stood back up, looking angry. I held up my tray again, now with a dent in the middle of it.

Then Alex's eyes crossed, and he slumped to the ground. Behind him, Nate and Oscar both had their tranquilizer pistols out, pointed where Alex had just been standing. Besides the sound of the metal tray hitting his head, the entire short battle had been eerily silent.

"Two shots will be potent, but that kid has a fast metabolism," Nate said. "We better get moving." He leaned down and tucked a Doctor Oracle calling card into Alex's belt. Then he offered a hand to Jin, who was still on the ground. She reached up and let Nate help pull her to her feet, but as soon as she stood, she winced and stumbled. I grabbed hold of her.

"I'm pretty sure my ankle is broken," she said in a matter-of-fact tone. I looked down at her legs; she stood on the left and had the right held up slightly. I couldn't see the extent of the damage, since everything was still held in place inside her boot.

"Okay," Oscar said. "We got you." He and Nate ran over and carried one of the picnic tables over, setting it down just under the ropes. Oscar climbed onto the table quickly, jumped up to get on the roof, then lay on his stomach, holding down his hands. Nate and I helped Jin hop up on the seat of the picnic table, then on the main surface. She reached up, and Oscar pulled her up onto the roof.

Nate bowed and waved for me to go up next. I handed him my dented tray. "I'm keeping that as a souvenir," I told him. Then I bypassed the rope entirely and jumped for the edge of the roof, just to see if I could.

I was right when I made my plan—I just barely made the jump. I swung my legs over and hooked a foot on the edge of the roof, then pulled myself up. Nate handed my tray up, then jumped up last, bypassing the ropes and getting on the roof the same way I did. Oscar unhooked the ropes and stuffed them into his backpack, while Nate held on to Jin.

"This will probably be easier if I just carry you," he said. "Fireman-style, or bride across the threshold?"

"Bride," Jin said. "Mark never did carry me on our honeymoon."

"Rude," Nate said as he leaned down so Jin could hop up into his arms. "Remind me to have a word with him when we get back."

We hustled across the rooftop as quietly as we could, meeting no more resistance. Oscar brought the ropes back out when we reached the far corner of the roof, and we made our way down, Oscar gently passing Jin down to Nate. The outside of the property was surprisingly well kept and lush compared to the awful courtyard inside. We crept around behind some bushes and across a small patch of grass to a chain-link fence.

The team had cut the fence open on the way in, which made escape easy. The fence was tall enough that it would have made a hell of a climb for me, and had coils of razor wire at the top. I wondered again if the building had been a prison in a former life.

A black van was parked along an unlit road. We loaded Jin into the back, and Nate and I climbed in there with her. Oscar got behind the wheel and drove for a while with the headlights off. When we turned onto the main road, he switched the lights on.

Jin grimaced as we rode along.

"Does it hurt?" I asked.

"It's not the ankle," she said. "It's what Oscar is doing to my van."

"I'm a little rusty on a stick shift," Oscar's voice said in my ear. We still had our channel open. I popped the earpiece out and put it back in the ChatterBox, then looked across at Nate.

"So," he said, "how does it feel to be kidnapped by Doctor Oracle *twice*?"

"I've never been happier," I said.

TWENTY-FIVE

We only stopped once on our way to the airport, at a twenty-four-hour fast food restaurant. I fished my bobby pins out of the pocket of the scrubs and tucked them safely into one of the zippered pockets of my black tactical outfit. We threw the scrubs in the trash, in case there was a tracking device of any kind. Then we got soft drinks and french fries—it was the best-tasting meal I'd had in a couple of days.

Oscar managed to get the van to the airfield without causing Jin too much more aggravation. Once we got about fifteen minutes away from the Ultimate Faction's trainee compound, I started recognizing landmarks. We weren't in Seattle itself, but we were in one of the many smaller cities surrounding it.

We didn't go to the big international airport; instead, we headed for the smaller county airport a few miles away. I'd seen it from the freeway on occasion but had never visited before. Oscar pulled up to a hangar. Nate jumped out and unlocked the doors, and in we went, van and all.

The hangar was huge and contained an interesting assortment of vehicles. Besides another van and two black sedans, there was a helicopter and the same small, insanely fast jet we'd taken from the island to get to Los Angeles the other day. The pilot was walking around the jet, performing his preflight check.

Oscar parked the van off to the side and we all piled out, helping Jin as much as she would let us. She refused to be carried again, so it was a matter of providing an arm to hold as she hopped around. She gritted her teeth, and I figured she must have been in a good deal of pain, but she didn't complain.

We all got onto the plane, and a few minutes later we were in the air. Jin reclined her chair and closed her eyes for a nap. Oscar also stretched himself out. It was, after all, around four in the morning by that point. We were all pretty tired.

"Want to catch a few winks?" Nate asked. "I'd like to hear all about your stay, but I can wait."

"I might still be a little too keyed up to sleep."

"It's up to you," he said. So I stayed up and told Nate about the past couple of days. I didn't hold anything back, so he soon knew about poor angry Bethany, as well as the full purpose of the facility (as much as I was able to figure out, anyway) and the conversation between Commander Alpha and Firewolf.

Nate grimaced. "I can't believe those guys," he said. "That kind of treatment goes against anything we've historically done."

"It's like he's taking everything with you really personal," I said. "I wouldn't be surprised if he bends even more rules to get you."

"But that's me," he said. "Not my people. Even though he didn't know you were on our team. He should never have kept you in such an awful place, or even thought about torture. Or worse."

"Do you think he suspects that I'm working with you?"

"I don't know," he said. "He told Firewolf that he thought you were holding something back, but he also said he didn't think you lying to him, right? So in his mind, you might have been keeping something from him out of fear of retribution from us."

"He thought he had the perfect informant," I said. "Someone who had been on the inside."

"And now we've stolen that informant away again. Which might make him think that you really *do* know important information and we risked capturing you again to keep it safe."

"Jeez," I said. "This just doesn't look good for me either way."

"Well, since we got rid of the mole, the leak should be

plugged. He shouldn't be able to get the drop on us again."

I thought about the mole problem. "Alpha said to Firewolf that their information source was feeding information to someone named Mel, who I assume is the Green Lady. Why do you think Catalyst would be working with her? Aren't they on opposite sides?"

"I don't know," Nate said. "I have a feeling there's some connection we're missing. There are still plenty of things we don't have in our database, things that have been kept secret too well."

"We'll figure it out," I said.

After a couple of hours of flight, we started our descent to the island. We'd flown southwest, away from the sunrise, but there was just enough twilight to see some of the details of the island as the pilot flew his landing pattern. It was cool to see the island from above, something I'd missed when we left due to it being pitch dark.

It was really beautiful, and I'd genuinely missed it. I knew I was pretty hopelessly stuck on the place.

We landed and taxied down the runway toward the hangar. I saw some lights up ahead; as we got closer, I saw two transport balls waiting on the side of the runway with their headlights on. Someone was sitting in one of them.

I reveled in the warm air when we got off the plane. That couple of hours traveling farther south than Seattle had made a world of difference in the ambient temperature. It was also a different level of humidity, and I was delighted to smell the sea again.

Oscar held on to Jin as she hopped her way down the stairs off the plane. By the time she got to the ground, Scar had run up from where he'd been sitting in the transport ball.

"What have you gone and done to yourself now?" Scar asked.

"Eh, 'tis but a flesh wound," Jin said.

"Right," Scar said, and he promptly hoisted Jin up in his arms. He carried her to one of the transport balls and gently sat her in the passenger seat. Nate and I took the other ball, and I got to see the jump seat in back when Oscar wedged himself into it. It didn't look awful, but it didn't look terribly comfortable.

We all trundled around the island to the hospital wing, and Scar carried Jin inside. Jake the night-shift nurse was there, and he still looked vaguely embarrassed when he saw me. He got Jin comfortable on one of the beds, got a special pair of shears to cut the leg of Jin's tactical trousers up to the knee, then paged Dr. Adams. He grabbed a device that looked a little like a Taser, then pressed it against Jin's neck. The gadget made a hissing sound, and Jin visibly relaxed. It must have been some kind of pain medication.

We all kicked around the hospital room as we waited for Adams to arrive. She made it in a little over five minutes, fully dressed for action but with her hair smashed flat on one side. Which was fine by me; I'd rather have a doctor ready to patch me up than have her delay by dealing with bed-head.

I was still fascinated by the medical advances on the island, so I stood behind and watched. First, Adams prodded and poked at Jin's ankle. Then she got an object that looked kind of like a tablet computer but a little thicker. She turned it on, and it glowed green. She held it over Jin's ankle, and an X-ray image appeared on the screen. We could all clearly see the break, near the bottom of the skinnier bone of her leg.

"Clean break of the fibula," Adams said. "An easy fix, thank you."

"My pleasure," Jin said. "Ready when you are."

Adams looked at the break from all possible angles with her device. "We're looking at surgery to install a metal plate and pins to hold the bones back together, and a cast."

"Let's get moving, then," Jin said. "We have some work to do next week."

"Oh, no," Adams said. "No, we're talking about a recovery time of four to six weeks before the cast can come off."

Jin looked crestfallen. "Don't you have some nano-stuff that can fix it?"

"I do," Dr. Adams said. "That's why it's four to six weeks instead of eight to twelve weeks. We're advanced, but we're not miracle workers."

"Crap," Jin said. She looked at Nate, then at Oscar. It was the most upset I'd ever seen her, practically on the brink of tears.

"It's okay," Nate said softly.

"No, it's not," she said. "I'm going to miss all the *fun*."

Scar took her hand in his and gave us a look. We all picked up on it pretty quickly, made our excuses and said our good-byes, and left the room.

"Man, she was so upset," I said.

"I don't blame her," Oscar said. "This one is going to be really cool."

"It sure is," Nate said. He looked at me. "Although I don't suppose . . ."

I waited for him to continue, but he just pursed his lips. "What? What don't you suppose?"

"I don't know, Sarah. We just got you back; you've had a hard couple of days. I was going to suggest that we find another angle, so you don't have to go to this party at the Green Lady's. I don't want to throw too much at you, after what you've been through."

"Are you kidding?" I said. "How often does a girl get invited to a ball?"

"You still want to do it? I could go alone. I've done recon alone before."

"Nate, whatever they were going to do to me was going to be bad stuff. Even though they didn't get a chance to do it, I still think a little revenge is in order. We could call it pre-venge."

"In that case," Nate said, "we're going to need to get you a gown."

TWENTY-SIX

Nate and I walked through the massive doors of Sedgewick Manor arm in arm. Nate wore a beautifully cut tuxedo, which was complemented by his dapper salt-and-pepper hair, little round spectacles, and completely reshaped face. I almost didn't recognize him, which was the whole point of the disguise.

I felt like tugging at the gown to make sure I was covered, but channeled that energy into standing up straighter and taller. The thing was clingy in places I wasn't used to things clinging, and I felt like a total goofball in it, despite Nate's and Rupert's declarations that I looked beautiful. (The look on Oscar's face was also pretty priceless.) It was a lovely shade of blue, and a bit chilly in the rear, where most of my back was exposed. Nate put his hand on my bare skin there. I was so nervous, I didn't even think about how delightfully intimate it was; I was just grateful for the warmth.

I did tug a little bit at the elbow-length gloves I wore. At least I didn't have to worry about leaving any fingerprints anywhere to indicate that twice-kidnapped Sarah Valentine was in the house.

I wore a wig so dark brown it was almost black, the hair pulled back and twisted in a dozen intricate ways at the nape of my neck. A few extra pieces of latex and a face full of glamorous makeup meant I was pretty much unrecognizable. Which was good, in case I ran into anyone I'd just spent a couple of days with. We didn't think any of the Ultimate Faction besides the Green Lady would be at the party, but it was best to not take chances.

Jin had given me some beautiful jewelry to wear on the mission, some pieces she'd worn on similar jobs before. The sapphire earrings were big enough to be impressive but not too heavy. The diamond and sapphire necklace was intimidating as hell, since it was probably worth a couple of million dollars. Nate assured me that everyone would be wearing similar jewels to flaunt their wealth.

I just hoped that it if was stolen, its original owner wouldn't be at the party.

Nate handed our invitation to the doorman, who only gave it a perfunctory glance. He gave me a much longer look. I wondered if we'd even needed to go to the trouble to get the invitation from Nate's contact. Clearly, I could have just worn this dress and given the guy a Post-It with crayon writing on it.

We went through the foyer and down a hall lined with chatting couples and then entered the ballroom. It was amazing, like something out of a movie. I'd thought that kind of lifestyle was totally made up and that no real people actually lived that way. Guess I was wrong. There were oil paintings all over the walls, a mix of portraits, landscapes, and still lifes. Everything seemed to be embellished with extra curves or gold leaf or both.

A small band was in the corner, the exact opposite of the band at Chalmun's in every way. These guys wore white tuxedoes, looking like the epitome of elegance, and played standards and American songbook stuff. Nate grabbed a pair of champagne glasses from a passing waiter and gave me one. Then he led me out to the dance floor.

"What am I going to ask?" he whispered in my ear as we danced.

"Four, possibly five," I said. "Though if I count all of the windows, which I could probably smash with one of those heavy-looking chairs, my escape options go up considerably."

"Good," he said. We turned slowly on the dance floor so we could both get familiar with the room. We'd looked at the blueprints of the manor, but it was different seeing the place in person instead of as lines on a sheet of paper.

"The stairwell should be back behind the band," I said. "Upstairs, right turn, and the gallery is on the left."

Nate pressed his warm hand against my back again. "Exactly," he said.

"But how do we get up there to check things out?"

"We'll come up with something," he said. "If nothing else occurs, there's always the old 'Oh no, I got lost on the way to the bathroom' ploy."

"Yeah, let's shoot for something a little classier than that," I said. I sipped the champagne for show. It was actually pretty good, and I guessed that it was terribly expensive. I wondered what Melinda Sedgewick would think of my favorite wine, which was usually on sale for five bucks a bottle.

Nate and I weren't the only members of the team in the manor, but we were the only ones dressed to the nines and dancing around in the ballroom. I knew that Oscar was scouting out a drainage pipe that supposedly led into the basement. For all I knew, he was underneath us at that very moment. It was the perfect time for him to snoop around, since most of the alarm systems were deactivated for the party.

We danced around, eavesdropping on everyone we could. People were surprisingly open with their conversations out on the dance floor. Finally, we ended up near a couple who were quite interesting.

"I can't wait," the woman said. Looking her over, I thought her hair was pulled back a little too tight. To be honest, her gown was a little too tight as well.

"Neither can I," the man said. "I've heard she added a Picasso."

"Picasso, schmicasso," the woman said. "I just want to see the diamond."

"Of course you would. You always do." The man snorted.

Nate interrupted. "I'm sorry, are you talking about a tour of the gallery?"

"Yes," the man said. "Is this your first time here? Melinda often offers tours."

"It *is* our first time," Nate said. "I'd heard about the tours, though. I just wasn't sure when they happened."

"Why not go with us? We're heading up in about ten minutes," the woman said.

Nate ran his hand up and down my back, as if his hand was nodding. I took my cue. "That would be delightful," I said, using the posh English accent Evie had helped me refine. "Where shall we meet?"

"There's a small alcove behind the band," the man said. "Melinda will meet us there."

"As long as you're sure we won't be in the way," I said.

"Nonsense," the man said. "The more the merrier!"

We danced another song, sampled a few of the hors d'oeuvres (Jin was right: lobster and shrimp were both in heavy rotation), and made our way to the alcove behind the band. There were five people already there, including the couple we'd danced next to. We were right next to the stairwell I knew would be there from the blueprints.

Suddenly, Melinda Sedgewick was there with us. I hadn't seen her approach. She spoke slowly, with an upper-crust delivery. "Welcome, valued guests. I'm delighted to be able to show you all my treasures." She lifted a hand in a lazy gesture, which we all took to mean that we were supposed to follow her up the stairs.

Up we went, as I compared the layout of the house to the blueprints I'd studied. We took the right turn at the top of the stairs, but then went into a room on the right instead of to the left. I worried for a minute that the blueprints had it wrong.

My worries were unfounded. The room we went into was large, but not the huge gallery I was expecting. There were a number of paintings on the walls, but they seemed more like family heirlooms than priceless treasures. In the middle of the room was a golden clothing rack with a dozen large, down-filled parkas hanging on it. They all had luxurious fur collars and looked like they each cost more than my car.

I looked at Nate, who just winked at me. He grabbed a parka and put it on, so I followed suit. It didn't really go with my gown, but it was certainly toasty on my bare back.

We trooped across the hall, overstuffed and a little sweaty. Melinda opened the door ahead of us, and a blast of arctic air poured out. A couple of the ladies in our group gasped in shock. We herded in, and I buried my gloved hands down in the deep pockets of the parka.

Melinda waited for all of us to go through, then closed the door behind her. She wasn't wearing a parka herself but didn't seem bothered at all by the brisk temperature.

"Ladies and gentlemen, please feel free to look about. I'm happy to answer any questions you may have."

"Why is it so cold in here?" asked one of the women who had gasped.

"This room is kept at a steady fifty-two degrees Fahrenheit and thirty percent relative humidity, because that is the ideal archival temperature for artwork preservation," she said.

Nate linked his arm through mine and pulled me close. "Eyes open for everything," he said. I nodded.

The Midnight Star diamond was hard to miss; it was on a pedestal in the middle of the room. I opted to check out the rest of the room first and save the diamond itself for last. As I cruised around I saw the aforementioned Picasso, next to a Rembrandt and a Monet. Several other paintings looked vaguely familiar, but my knowledge of classical artists was scant, based mostly on a couple of required introduction to art history class from college. Most of the stuff I enjoyed was far more modern.

The room itself was six sided, just as the blueprints had shown. I wasn't sure why, but I found it pleasing to the eye. Maybe because there weren't any square corners to cast heavy shadows. Or something.

In three of the six corners, I saw the tiny telltale spots that were cameras. They were definitely smaller and better hidden than the ones in my room at the dormitory. I bet they had infrared night vision and probably other spectrums I didn't even know existed.

As we toured around the room, I kept one ear cocked for any interesting information as Melinda Sedgewick answered questions from her guests. Nate even joked that he'd never seen a black diamond outside of a ski resort, so we didn't stand out as the couple who didn't say anything.

I took in the diamond last. The pedestal was in the dead center of the room, made of beautiful polished mahogany. There were no wires going up the side, nor could I see any contacts anywhere on the glass dome. Inside, the diamond sat on a red velvet cloth. A few spotlights above were trained at the perfect angles to make the diamond sparkle.

Nate finished his lap of the room, then settled in next to me. "Much to discuss," he muttered in my ear.

We looked at the diamond for a few moments, and I felt someone step up next to me.

"Beautiful, isn't it?" Melinda Sedgewick asked.

"It is," I said. "Truly the centerpiece of a wonderful collection." I looked up at her. She didn't seem overly interested in scrutinizing me, which I was thankful for. She beamed with pride.

"Thank you," she said. "I've spent a lifetime collecting lovely things, but this is definitely my favorite."

I looked at her skin. Nate and I were the only people in the room who knew that she was green underneath the thick layer of makeup, and it was done so well I almost second-guessed myself that she was really the Green Lady. It was more than a little creepy, knowing that she was wearing such a heavy mask. Then again, I had on a wig and prosthetics and a paste of makeup myself, so who was I to talk about wearing a mask?

She glided away to tend to other guests, and shortly after that we were gently herded out of the gallery. Even wearing the cozy parkas, we were all starting to shiver. We went back to the room across the hall, where everything felt delightfully warm, and hung our parkas back up.

Nate looked lost in thought as he placed his hanger on the rack. I looked around the room; even though the paintings were nowhere near as valuable as the artwork across the hall, I found some of them quite lovely. There were a number of portraits, though I couldn't tell if they were relatives or what.

One of them caught my eye, and I stepped closer to look at it. It was a portrait of a young woman, with a smile on her face as subtle and gentle as the Mona Lisa's. Her bright red hair was pulled back into a bun. It took me a moment to figure out why she looked so familiar, because the smile was so unlike the expression on the face of the actual subject when I'd last seen her.

I went back over to Nate and linked my arm in his, then glanced around to make sure our hostess was nowhere nearby. I leaned in and rested my head on Nate's shoulder.

"I've figured out why our mole's information was being sent to the Green Lady," I whispered.

He inhaled sharply but otherwise gave no indication that he was startled. "How?"

I turned him around so he could see the portrait of Catalyst hanging on the wall.

TWENTY-SEVEN

"So how on earth did we not know about this?" Nate asked.

Evie shrugged. "Like I said, there's a *lot* we don't know, Nate."

"But now we know. And knowing is half the battle," Oscar said. He grinned and waited for someone to call out his G. I. Joe reference. Nobody was in the mood.

Nate ran his hands through his hair. "Evie, please check on Catalyst when we're done here. Clearly she's not the small-timer we thought she was." She nodded.

The eight of us were gathered around Nate's conference table. The purpose of the meeting was to go over our findings at the manor and refine our plan for the heist, but so far we'd only talked about the fact that Melinda Sedgewick had a portrait of Catalyst, also known as Catherine, on her wall.

"What's Catalyst's power?" I asked.

"She can metabolize anything she ingests," Nate said, without consulting the database. He would know, I supposed. He'd dated her and been stalked by her, after all.

"Anything?" I asked. "Drugs? Poison? Paint thinner?"

"All of that," he said. He slapped his hand down on the table. "And the Green Lady is immune to poisons and gases. Damn, they could be related."

"It's the right age gap for mother-daughter," Rupert said.

"I can't believe I missed it," Nate said.

"Dude," Elliot said, "they're on opposite sides. And there are probably at least twenty other people in the database, on both sides, who have powers that are similar. Nobody caught it."

"At any rate," Jin said, "there's nothing we can do about it now except file Catalyst away in the Ultimate Faction camp and get back to work on the plan." Her crutches were leaned up against the wall, and she sat sideways so her cast could be up on a chair.

Nate drummed his fingers on the table and sighed. "All right. Okay. We have the night all set; next Thursday, all of Ultimate Faction, including the junior members, will be out of state attending a dinner at the White House. Normally, I'd say we should delay this heist, but our minions are desperate for the new power source, and it may be a long time before we get a chance like this again."

"What's so special about this trip of theirs?" I asked.

"We've tracked the Faction for years, and the number of times that they've all left town at the same time can be counted on one hand. This is the first time it's happened in the last three years. If there are going to be guards, they'll just be plain, ordinary humans."

Oscar unrolled the blueprints on the table. "So we know that the floor plan is correct. We can get in just like normal visitors, once we take out any guards and regular security. We'll go in through the front, then take the staircase up the same way you did at the party."

"Evie, you'll be overriding their camera feed," Nate said. "Oscar mapped out the trip through the drainage pipe into the subbasement and marked off where all of the electrical junction boxes are. I'll be able to patch your transmitters in there."

"Once I'm patched in, I can also cut the lights and the easy parts of the alarm system," Evie said. "But the power has to stay on."

"Why is that?" I asked.

"The security system for the gallery is separate from everything else and tied into the power too extensively," she said.

"If we try cutting off the power, it goes to backup and sets off an alarm. That's why we're outfoxing the gallery system instead."

"Oscar," Elliot said, "I've worked up a refined version of our tranquilizer—it'll put people to sleep longer, and we've added in a mild amnesiac to the mix. They won't have any clear memories from a short time before they get knocked out, just in case you have to get up close and physical with someone."

"You'll be on the ground," Nate said to Oscar. "Or on the roof, or up trees, whatever you need to do. Take out anyone and everyone so Sarah has a clear path to get inside."

"I'm all set to monitor everyone from above," Elliot said. "Evie has me set up with a link to the satellite we hijacked. It's a nice one; this thing has camera resolution that puts Google Maps to shame."

"We'll be having a party out in the van," Evie grinned.

"That leaves me," I said. I'd already tried on the crazy outfit Jin would have been wearing on this mission so that Rupert could make a few adjustments. I made the most sense of anyone, since I was the closest to Jin's size. It would have taken too long to alter otherwise. The thing was like three layers of wetsuit, with what looked like miles of tubes between the layers.

"The main security system in the gallery is heat activated," Nate said. "She doesn't just keep it cold in there for the paintings; it's so that anything warm, like a human body, will set off the temperature sensors immediately. Sarah, the suit will keep the outside of you cold but will keep you warmer inside. You'll still feel chilly, but you won't set off the alarms."

"At least I don't have to go through the sewer pipes," I said. "Seems like that would be the proper initiation for the new kid."

"You'll do great," Oscar said. Everyone else agreed. We finished up with our meeting and adjourned. Everyone else left, and Nate poured a couple of glasses of Evie's excellent wine and led me out onto his wraparound balcony.

We leaned on the railing next to each other, looking out toward the jungle and the hills beyond. Aside from a few lights near the farms, it was pitch dark out there. A warm tropical breeze ruffled our hair.

"You're absolutely sure about this?" Nate asked, leaning over against me.

"You aren't?"

"I'm sure you'll do a fantastic job," he said. "I just want to make sure that *you* think you'll do well."

"With you guys on my side, and yammering in my ear, I'm sure I'll do fine."

He sighed. "I just feel like we're piling a lot on you in a really short amount of time."

"You are," I said. "But who else is going to do it? Even if we waited four to six weeks for Jin's leg to heal, she still wouldn't be at top speed or strength. And we'll have missed this perfect window of opportunity."

He linked his fingers with mine as we stood there.

"I'm glad you got hit in the head," he said.

"I'm not sure I like how you put that," I said.

"Well, I mean, of course I wish you hadn't been injured."

"How about this," I said. "I'm glad that you quit WonderPop and pulled a disappearing act so that I would be angry and want to take my mind off what a huge jerk you were."

"Not sure I like how you put that either."

"All right," I said. "Let's be glad that we bumped into each other after you set fire to my office building."

"Perfect," Nate said, raising his wineglass and tapping it against mine. "I'll drink to that."

TWENTY-EIGHT

Evie, Elliot, and I sat in the back of our van, surrounded by various computers and pieces of equipment. I tried not to touch anything unless I was told to. We all wore the standard black tactical outfit, with black ChatterBox units on our wrists. Our earpieces were in, and our private channel was open.

"You know," Nate's voice said in my ear, "the sewers really aren't as bad as you expect."

"You're just lucky it hasn't rained lately," Oscar said.

"Don't I know it," Nate said. "I'm at the back corner of the subbasement now."

We all watched the monitor that showed us a Nate's-eye view of the world, thanks to the camera built into his protective goggles. His flashlight showed a number of metal boxes on the wall, with huge trunks of cable leading in and out of them.

"Third from the left," Evie said. Nate's gloved hand reached up and opened the box. There were at least a hundred wires inside, in a crazy mishmash of colors, and it looked to my untrained eye like they went all over the place. "Lighting control will be the light blue and red next to each other, near the top right."

Nate carefully stripped the two wires, then snapped a small white box onto them. He pressed a button in the middle of the box, and one of Evie's other computer screens flickered to life.

"Checking the connection now," she said. She typed away on the keyboard for a moment. "Okay, I'm ready to test. Oscar, please hold your position."

"Got it," Oscar said. He was up on a roof of the manor house, looking up into a third-story window. We watched his feed on the monitor next to Nate's.

Evie scrolled through some options on her computer, then clicked on something with the mouse. The light that had been on in the upper window near Oscar winked out. She clicked again, and the light came back on.

"Excellent," she said. I knew that she was testing an out-of-the-way light that nobody would notice instead of something on the ground level. There were at least ten security guards patrolling the manor grounds, and we didn't want any of them noticing any flashing lights.

Nate grabbed another pair of wires in the same junction box at Evie's direction. Again, he stripped the wires and put some sort of transmitter on them. That was for the regular alarm system on the doors and windows. Another of Evie's monitors lit up with a map of the house, with green lights representing every sensor.

"Oscar," Elliot said, "I'd advise moving to the other side of that roof." Elliot was watching a separate monitor, which fed in the images from the satellite parked directly overhead. It had thermal infrared as part of its camera array, which meant that he could see orangey-reddish blobs that marked every warm object on the property.

Oscar's orangey-reddish blob, which was also marked on Elliot's screen with a flashing light thanks to a sensor clipped to his belt, moved from one corner of the roof to the other as another big blob slowly moved around underneath. It really was like a stealth video game. I would have found it even more cool and fascinating if I hadn't been terrified of my part in the job, which was still ahead.

"All right, Nate," Evie said. "Final box is the one on the far right." Nate opened up that junction box and revealed a tangle of cat-5 Ethernet cables. There were a ton of them, and they were only two colors: blue and white. Fortunately, they all plugged in and out of numbered slots in the panel.

"You're going to start with unplugging A25," Evie said. "Plug that into the A spot on the box I gave you." Nate followed her directions, and we watched it happen on the screen. "Now take the outgoing cable under the A spot, and plug that into A25 in the box. Same thing, this time with C13. Unplug, plug it into your box in the spot labeled 'C,' then take the outgoing cable from C and put it back into C13."

"Done," Nate said. He closed both junction boxes and latched them, hiding his work from view.

"Perfect," Evie said. "This will be a couple of minutes."

Nate stepped back from the electrical boxes and looked around; from what I could see in the murky light, the basement was full of crap that hadn't seen the light of day in decades: broken furniture, stacks of soggy old newspapers, and tons of unmarked boxes, all covered in a thick layer of dust and grime.

Evie switched on another pair of monitors, which showed the camera feeds from all around the property. She carefully went through them, one by one, and took on-screen snapshots of each feed, labeling the image files with what camera they'd come from. Then she put the files into a program she'd written back on the island. One by one, the camera feeds were replaced with still images from those same feeds. She had to wait on a couple of them as guards walked by. But it took less than five minutes for her to replace around thirty camera feeds, including the three in the gallery. If anyone was monitoring the video feeds remotely, they wouldn't see anything that happened next.

"Good to go," she said.

"Oscar, you're up," Nate said.

On Oscar's monitor, his gloved hand pulled out a tranquilizer gun with a silencer attached. I looked over at Elliot's monitor to watch Oscar's progress across the roof.

"All right," Elliot said. "Your nearest guard is to your left, about a hundred feet along the roofline."

We watched Oscar's thermal blob move toward the edge of the roof. I looked over to see Oscar's point of view on his monitor.

He leaned over the roof to check the guard's location, then moved back. He raised his gun, leaned gently over, took quick aim, and shot the guard. The tranquilizer was effective almost immediately.

Oscar put his hand in front of his face in a thumbs-up.

Elliot guided him around to take out the other guards. When every blob but Oscar's was still, I knew it was my turn. I felt a little queasy from nerves, but I knew exactly what I had to do. I'd practiced all week with the suit, so I was as ready as I'd ever be.

While Elliot kept an eye on the screens, Evie and I stepped out of the back of the van and went to the trunk of a black car parked nearby. My cold suit was inside. I stripped down to my underwear and then put on the first layer, a kind of wetsuit-type of thing to insulate my body against the cold.

Evie helped me into the second layer, covered with a webbing of tubes. Then it was an even more difficult task to get into the third layer, with another webbing of tubes all around it. She bent down to help me step into insulated shoes, then put an insulated hat on my head and topped it off with another insulated helmet, lined on the inside with more tubes.

We opened up the back doors of the van, and I sat on the ledge. Elliot reached down and snapped a rope line to a hook on the back of the suit so I wouldn't fall out. Then Evie slowly drove the van up the long driveway to the manor, where Oscar met us at the gate. He opened the gate, and we drove in.

We were lucky that Melinda Sedgewick lived in a part of town mostly populated by software billionaires—the houses were all far apart and separated by thick greenbelts, and the driveways were long to ensure privacy. Evie pulled around so that the rear doors of the van were near the front doors of the house and I would have the shortest distance to walk in my giant Michelin Man suit.

Elliot unsnapped me, and I slid out onto the ground. Oscar helped me fit an insulated mask over my face so my warm breath wouldn't set off the temperature sensors. Then he put my goggles on for me, complete with a camera feed of my own that went back to the van.

While Oscar got me all set up, Evie was back in the van, tapping away on her computer to turn off the basic alarm system, the one connected to the doors and windows of the manor.

Oscar connected all the various tubes to a pump in the back of the suit and turned the whole contraption on. I could feel a mild humming in the middle of my back, but it was nothing I couldn't ignore. I watched Elliot's thermal-image screen from my spot outside the van; we were a grouping of four orange blobs, but one of them was fading to yellow. Oscar switched something else on, and now my thermal blob had a flashing light on it, just like Oscar's had.

My blob went from yellow to green, then to blue, then to a dark purple. Then the only thing visible was the flashing light; the thermal cameras weren't picking me up at all. I felt a little chillier than usual, but it wasn't too bad.

"Sarah has gone dark," Elliot said.

"Get a move on," said Nate said's voice through the earpiece. "The insulation inside the suit will only work for so long before you start to get cold."

Evie tapped on another of her keyboards. One by one, the lights on the manor winked out. Now nobody passing by would be able to see anything at all. And if any of the cameras went back online for any reason, they'd only see black.

I flexed my thick gloves and shuffled forward; it was how I imagined that astronauts felt in their enormous suits. But they had the luxury of weightlessness, while I had the complete opposite. Oscar opened the front door of the manor for me, reached out to turn my goggles to night-vision mode, then shut the door behind me and went on to his next task, patrolling the perimeter.

It was eerie, walking the same path I had just a few nights ago. There was no doorman to accept my invitation or ogle my outfit this time. I trudged down the hall toward the ballroom, which was giant and spooky in the dark. It didn't help that I saw everything in shades of green, thanks to my night-vision goggles.

I caught sight of myself in a large, ornate mirror. What with the big black suit, and my head entirely covered with hat, mask, and goggles, I really did look like something out of a video game. Even in my nervousness, I thought it was pretty cool.

"I look like I'm wearing a giant Fremen stillsuit," I said.

"What on earth is that?" Evie asked.

"*That*, my friend, is a reference to the movie *Dune*, and now I know what I'm going to get for the next movie night," Elliot said. "Sarah, you just earned ten geek points."

I saw a flicker of movement to my right and jumped as much as the bulky suit would let me.

"Just me," Nate said. He was mostly a dark blur, even though I had my night-vision goggles on. The fabric of the tactical suit, already black and hard to see, seemed to scatter the small amount of available light so that Nate was more a murky cloud than a person-shaped object. He was grinning at me, and I realized what had caught my eye was the solid glow from his teeth.

I took a deep breath, then continued on my way. I crossed the ballroom where we'd danced so recently, found the staircase on the far side of the room, and started up the stairs. If I thought it was hard to walk in the suit, it was *way* harder to climb stairs.

"A little help here?" I said.

"My pleasure," Nate said. I couldn't see him smiling, since he was behind me, but I could hear it in his voice. I felt his hands on the gigantically padded butt of my cold suit, and he pushed gently but firmly to help me hoist the weight of the suit up the stairs.

"I hope you're enjoying this," I said.

"It would be nicer if your ass wasn't so cold," he said. I heard Oscar snicker in my ear.

We made it to the top of the stairs, and I trudged my way down to the gallery.

"I'm glad I don't have to dodge lasers in this thing," I said.

"Laser security systems only exist in the movies," Nate said. "*MythBusters* took that one on."

I stood in front of the door. "Ready up here, guys," I said.

"Elliot? Still in the black?" Nate asked.

"Good to go," Elliot said. "I'm picking up Nate's heat signature, but Sarah, you're just the flashing tracker light."

I took another deep breath. "Here we go," I said.

Nate slipped into the room across the hall so that the heat sensors in the gallery couldn't pick up any of his body heat. I opened the door and felt the rush of pressurized air come out at me. It didn't feel particularly cold this time, because I was already feeling a bit chilled. I knew the clock was ticking.

I shut the gallery door behind me so that the cold air would stay in the room. No alarms went off, and no lights flashed, so I figured I was doing all right.

The pedestal was in the center of the room, draped with a velvet cloth.

"Nate," I said, "just so you know, there's a cloth draped over the case."

"Hmm," Nate said. "I wasn't expecting that."

"Should I keep going?"

"Hold on," he said. "Evie, no alarms going off? No signal leaving the estate?"

"Nothing," she said. "We're fine out here."

"Okay, Sarah, keep on going," Nate said. "I'm right outside the door if there's a problem."

I shuffled toward the case, feeling extra nervous. We'd all expected the case to be uncovered, exactly as it had been when Nate and I had taken our tour at the party. Anything that deviated from the plan was a concern.

I got close enough to touch the case, then walked a slow lap around it, looking for any new wires, cords, sensors, or anything unusual. I saw nothing.

"I'm in touching distance," I said. "I can't see anything weird. Is everyone ready?"

"We're good out here," Evie said.

"Perimeter is still secure," Oscar said.

"Ready outside the gallery," Nate said. "Go ahead and take off the cloth."

I reached out with one of my giant gloves and managed to pinch a corner of the cloth. I pulled it away and just stood there silently for a moment, looking inside the case. I blinked a few times and realized I was shivering slightly.

"Um. Okay," I said.

"What?" Nate asked.

"There's no diamond here," I said.

"*What?*" Nate asked.

"Nate, it's gone. There's a card or something propped up in its place."

"Don't open the case," Nate said. "Lean in and look at the card. What is it?"

"It's hard to see," I said. "I think there's writing on it, but it's not written dark enough to stand out. It's all blasted out solid white in the night vision."

I couldn't take off my goggles, because they were insulated to keep my body heat inside the suit where it belonged. I also couldn't easily switch off the night vision, because the button was very small and my gloves were very large and clumsy.

"Get in close anyway. Evie, can you get something on the video feed?"

"Got it," she said. "It's hard to make out, since it's so dark in there; I'll have to run it through some filters. Or, no, wait. Sarah, I can turn the lights on, but you'll have to shut your eyes so you don't get blinded through the night-vision goggles."

"No problem," I said.

"Okay, lean in like you were before . . . Perfect. Eyes shut?"

I squeezed my eyes shut. "Go for it," I said. I could still tell when the lights came on. Everything glowed pink behind my eyelids. A moment later, the lights went dark again.

"Now, Sarah, if you'd move around to the other side of the case and squat down as best you can, I'd like to get as much of the back of the card as possible, in case there's something on it." I followed her instructions and tilted my head at the right angle, then shut my eyes again as she turned the lights on and then off.

My teeth were starting to chatter, and I was feeling really, really cold. "S-s-so are we d-d-done here?"

"Yes!" Nate exclaimed. "Your time in the suit is almost up. Get out of there as fast as you can. Oscar, can you come up here to help?"

He didn't have to tell me twice. I turned around and shuffled my way back to the door of the gallery. I opened the door, shut it behind me, and then started to make my way back down the hallway. I thought Oscar was coming up to help me get out of the house, but as he bounded up the stairs, Nate held out a hand for me to stop. He started unhooking all the machinery from the pump on my back.

Oscar pulled off my goggles, helmet, hat, and mask. They helped me get out of the outer layer of the suit and helped again to get me out of the middle layer. That left me in the base insulating layer. I should have felt warmer without that cold suit on me, but I was chilled to the bone.

"Here," Nate said. "A souvenir." He held out one of the beautiful fur-lined parkas from the room across the hall from the gallery. He helped me into it and zipped up the front. It was a slight improvement.

Oscar picked up a layer of cold suit under each arm, as if they weighed nothing. Clearly, I had a lot farther to go at building up strength. Nate wrapped an arm around me and helped me down the stairs, since I was still shivering. I noticed that he was carrying something in his other hand.

"What did you take?" I asked.

"A little souvenir of my own," he said. "Not as nice as that parka, although you won't have much use for it on the island."

"You'll have to take me somewhere cold, then," I said. "Maybe there's a ski chalet to rob somewhere."

"I like the way you think," he said.

"So what is it?"

"Cat's portrait," Nate said. "At the very least, it should make them think twice about using her again."

"I hope you left a calling card in its place."

"Of course," he said. "A card for a card, as the saying goes."

We loaded all the various cold-suit parts into the back of the van, and Evie drove it back out through the gates, with Elliot riding shotgun. Oscar ran down to the car and drove it up to meet me and Nate. We both climbed into the backseat, where Nate piled blankets on top of me. Oscar pulled through the gate and got out to close it; then we followed the van away from the manor.

A few miles down the road, we stopped at a twenty-four-hour doughnut place. Elliot jogged inside while Nate helped me out of the car, wrapping me so securely in blankets that I was back to slow, shuffling footsteps. I watched as Nate and Evie unloaded the parts of the suit from the van back into the trunk of the car so she could climb back up inside with all of her computers and monitors.

Evie tapped on her keyboard to turn all the lights back on. She turned the basic alarms back on, and then she shut down her program that displayed static images on all the camera feeds. With a brief flicker, they were all back to a live picture.

In one corner of one screen, I could see a shoe. I hoped that the guards would wake up before anyone from the Faction came back, and that they'd agree among themselves that nothing had happened. I'd hate to see the kind of punishment the Ultimates would dish out.

Elliot brought up a cardboard tray with hot coffee for everyone. I wrapped my hands around the paper cup, and the tingling in my fingers was both painful and fantastic. I sipped as fast as I could without burning my tongue.

Evie turned one of the screens so we could all see it. "So, here's the note."

It was a plain white card, about the size of a business card. In fact, it was quite similar to the logo calling cards that Doctor Oracle left behind.

There was just one sentence written on it: "Nice try, Doc. Not this time. —Alpha"

TWENTY-NINE

I dozed for most of the flight back, wrapped in a half dozen blankets, and exhausted from the combination of plodding around in the cold suit and being a big anxious panic monster. By the time the plane landed on the island, I was starting to feel normal again.

Jin was at the airfield to meet us, leaning on her crutches next to a trio of transport balls. We piled in and headed back to the residential sections. Most of the equipment would be brought back over for us later, although Nate carried the stolen portrait of Catalyst by hand.

We agreed to all get some sleep, then have a breakfast meeting in the morning. Nate walked me down to my door.

"Are you feeling all right? Warmed back up?"

"I think so," I said. "I'm just worn out."

"It's not just the exertion. The adrenaline rush always has a crash afterward."

"Good to know," I said. "I certainly feel like crashing."

"A few more hours of sleep and you'll be good as new," he said. He squeezed my shoulder and headed down the hall to his own apartment, looking fairly tired himself.

I pressed my ChatterBox against the panel next to the door, and it opened for me. I slumped my way inside and finally shrugged my way out of the insulated inner layer of the suit, trading it for a loose pair of shorts and a T-shirt. I brushed my teeth, washed my face, set an alarm on my CB, and collapsed into bed.

Before I knew it, the alarm was going off. I'd slept hard and dreamlessly, which was great. I got up and took a really hot shower. Nate was right: besides being a bit sore, I felt pretty darned good.

I threw on my most comfortable exercise pants and hoodie, along with a pair of flip-flops, and shuffled my way down the hall to Nate's apartment. The door slid open for me, and I went straight for the pitcher of orange juice on the counter. There was also a nice selection of doughnuts and other breakfast pastries, and some fresh fruit. I filled a plate and carried everything into the living room, where almost everyone was already sitting and eating.

Scar and Jin came in shortly afterward, got their own plates, and sat down. Jin handed me a wrapped package about the size of a book.

"What's this?"

"Open it," she said.

I tore off the paper and found a picture frame inside, silver with a beautiful cream-colored mat. Mounted in the frame were my two bobby pins, one bent in an L shape, the other bent open into a straight line.

I felt a little bit emotional. I hadn't mentioned to anyone that I wanted to keep the pins as a souvenir. Jin must have watched me carefully retrieve them from the scrubs and had guessed.

"I'm so proud of you," Jin said. "They're just perfectly done."

I hugged her tight, wiped away a little something that got caught in my eye, and set the frame on the coffee table, where I could look at it while I ate my doughnut. The silver of the frame she'd chosen was almost a perfect match for the metal cafeteria tray with the dent in the middle, I realized. The tray was currently sitting on the kitchen counter in my apartment. Now I had a matching pair of souvenirs to hang next to each other from my first big adventure.

We finished up with breakfast, and Evie turned on the TV. She plugged a thumb drive into the side and called up the image of the note that Alpha had left.

"So first off, before we get to the note," Nate said, "great work, everyone. The whole thing went off without a hitch, and I couldn't be more proud. And how about Sarah? How was that for her first big job?"

Everyone applauded for me, which felt really weird. And good. But mostly weird.

"You did me proud there, too," Jin said.

I hugged her again and had a little something more in my eye. Stupid dust.

Nate smiled and winked at me, then turned to the TV. "All right, then. So clearly, they knew we were coming."

"I thought about that," Evie said. "Tammy was part of my team, but we did help out a little bit on the project with the small test diamond. My guess is, she told them we were working with a black diamond, and they all assumed we might go after Sedgewick's."

"But if they knew we were coming, why weren't there extra guards?" I asked.

"They may have guessed at the *what* but didn't know the *when*," Nate said. "After all, we didn't decide on the perfect robbery date until just after we sent Tammy away."

"I don't think that's all of it," Rupert said. We all turned.

"What do you think?" Nate asked.

"I'd think they would be able to guess the when pretty well, since they all go out of town so seldom," Rupert said. "Yesterday was the perfect time for us to try. But I think the reason there weren't more guards was that it's personal for Alpha. He wants to catch you himself, not have a bunch of hired muscle try to take you down. He wants to catch you with his own hands."

"So that's why he took the diamond himself and left a personalized card," Scar said.

"Exactly," Rupert said. "When they get back later today, they'll know that we've been there, and Alpha knows that we know that he has the diamond. Now he'll be waiting for us—or more precisely, Doctor Oracle—to come to him."

"But where?" Evie asked.

"Where, indeed," Nate said. "At least he's giving us credit for being smart enough to figure it out. We just have to actually do the figuring."

"What if we don't figure it out?" Jin asked.

"Then there will probably be a good bit of gloating and taunting," Nate said. "What else can he really do? On the one hand, I'm sort of tempted to let it slide, and let him stew about things for a while. On the other hand, we're holding off on over a dozen projects right now because we don't have the power available for them—we could really use the Midnight Star. And it'd be an extra bonus to figure out Alpha's plan fast, just to show him how good we are."

"What do we know about him?" I asked.

"We'll have to go to the database for all of the information," Nate said, "but I know most of his origin story. He was a janitor at that nuclear power plant. The core started to melt down, and he went in and shut it down from the inside."

"Why would he do that?" I asked.

"Heroics," Nate said.

"Showing off," Elliot said.

"Stupidity," Oscar said.

"Suicide?" I asked, thinking about what I'd seen in his file.

"What?" Nate asked.

"His picture from before the accident," I said. "I remember it from his file. He was scrawny, geeky, and he looked really weak."

"So he wanted to kill himself because he was skinny?" Elliot was confused. "I'm skinny, and I'm perfectly happy."

"It was more than skinny," I said. "He looked *scary* skinny. Like he had a health problem or something."

"Enough to make him want to kill himself?"

"If it was already killing him, maybe? I don't know," I said.

Nate ran his hand over his chin. "It's as good a theory as any. We'll have to do more research in the database."

Nate asked us all to put some thought into Alpha's possible hiding places and adjourned the meeting. He and I went down to his office, accompanied by Evie and Jin. The room off to the side of Nate's office where the database computer lived was certainly not large enough for all eight of us. Besides, the rest of the guys knew we'd fill them in if we discovered anything.

We fired up the computer and scrolled forward and backward through Alpha's entry, reading everything over multiple times. It felt like there wasn't a lot of material from before his accident; most of the data on him was from after he'd gained his superstrength.

I went out to the computer in Nate's main office and started searching for Tyler Royce, Alpha's name from before. I opened up a few likely looking web pages and did a bit of reading before I came up with something interesting.

"Hey, guys," I said. "I found his high school yearbook."

Jin peeked around the open door. "Where?"

"One of those classmate-finding sites," I said. "It looks like someone scanned the whole thing in."

The yearbook, from a Custer High School, was kind of an awesome time capsule of hairstyles and clothing. I found Tyler's senior picture, in which he looked just as skinny but a bit younger than his ID from the nuclear plant. I scanned through the rest of the pages and found him mentioned on two of them.

"Oh boy," I said. "This kid was not popular."

"How so?" Nate asked.

"Some guys hoisted him up a flagpole," I said.

The other three came out quickly to take a look. There, in black and white, was a picture of three big jocks standing around the flagpole, clearly laughing their asses off. Poor skinny Tyler was up in the air, the clip that normally held a flag attached to the belt loop on the back of his trousers. It must have been a hell of a wedgie.

"Wow, they sure did," Evie said. "The cruelty of children knows no bounds."

"Hardly children," I said. "They were practically adults."

"In physical age only," Jin said. "So, I'm going to assume that this wasn't the only time he was picked on."

"Oh," I said. I turned to Nate. "You're the new bully."

"What?"

"He's huge and strong now, but crap like this can stay with a person for a really, really long time. No wonder he has a personal vendetta against you. You've outsmarted him more than once, so in his mind, I bet you're just the same as the bullies that sent him up a flagpole."

"But he's twice my size!" Nate said.

"Doesn't matter," I said.

"Too true," Evie said. "Once you're bullied, that mindset sticks with you. It wasn't until I was almost forty that I stopped thinking of myself as fat and ugly all the time."

Jin put her hand on Evie's arm. "I'm glad you stopped that, Evie. You're beautiful."

"I said *all* the time," Evie said. "Doesn't mean I don't still think it sometimes."

I scrolled back to Tyler's senior picture and read the text underneath: "Thanks to Mr. Purcell, Miss Green, and Mr. Hasselbeck. And special thanks to the best mom in the world."

I flipped up to the faculty section of the yearbook. Purcell and Green were teachers, and Hasselbeck was the vice principal. I scrolled back to Tyler.

"He didn't say anything about his friends," I said. "Most of the other kids mention their friends."

"Maybe he didn't have any," Jin said.

The guy was a total dick, and had discussed having me killed in a roundabout way. Still, I felt kind of sorry for him.

"He thanked his mum," Evie said. We all looked at her. "Right? A guy thanks his mum in his yearbook, I bet he's still close to her."

At her direction, I looked up the location of Custer High School. It was in Richland, Washington, a small city in the southeast corner of the state. I called up the white pages on the Internet and searched for anyone with the last name Royce in Richland. There were five hits.

"Yeah, that's what I thought," Evie said.

"About what?" Nate asked.

"I'm thinking that the Columbia Generating Station, where Tyler worked and where his accident happened, is only ten miles or so from Richland. He could have still lived at home while he worked there."

"He would have been in his midtwenties," Jin said. "Surely he would have moved out?"

"Yeah, but he thanked his mother in his yearbook," I said. "Teachers and mom—that was all. I see where Evie is going with this. No, I bet if we find out which Royce we're looking for, we'll find that he might even still have a room in Mom's house. Or maybe a little apartment set up in the basement."

"You think he took a diamond worth millions of dollars to his mom's house?" Nate asked.

"If it's the place where he feels safest, yes," Evie said.

"Fair enough," he said. "This one is your baby, so roll with it. Check in with all of the Royce families, see if Tyler belongs to any of them and if they still have his pennants and pinups on the walls of his room. We'll keep scanning the database for any other options."

"I'll make the calls, Evie," I said. I emailed links to all the web pages I'd used in my research to myself, then went to my own office down the hall to use the phone. I presented myself as a member of the high school reunion committee, trying to track down Tyler as we planned our twentieth reunion.

I reached people at three of the numbers, but they said they'd never heard of a Tyler. One of the numbers was disconnected. I got an actual answering machine on the last call, not even voice mail. The tape made a quaint clicking sound as it started to play. It was an older woman's voice.

"You've reached the Royce household," the recording said. "We can't come to the phone right now, but please leave a message at the beep, and we'll call you right back." The machine clicked, beeped, and I took a breath to speak. Then there were a couple of additional soft clicks on the other end of the line.

I hung up immediately.

Hustling back to Nate's office, I poked my head into the little room with the database computer. "Hey, Evie," I said. She stepped out of the smaller room into the larger office with me.

"Yes, love?"

"You remember answering machines, right?"

She wrinkled her nose. "Yes, Sarah. Are you trying to point out how old I am?"

"No, no, not at all," I said. "I just got an answering machine, and . . . well, the tape clicked, and the beep sounded, right? And then I heard a couple more really quiet clicks."

"What did you do?"

"Hung up fast," I said.

"Good girl," Evie said. She raised her voice toward the secret room. "Nate, I think this is it."

Nate came out to join us. "What did you get?"

I told him about the answering machine and the sounds it made. "Tracers," Evie said.

"I hung up right away," I said.

"Don't worry," Nate said. "We ping our phone signals around a number of relays. It'd take at least a minute or two to get a trace."

"So what do we do?"

"We're going on a little field trip," Nate said.

THIRTY

Half of us would be going on the road: Nate, Evie, Oscar, and me. Meanwhile, Scar would hold down the fort overall, and Elliot, Rupert, and Jin would pick up any slack for the other departments missing their leaders. This would be a longer trip than usual; instead of an overnight hop, we were planning for at least a couple of days. The minions were told about a corporate retreat that included team-building exercises and a ropes course. For most of the introverted geeks on the island, including me, it sounded like a terrible thing to have to do.

We flew into the little municipal airfield outside Seattle, where Nate had more than one safe house to choose from. He opted to take us to a converted warehouse near the airport, since it was closer to our jet and more well equipped than the group's high-rise apartment in the city. It also had a storehouse of all the equipment we could possibly need.

The hangar we parked the plane in had all the same vehicles as before, with one addition. Sitting among the black vans and black sedans was my little junky car, complete with all the bumper stickers holding it together.

"You rescued my car?" I asked Nate.

"I know how much you love it," he said. "Plus, now you can use it whenever you fly into town. Though I warn you, Jin said she'd be out here as soon as Adams clears her for travel so she can, and I quote, 'make some improvements.'"

It seemed a shame to call the place we stayed that night a warehouse; everything was redone inside in sleek modern lines, white and bright and beautiful. But on the outside it looked just enough like a ramshackle mess to hide its value, while still looking decent enough to deter would-be squatters. I was fine with the lack of curb appeal, since the interior amenities were great.

Oscar showed off another hidden talent by cooking dinner for all of us, and we had a good night's sleep before taking the short flight over the mountains to the eastern side of Washington State the next morning. We didn't have a safe house out there, but Nate had lined up rooms in the nicest hotel in town. It wasn't exactly deluxe, but it wasn't a dump.

We split up all the Royce addresses from the white pages, just in case. The location with the mysterious clicking answering machine was the home of Eleanor Royce, on the south side of town, but it would be foolish to not look at all of them.

Three of the houses were to the north, so Oscar and Evie took those addresses. Nate and I took Eleanor Royce, as well as a Harold Royce, on the south side of town. He asked if I'd mind driving while he navigated, primarily because while he drove transport balls all the time, it had been quite a while since he'd driven an actual car.

"How long has it been?" I asked.

"I think about two years?" he said. "Something like that. Jin gets twitchy when someone else drives her cars."

"Well, at least we're in rentals right now. Hopefully she isn't having a panic attack." We'd picked up two plain silver family sedans at the airport. They blended in perfectly with all the other cars on the road. We didn't have a hangar full of cars out here; besides which, a sleek black van with tinted windows would probably be a little more obvious than necessary. Our intention was to hide in plain sight while we did reconnaissance.

I drove us to the wrong Royce first, just to get it out of the way. We looked at the tiny house from across the street. Nate checked out some details with a pair of binoculars.

"Single story, on a slab," he said. "No basement windows, and the house is pretty small."

"Most likely not the place," I said. "Still, we must do our due diligence."

I dialed the number we'd pulled out of the white pages for Harold Royce. It rang three times; then the line was picked up. A gruff male voice said, "Hello?" It was one of the people I'd spoken to before, who said there was no Tyler in his family.

"Hello, sir," I said in a fake cheery tone at least an octave above my normal voice, "My name is Mary Lou Baker, and I'm calling from the City of Richland Energy Services. We've received a report that there may be an issue with your electricity meter."

"What's the problem?" he asked.

"We're not even certain there *is* a problem, sir," I said. "I'm wondering if you can do me a favor and take a look at your meter? If it's working properly, there should be a flat disc in the middle of it, slowly spinning around."

"You're not going to charge me for any repairs, are you?"

"Not at this time, sir," I said, upping the friendliness as much as I could. "In fact, if there's something wrong with your meter, it's a possibility that we may have overcharged you, and you would be due a refund. But before I can determine that, I'll need you to check that meter to see if that little wheel is spinning."

"All right, let me go check," he said. He sounded a bit less gruff since I'd mentioned a refund.

We watched his house from across the street. The front door opened and an older black man holding a portable phone shuffled out and around to the side of his house. He went to the electricity meter, wiped some grime off the front, and peered inside.

"So, definitely not Tyler Royce's mother," I said, holding my hand over the mouthpiece of my cell phone.

"Nope," Nate said.

We watched Harold Royce lift the phone to his ear. "It's right there, like you said it was," he said. "Flat wheel, turning around. It's going really slow."

"Perfect," I said. "The slower it spins, the less energy you're using. We'll have a meter reader out to you within the next few days to take a fresh reading, but it looks like we have an error on our side. You should see a refund on your next bill."

"Oh, good," he said as he shuffled back to his front door. "Okay, right. Thank you, miss."

"No, thank *you*, sir," I said. "You have yourself a wonderful day, now."

I hung up. "Your phone voice is really sickening," Nate said.

"Shut up," I said, starting up the car. "It gets results."

Nate wrote himself a note. "I'm going to make sure that Evie hacks the power system and gives Mr. Royce a decent refund," he said.

"You see?" I said. "This is why I like you evil geniuses."

"They're not all as nice as I am," he said.

"That's why you're my favorite."

We drove on to the house we suspected was our target, the home of one Eleanor Royce. I drove a slow lap around the block, looking at the house and scoping out a parking spot. Coming back around, I pulled up to the curb across the street from the Royce house, about two car lengths down. Nate got his binoculars back out. I could see that it was a much larger house than Harold Royce's; the footprint itself was larger, and this house was two stories.

"Definitely a basement," he said. "You can see the windows along the bottom edge of the house."

I got my own binoculars out. "Mailbox says Royce," I said. "Plus, look at the front stoop. It's well after noon, and the newspaper is still sitting out there."

"Nobody home right now, you think?"

"Probably not, but I don't necessarily want to go knocking."

"How about this," Nate said. "Let's make sure the phone number we have is going to this house."

"How?"

He grabbed a baseball cap out of the backseat and pulled it low over his eyes, then opened his door. "Get ready to make the call on my signal."

I watched him stroll across the street, casual as anything. He walked straight up the driveway, but instead of taking the left turn that would take him to the front door, he continued along the side of the house until he was near a side door. Considering the layout of all the houses I'd ever been in, I figured the side door led into the kitchen.

He gave me a thumbs-up, and I dialed the number I had for Eleanor Royce. It rang four times, then went to the answering machine again. I hung up before it even made it to the mysterious double click.

Nate casually strolled back down the driveway, looking up at the wires connected to the house. Hands in his pockets, he sauntered back across the street and got back in the car.

"Definitely the right house," he said. "I heard the phone ring inside. Nothing looks obviously booby-trapped, but you never know. I don't see any newer phone lines or cables coming out of the house, so if there's a wiretapping device, it has to be on the inside. Which means that the person who set it has free and open access to get into the house."

"This theory is sounding better all the time," I said.

"It sure is," he said. "I do have one more idea I'd like to try."

Nate called up a map of the area on his cell phone, scrolled around a little, then had me drive two blocks south. There was a small convenience store on the corner, the kind of mom-and-pop shop that the bigger cities had all put out of business years ago. He tossed his baseball cap back in the rear seat.

"What are we doing here?"

"You want to know about a neighborhood, you go to the corner shop," he said. "Come on."

We went into the little store, and it was like stepping back thirty years in time. The shelves held a little bit of everything so people in the neighborhood wouldn't have to go all the way to the big grocery store to get that one little item. There was a tiny white-haired man sitting behind the counter.

"Excuse me," Nate said. The little old man looked up and squinted at Nate through his thick glasses.

"Good afternoon, sonny," the man said.

"Good afternoon," Nate said. "How are you?"

"Been better, been worse," the man said. "Yourself?"

"Not too shabby. Though I'm wondering if you can help me."

"I'll see what I can do," said the man.

"I'm trying to track down a friend from high school, and I know I'm close to his old house. His name was Tyler Royce—he lived somewhere around here?"

"Oh, yeah, Tyler. I remember him. Good kid. Kinda sickly. Something with his stomach, I think."

That explained his anemic-looking pictures. A lot of those gut diseases make people tired and thin.

"Such a shame, what happened," the old man said.

"Oh? What's that?" Nate said.

The old man sat up a little straighter, smiled, and rubbed his hands together. Nate had led him straight into the trap of being the one to fill in strangers on bad news. Like most people, the old man was delighted to take on the job.

"It musta been ten years ago at least," he said. "Young Tyler was living at home and working out at the power plant. There was some kinda accident. I heard he saved at least a dozen other guys but got hurt up real bad."

"Oh no," I said. "That's horrible! He . . . he didn't *die*, did he?"

The old man leaned back on his stool. "Not that we know of, no. But I hear tell he was messed up real bad by the accident and had to go into a special home. He never did come back around here."

"That's a terrible shame," I said.

"Ah, but," said the old man as he leaned forward, "Ellie must get some nice checks from the power plant because of the accident. Got that nice new car a couple of years back. Always pays in cash, never needs to run a tab anymore."

"Good for her," Nate said. "I wonder if you could tell me, in which direction would I find her house? I'd like to pay his mother a visit and offer my condolences on Tyler's terrible accident."

"I could tell you, but she ain't there right now."

"Oh? Where did she go?"

"Came by yesterday morning," the old man said. "Got some gum and snacks. She told me she'd won a trip from one of those Publishers Clearing House types and she was going away to Branson for a couple of weeks. I told her to check out that Dixie Stampede for me. Always been a fan of Dolly Parton." The old man made a kind of half squint, half wink at Nate, which made it clear what part of Dolly he liked.

"Wise man," Nate said. We picked out two bottles of soda and some chips. The old man rang us up, and Nate pressed a twenty into his hand. "Keep the change, my friend. Have a good day."

The old man beamed. "You, too, sonny and miss."

We drove back by the house one more time on our way out of the area. The newspaper was still on the front porch.

"I'm feeling good about this one," Nate said. "Mystery trip out of nowhere? Classic technique."

"So that means he expects us to come by?"

"Probably," Nate said. "But if she just left yesterday for a two-week trip, we may be able to catch him by surprise. He won't expect us to have figured out his location this quickly."

"I hope you're right," I said, driving back to the hotel so we could rendezvous with the others.

"I hope so, too," he said.

THIRTY-ONE

We flew back to Seattle that evening in order to plan and pack up everything we needed. The warehouse was fully stocked with field equipment, and it was much more comfortable and luxurious than the best hotel in Richland, Washington. We wanted to get rolling the next day, to give Alpha as little time as possible to put his defenses in place.

I knew that Alpha was making this one personal, and I was pretty sure Nate was taking the whole thing more personally than usual, too. They weren't the only ones—the guy had stowed me away in a windowless room and talked openly about making me, a "useless civilian," disappear. I wanted to take him down, and take him down *hard*.

That evening in the warehouse, Oscar was hunched over a computer with two monitors. On one, he was looking over aerial maps of the neighborhood to scout out all possible approach and escape routes. On the other, he had the blueprints of Eleanor Royce's house, which Evie had acquired from the city's encrypted files. He was busy filling up a notepad with thoughts and ideas.

Evie was on another computer, hacking into the local utilities. Her main intention was to see if she could get access to the power at Eleanor Royce's house remotely, or if we'd have to patch in like we did at Melinda Sedgewick's manor. While she was in the system, Nate asked her to give a refund to Harold Royce. She not only gave him a refund for the past two months of payments but also reduced his rate by half.

Nate and I stacked up equipment and talked about possibilities. We figured if we came up with a couple of different plans, one of them might fit in with Oscar's findings about the neighborhood. Most of the equipment was fairly standard: black protective tactical suits for everyone and the black ChatterBoxes we used for missions, all tied into each other. We put out an assortment of gadgets on the huge living room floor so we could see what we had on hand.

"So, we're thinking basement?" Nate asked, setting a pair of grappling hooks down next to coils of thin, black, ultrastrong rope.

"Likely," I said. "But there's also a chance he has something upstairs. The plans show a three-bedroom house, so what if they combined two of those into his bachelor apartment?"

"We'll check everywhere, of course," he said, "but I'm betting on the basement."

"Agreed," I said. I also felt good about the basement. When Tyler had the accident that turned him into Alpha, he would have been twenty-five. A midtwenties young man still living at home would have wanted more privacy than having a bedroom on the same floor as his mother, even though they were close.

"I have access to the power grid," Evie called across the room. "You'd think these people would use better security."

"Even if they did, Evie, you'd tackle that, too," Nate said.

"Such a flatterer, you," she said.

I tested out four pairs of night-vision goggles and put one on top of each of the tactical suits. "Nate," I said.

"Yeah?"

"Thanks for bringing me along on this one."

"Sarah, even if Jin weren't out with a broken leg, I'd have brought you on this one."

"Really?"

"Yes, really." He checked over a case full of tiny tranquilizer darts. "Besides the fact that you come up with good ideas and can handle yourself in a crisis, you've actually had more exposure to Alpha than all the rest of us combined. That's a huge asset."

"I'm just glad to be useful," I said.

"Plus," he said, "the bonus for me is how much I like having you around."

Oscar sauntered up to us. "I hate to break up the lovefest, but I just got an email from Jin."

"What's up?" Nate asked.

"A notice went out to police and government agencies, very under the radar. Commander Alpha is taking a couple of weeks off, so they shouldn't expect him to show up at any crisis they may be experiencing. The rest of the Ultimate Faction assures everyone that they'll be extra vigilant and helpful."

"Sounds like we're definitely on the right track, then," Nate said. "Unless it's an incredible coincidence that he's taking two weeks off, while his mother just shipped out for two weeks in Branson."

"Yup," Oscar said. "Hey, can you make sure to pack my shoes with the toes?"

"Got 'em," I said, pointing at them next to Oscar's tactical suit. I'd tried a pair myself but didn't like the feeling of having my toes individually separated inside my shoes. I stuck with a pair of lightweight running shoes with heavy-duty traction.

"Awesome possum," he said, and went back to his computer screens.

Nate and I looked over all the equipment we had laid out on the floor. "We can't fit all of that in the trunks of two rental sedans," I said.

"I've made a reservation for a cargo van," he said. "So we can bring anything we need."

"So prepared," I said. "I bet you were a Boy Scout."

"Camp Fire," he said. "Similar, but they had a cooler summer camp."

We took a break from our preparations, and Oscar drove out to get pizza. When he returned, we gathered around the dining table and listened to his ideas.

"The neighborhood is pretty standard," he said. "A grid of streets, with houses backed up on each other. The Royce house is third from the west end, so of the four directions, the easiest escape routes are out the front, or out the back and through the rear neighbor's backyard, then front yard. There are also two neighboring backyards to the west, to get to the side street, but it looks like the house on the end has a really high fence."

"Let's hope we can keep it simple and just go in and out the front," Nate said.

"So, inside the house," Oscar said, pushing the blueprints across the table. "A pretty standard three-floor layout: the main floor, with living room, dining room, kitchen, and a small bathroom. Upstairs are three bedrooms and an additional bathroom. Down from the main floor is the basement, which the blueprints show as mostly open space. There is what looks like a laundry area in the corner but nothing beyond that."

"There's no record of any extra work down there? No walls put up, no bathroom installed?"

"No, but you can put in interior walls without a permit. It may not be legal or up to code, but if you're building in your basement, who's going to stop you? There's already a wet wall down there for the laundry, so someone could have done some plumbing for a bathroom, too. There's just no way to know without seeing it."

"Got it. Okay, what's our path to the basement?"

"It's pretty easy. The side door leads to the kitchen, and the basement door is also in the kitchen, just across from the door to the outside. It's not a private entrance to the basement, but it's the next best thing."

"I'll still want to check upstairs," Nate said, "but the basement is looking more and more likely."

"If we get into trouble, there are some options," Oscar said, turning back to his computer monitor and pulling up an area map. He pointed at several spots on the screen. "Here's the house. Two blocks to the west, we have a park. It's mostly open green space, but there's also a wooded area. It could be useful. Over here is an elementary school, and this over here is a supermarket."

"What's that big building to the east?" I asked.

"YMCA," Oscar said. "It's pretty big, but it's likely to be locked up. Still, it would have a number of good hallways to get lost in." He pointed at a couple of other helpful locations, including the little convenience store, a gas station, and a couple of restaurants. "These will all likely have alarm systems, so a smashed window will get the police rolling. If all else fails, we may be able to escape during the confusion."

"Let's hope it doesn't come to that," Nate said. He looked around at all of us. "This is a tough one, guys. It's in a huge rush, we haven't been able to put in the usual due diligence in researching the location, and we don't really know what we're headed in for, except that we know that there's a guy out there who's really strong, can punch any of us into next week, and has a personal vendetta against me. If any of you want to opt out, I won't hold it against you."

"Hell no," Evie said. She looked at me. "He took away one of our own and was going to do heavens knows what with her. Whatever he was planning, I'm sure it would make me quite angry."

"Agreed," Oscar said. "That guy thinks he can outsmart us, he's in for a surprise."

Nate looked at me. "I'm in," I said. "My mother always said, if someone cares enough to kidnap you twice, they're worth sticking with."

"Right, good," Nate said. "Let's figure out who's doing what."

* * *

We parked the van across the street from Eleanor Royce's house the next night, just shy of eleven o'clock. Evie had a couple of laptop computers set up in the backseat of the rental van, and would be monitoring our goggle-mounted video feeds from inside. She also had access to the power in the area, both inside and outside the houses.

We all had our tactical suits on, with the hoods up to cover our hair and parts of our faces. Oscar, Nate, and I pulled on our gloves and checked out our goggles, while Evie turned off a couple of the streetlights on the block, as well as a couple on each of our main escape routes. We would be able to be in shadow no matter which way we had to go.

The neighboring house that shared a driveway with the Royce house had a motion-activated light on the outside; Evie turned it off in advance. Our target house was completely dark already, but Evie shut off the main power anyway, so we wouldn't be surprised by someone turning on a light switch.

She ran a few scans of the house and determined that there were no active audio or video feeds and no wireless networks. It looked as if the owner had gone on vacation and left everything turned off. Thanks to our hijacked satellite, her monitors also showed no orangey-reddish blobs that would indicate a person inside the house. She gave us the all-clear, and we checked our equipment.

We had a weird assortment of gadgets on us, because we weren't sure what we were in for. We all had grappling hooks and black rope attached to our belts, in case climbing was necessary. Nate and I each had a full lock-picking kit, and we all had infrared flashlights, so we could see easily in the dark with our night-vision goggles.

I had a couple of carabiners hooked to my belt loops, and the guys each had a holster with a tiny silenced pistol loaded with tranquilizer darts. Wire cutters, a lighter, a mechanical pencil, a pad of paper, and wet wipes were among the other things in our pockets. It was a heavy load, but it was like pockets full of feathers compared to the multilayer cold suit.

Evie kept a stash of extra equipment back out in the van: two of every common tool, including hammers, screwdrivers, and wrenches; a crowbar, a tire jack, and a small arsenal of knives. We were ready for almost anything.

We slipped out of the back of the van quietly. The street was lined with large trees, which helped block any moonlight that might have given us away. Nate went straight for the kitchen door and picked the lock. I raised my goggles to check if I could see him in the dark; with the streetlights out, it was hard to see anything. I slid my goggles back on and watched as he looked all around the door, checking for traps.

I scanned the front of the house and noticed that the porch was bare. So either the newspaper we'd seen the day before was stolen, or someone had taken it into the house.

Nate opened the kitchen door, looked around more, then slipped inside. The neighborhood was quiet. Even if there was a security system, Evie had cut all power to the house.

I went across the street next, hidden in the shadows of the big trees. I slipped inside the house and squatted down beside the kitchen counters, next to where Nate was already waiting. A few moments later, Oscar came in after us.

Nate gave us a thumbs-up, our signal to go about our tasks. Oscar headed upstairs to check out the top floor. My job was the main floor, and Nate was taking the basement. We all went very slowly, looking for traps along the way.

I slowly walked the perimeter of the living room, checking every possible nook and cranny with my flashlight. The house was pretty old, with creaking hardwood floors that looked like they were original. There were some gaps in the floorboards, and they needed a serious refinishing. The furnishings were in line with older-woman chic, with lots of floral patterns and doilies.

I got to the front door and realized that Alpha might be dumber than I thought.

"Found a booby trap, guys," I said quietly.

"What is it?" Nate asked in my earpiece.

"A wire, very low across the front door frame."

"Wait, but he didn't put one on the kitchen door?"

I looked at the front door. "The door is unlocked. I guess he figured we'd go for the easy way."

"What a moron," Oscar said.

"Not necessarily," Nate said. "Maybe he put the obvious trap there so we'd be lulled into thinking that he's a moron. Then something else will hit us. Stay sharp."

I continued my lap of the living room, finding nothing. I checked behind the pictures, under the sofa cushions, and inside the covered candy dish. No booby traps, but also no diamond.

"Found another one," Oscar said. "Another wire in the doorframe, on an upstairs bedroom. Looks like it'd trigger a net to fall from the ceiling."

"The good news is, we were right. This is totally a bachelor-pad basement," Nate said. "The bathroom was first, right next to the laundry room. All clear in there."

I made my way around the outside of the kitchen, checking all the cupboards. Nothing. I looked at a rug in the middle of the floor; it looked kind of lumpy.

I got down on the ground, put my head on the floor, and lifted one corner of the rug just high enough to peek under.

"Wow, guys," I said. "I'm not entirely sure, but I think there's a pressure-sensitive switch under this rug in the kitchen."

"Okay, that's sneaky," Oscar said. "I take back my moron statement."

"I'm being extra careful down here," Nate said. "Slow and steady wins the race."

I only found one more booby trap on the main floor, which would have been triggered by someone opening the window of the tiny bathroom. That one was barely hidden; it was a plank of wood with nails sticking through it, mounted on a hinge. Anyone opening that window from the outside would have received a face full of nails.

"I'm liking this less and less," I said after describing the trap to the guys.

"Just think, he isn't done yet," Nate said. "This is just the first stuff he put up." He'd found a pressure plate of his own in the basement and reported that he was creeping along at a snail's pace.

I looked down the stairway to the basement. There was a door at the top of the stairs in the kitchen, and weirdly enough, I saw that there was another doorway at the bottom of the stairs.

There were hinges on one side, but I couldn't see the door itself; it must have been standing wide open. The extra door made me uneasy.

"Nate got the best floor, guys," Evie said in my ear. She was watching all of our video feeds back in the van. "It's like an epic shrine to the midtwenties male."

"Judging by the age of the movie posters on the walls, I bet this room hasn't been touched in the dozen years since the accident," Nate said. "It's a time capsule of Alpha before he was Alpha."

"Good lord, it's every cliché in the book," Evie said. "Billiards table, neon beer signs, pictures of girls in bikinis on the walls. There's a neatly made twin bed against the wall, and a little bitty fridge."

"We didn't *all* have a pool table in our midtwenties," Nate said.

"Of course not," Evie said. "But then again, when you were in your midtwenties, you had an island."

"Touché," Nate said. I could hear the tension in his voice. He had the hardest room in the house; the only means of escape from the basement were the very small windows and the staircase with two doors.

"I'm checking out the pool table," Nate said.

"Upstairs is clear," Oscar said. "I'm coming down to the main, Sarah."

I went to the foot of the stairs that led to the second floor and met Oscar. "If it's anywhere, it's in the basement," he said. We went around to the kitchen and looked down the stairs to the basement.

"I found it," Nate said.

"Where?" Oscar asked.

"Under the eight ball, corner pocket." A long pause. "It's one of those old-style pool tables, with the mesh bag pockets. I can see all around, and I'm not seeing anything attached to the pocket."

"Careful," I said. "It feels too easy."

"I know," Nate said.

"You're sure you don't want one of us to come down there with you?" I asked.

"Best that only one of us is in danger, in case something happens. Stick to the plan," Oscar said.

Another long pause as we waited for Nate.

"Okay, I have the eight ball out," Nate said. "I'm looking straight down at the Midnight Star. Nothing is attached to it. Checking it out from all possible angles."

"Looks clean to me, too," Evie said from out in the van.

Oscar reached out and grabbed my hand. I squeezed his back. We kept looking down the stairs, even though we couldn't see anything. I wanted to be down there with Nate. I wanted to be out in the van watching his video feed. But I stayed where I was, because that's where the plan dictated that I stay, until Nate came back upstairs.

"Okay, I have my hand on the diamond," Nate said. Nothing happened.

"Don't rush back up," Oscar said. "Take your time."

"You know it," Nate said. "Okay, here goes."

There was a split second where I thought we were going to get out of there just fine. Then there was a muffled bang, the house shook a tiny bit, and that mysterious second door at the bottom of the basement stairs slammed shut.

Oscar and I looked at each other, already trying to figure out what to do. He opened his mouth to speak, then snapped it shut instantly when we heard a voice. It was muffled in my open ear and more clear on the side with the earpiece. The voice was down in the basement with Nate.

"So nice of you to visit my family home, Doctor Oracle," Commander Alpha said.

THIRTY-TWO

Oscar and I looked down the stairs, then at each other again, then back down the stairs at the basement. Was Alpha actually here?

"Why not come out and show yourself?" Nate said in his deep Doctor Oracle voice.

"Oh, I will," Alpha said. I plugged my free ear so I could listen to the feed over my earpiece. He didn't sound as clear as Nate. "I'm just a few minutes away, but I have you on the Bluetooth in my car. I wonder, do you have Bluetooth in your car, Doctor Oracle?"

"In my private jet, too," Nate said.

"Hey, chums," Evie said over our headsets. "Nate has written a note: 'Foot stuck, try door and windows.'"

"Nate, we're on our way," Oscar said. "Evie, can you turn off his earpiece so we don't distract him?"

"You got it," Evie said. Now we could hear Nate and his conversation with Alpha, but he wouldn't hear anything we said, so he could concentrate on talking to Alpha.

"A note instead of talking," I said. "He doesn't want Alpha to know there's anyone else here."

"Exactly," Oscar said. "If Alpha thinks that Doctor Oracle is trapped in the house without help, he may take more time getting here."

Oscar and I went down the kitchen stairs and checked out the door. There was no keyhole, so we couldn't pick the lock. The hinges were either on the inside or hidden away completely, so we couldn't take the pins out to open the door that way.

"You certainly got there fast, Doctor. I have to admit, I'm impressed," Alpha said. "I still had a number of things I was going to install in the house over the next few days."

"Sorry to disappoint you," Nate said. "I was just too excited to see the childhood home of Tyler Royce."

Oscar and I went outside to look at the basement windows. They were awfully small, set low in the foundation. Just like the windows in the doors at the Ultimate Faction's trainee dormitory, there was a pattern of wire mesh sandwiched in the glass. We'd have to smash the glass to get to the wires so we could cut them, and after all that work, I still wasn't sure any of us would be able to fit through.

We shined our lights in and saw Nate bent over in the middle of the room, next to what looked, weirdly, like a pool table without legs. He waved at us, then went to work on another note with his pad and pencil.

"I'm completely aware that I should have been more secret about my history," Alpha said. "Though I did think it'd take longer for you to figure it out. But that's all right—I've already had time to make the most important upgrades. There's no escape for you. The kitchen stairs are the only way out, and that's a metal-core door in your way, without any locks to pick. The windows are a bit small, and even if you had something down there with you to break the glass, you'll see that they're impregnated with wire mesh."

"New message," Evie said. "'Boot caught, trying to get loose.'"

"We saw," Oscar said. "It looks like the pool table is resting on his foot."

Oscar and I went back to the kitchen. "Okay. No door, no windows," I said.

He knocked on the wall. "Pretty thin drywall, if we could find a way in from the side."

I stepped toward the living room, and the hardwood floors creaked under my feet. I stopped and was suddenly glad I watched so many fixer-upper shows on TV. "Or through the ceiling?" I asked.

Oscar's eyes got wide, and he dashed out the side door. "Evie," I heard him say in my ear, "can you please grab anything in the toolbox we can use to pry? The crowbar, claw hammers, anything."

I heard them both over my headset as Oscar grabbed what he could from the van. I started jumping around the living room in a way that probably made me look crazy. The old flooring squeaked and groaned under my feet in several places.

"Evie," I said once Oscar said he was on his way back, "I figure sneaking is done. Can you get me lights on the main floor?"

"On it," she said. I flipped the kitchen and living room light switches so the lights would turn on when Evie reconnected the power. I pulled off my night-vision goggles and slung them around my neck.

Oscar came back in with a crowbar and the biggest claw hammer I'd ever seen, his goggles pulled down like mine. The lights flickered on, and I kept jumping on the floor. I found the spot that squeaked the loudest, which meant it had the loosest floorboards.

"Here," I said. We were close to one of the walls. "Pry the baseboard off so we can get at the ends of the flooring."

Nate's earpiece was still shut off, so that our planning wouldn't distract him from bantering with Commander Alpha. "Evie," I said, "can you turn Nate's feed back on?"

"Done," she said.

"Nate, we're coming at you through the ceiling. Hold on tight." We left the channel open but stayed quiet so he could concentrate on talking to Alpha.

Oscar had the baseboard pulled up, and the old, old hardwood flooring was just as wonderfully uneven as I hoped it would be. Oscar and I used the claw end of the hammer and the crowbar to pry up the planks of wood. Most of them came up surprisingly fast, since the wood was old and a bit crumbly and the nails were already loose.

Alpha continued his mocking tirade as we worked. We had no idea how far away he was, but I hoped he'd brag about making the last turn into the neighborhood to give us warning.

"I'm surprised at you, Doctor," Alpha's tinny voice went on over Nate's open channel. "I thought you had rules about getting involved with your enemies' families. I wasn't entirely sure you'd come to my mother's house, but I guess you've shown your true colors."

"Well, first off, your mom isn't even *here*, Alpha. Secondly, you're the one who brought me here, so getting her involved is *your* fault. Third, you don't exactly play by the rules yourself," Nate said in his gruff voice. "Since you kidnapped my kidnap victim, I guess we're even."

"Ah, yes, the irritating Miss Valentine. Have you killed her yet? I hope so. She was annoying as hell, even for a civilian."

I wrenched a board up with a bit of extra vigor and tried to ignore the rest of their conversation.

Evie said, "I've shut Nate's earpiece back off for a second. So you know, I'm still not picking up any video signal, but there is a cell phone signal down there. Must have autodialed Alpha when his trap was triggered."

"So at least he can't see how many of us there are, as long as we try to stay quiet," I said.

Oscar looked down into the hole we'd made. "I don't know how quiet we're going to be," he said.

We'd made a big enough crater in the top layer of hardwood flooring to be able to get through to the basement. Our next obstacle was a layer of subflooring, which was fortunately made of narrow wooden planks instead of sheets of plywood. I took a couple of whacks at a plank with my hammer, and it crumbled.

"I think Mrs. Royce needs to have her home checked for termites," Oscar said.

We smashed away at the subfloor until we had another hole. The shattered pieces of wood sat on top of a layer of insulation— not the newer pink stuff; this was gray and lumpy. I was never happier to be wearing gloves. Oscar and I took turns scooping a handful of the stuff out and throwing it onto the living room furniture. I just hoped it wasn't made of pure asbestos.

In a few moments, the old-lady furniture was covered with a fine layer of gray fluff, and our hole was even deeper. This time the bottom of it was a smooth surface. Oscar stepped carefully down into the hole, braced himself on the side, and kicked one foot down. I grabbed hold of his belt just to be safe. He kept kicking until his foot went through the thin drywall ceiling of the basement.

We looked down but couldn't see much in the dark below. Since Nate was stuck in the middle of the room, he wasn't able to flip a light switch, even though Evie had turned the power back on.

"Sounds like you're smashing some things around in there, Doctor," Alpha said.

"Damn you, Commander Alpha," Nate shouted in his deep voice. "You've built an inescapable trap. But still, I must try."

Even in the panic of the moment, I had to roll my eyes at that one. It did, however, reassure Alpha that Doctor Oracle was still in his basement.

I switched the lights back off in the living room and kitchen. No sense in Alpha finding the house all lit up, and we were going to head into the pitch-dark basement anyway. Best to get ready for the dark. Oscar and I put our goggles back on.

"We're going in, Evie," Oscar said.

"Turning Nate's channel back on," she said. "Good luck."

Oscar kicked around a bit more, until the hole was big enough for someone to fit through. While he did that, I took my grappling hook and snagged it on a big metal radiator on the other side of the room. I pulled as hard as I could to test the line. The radiator groaned a little bit but seemed solid enough. I tossed the rope down the hole. Oscar held a finger up to his lips and slid down the rope. I quickly climbed down after him.

Nate smiled broadly and blew kisses at me when I reached the basement floor. Oscar was already kneeling next to Nate, checking out the table that had him trapped. The side of the pool table rested perfectly on Nate's foot. He'd untied his shoelace already but still wasn't able to get his foot free. And the angle he was stuck at meant he wouldn't be able to get much leverage.

Oscar caught my eye and mimed lifting the table. We flanked Nate, got a firm hold, and lifted. I never knew that pool tables were so heavy, but I guess that's what you get with a solid chunk of slate. Maybe this one was extra deluxe.

We didn't get the table up too high, but it should have been enough for Nate to pull his foot out. He tried, but there was still something stuck. Oscar and I dug in a little harder and lifted the table up another inch, and Nate was able to slide his foot free. The entire toe was dented in; it looked like the table had mangled the steel toe in the boot and then become caught behind the steel plate.

Nate tried his weight on the foot, and winced but gave us the thumbs-up. He tied his boot back up as fast as he could.

"Almost there, Doctor," Alpha said. "I can't wait to see who you really are. Though instead of referring to you by your title, I could call you . . . *Jeremy.*"

That perplexed me for a minute, until I remembered that Jeremy was the fake name Nate had given Catalyst when they were dating. If we needed another piece of evidence that she was behind all the leaks, Alpha's self-assured error was definitely it.

"I can't wait to take you down, Alpha," Nate said. He limped toward the rope. Oscar had been listening to Alpha's voice and went over to a corner of the room. He plucked a cell phone off a bookshelf and tucked it into his pocket.

Nate waved for me to go up the rope first. I rolled my eyes at the chivalry but shinnied up the rope as fast as I could. Oscar quickly followed. Nate grabbed the rope and tried to go hand over hand to protect his foot, but it was much too slow. Oscar and I grabbed the rope and pulled, and once again I was glad beyond measure to have gloves on. They truly were good for a thousand and one nefarious uses.

Nate grabbed hold of the rough edge of the hole, and Oscar and I reached down to grab his arms. We pulled him up and over the edge of the hole, until finally we were all back in the living room together. Nate slapped each of us on the arm with a grin, then took the cell phone from Oscar.

"Oh, would you look at that," Alpha said. "A mysterious van across the street from my mother's house."

"Crap," Evie said over the headset.

Nate covered the microphone on the cell phone so it wouldn't pick up his voice. "Get out of here, Evie," he whispered.

"I wonder," Alpha said, "if there's anyone in there. Perhaps I should go tear the doors off their hinges."

"There's nobody else but me here, Alpha," Nate said.

Alpha laughed. "Which tells me you *do* have an accomplice."

At least we didn't have to tell Evie that we'd managed to get Nate out of the basement; she would have been able to watch it on her monitors. I hoped she already had the engine running and the van ready to go.

I picked up my claw hammer and stuck the handle down through one of the carabiners on my belt. The hammer did its job well as a tool, but it would also be handy as a weapon. Oscar quickly pulled my grappling hook from the radiator and rolled up the rope.

We opened the kitchen door and peeked out. We could see the van across the street, with headlights shining on it. Our view of Alpha's car was blocked by the neighboring house. We ran as quickly as we could around the outside of the house to the backyard. Evie gunned the van's engine and drove away.

We ran to the back fence, Oscar's second-best option for getting away. There would be no easy escape out the front.

"Oh, what a shame," Alpha said. "Looks like your friend has deserted you." We saw a flash of headlights as Alpha pulled his car into the driveway, but we were in the opposite corner of the backyard, where he couldn't see us. His car came to a quick, jerky stop, the tires squealing. I almost laughed; if anyone had a heavy foot when driving, it would definitely be Commander Alpha.

"Sorry, all," Evie said in our ears. "I hoped he'd follow me."

Oscar and I boosted Nate over the back fence. He dangled on the other side, then dropped down. The fence wasn't that tall, maybe seven or eight feet, so at least Nate didn't have far to fall with his injured foot.

"Well, at least we have each other," I heard Nate say on the other side of the fence. He was still talking to Alpha, to gain us as much time as possible.

Oscar gave me a boost up to the top of the fence. I threw my leg over the top and fell down the other side, barely managing to stay on my feet. Oscar jumped up easily and threw himself over the fence, landing in a roll and standing right back up. It was a move so smooth I could never hope to match it. He sprinted up to the side of the neighbor's house and unlatched the side gate for us. I stuck with Nate, who was limping even more.

We crept down along the side of the house, expecting to see Evie drive up in the van at any moment.

"Oh no no *no*," Evie said in my ear. "Bloody hell. Guys, I just blew a tire. Damn it to hell!"

At almost the same moment, we heard a yell from the Royce house behind us. Clearly Alpha had just found a hole in his mother's living room floor.

Nate tapped the "End Call" button on the cell phone and tossed it aside. No sense in stringing Alpha along anymore. He cleared his throat and went back to his normal voice. "Evie, where are you?"

"A couple of blocks over," she said.

"You can put the spare on, right?" Nate asked.

"Jin would kill me if I couldn't," she said. "I can get the tire changed, but it'll take some time. Five, ten minutes?"

Nate looked at us. "So we need to kill a little time. Ideas?"

"Yeah," Oscar said. "Evie, meet us at the YMCA when you're done."

"The YMCA?" I asked.

Oscar grinned. "There's a pool there. Sink-or-swim time," he said. Nate looked puzzled for a second, then laughed.

"See, this is why I surround myself with the best people," he said.

THIRTY-THREE

Oscar and I flanked Nate as we hustled down the sidewalk. The YMCA was about three blocks away, so Nate had to limp as well as he could for a farther distance than I would have liked. We kept an eye out in front and behind, since we weren't sure what direction Alpha would approach from.

We passed a few parked cars, both in driveways and on the street. "Do we want to steal a car?" Oscar asked.

"I don't know about you guys, but I know my limits as far as breaking in and hot-wiring go," I said. "In the time it would take me, he'd definitely catch up. Besides which, driving away means he could go after Evie."

"Best to keep him on our tail," Nate said as he clutched my arm and limped along. "We can lead him right where we want him."

"Broken foot, you think?" I asked Nate.

"Feels like it," he said.

"What happened down there? What was the trap?"

"I think it was when I pulled the diamond out of the pocket," he said. "I felt a little jolt, like when you play the game Operation and hit the sides with your little tweezers. The legs blew off the table, and it smashed down on my damn foot." Nate hurried along at a good pace, but he was clenching his teeth and sweating profusely.

"So, Oscar, what's your plan?" I asked.

He described the layout of the YMCA and what he thought we could get done in the limited time we had. Nate and I each offered up a couple of refinements. Nate handed me his tranquilizer gun, since he was concentrating on just keeping up his speed. Oscar also had his gun out.

We hadn't tried this sleep formula on Commander Alpha, so we didn't know how (or even if) it would affect him. Still, I felt more comfortable with the pistol in my free hand, even though I wasn't the greatest shot. Alpha was large enough; I was pretty sure I wouldn't miss him if I needed to shoot.

On a normal day, we could have outrun Alpha easily. But with Nate's injured foot, sprinting away was out of the question. At least Alpha was apparently coming after Doctor Oracle all by himself, so we didn't have to worry about someone fast like Action Alex catching up with us.

We reached an intersection and turned the corner. I glanced back down the street just in time to see a bulky figure move in the shadows, down near the house that backed up against the Royce house. Since Evie had shut down the streetlights in that area, it was hard to tell if it was Alpha. But it was a big, bulky person, and he was wearing white. I was pretty sure.

"There he is," I said. We slipped around the corner as quickly as possible and tried to keep to the shadows.

"Did he see us? Is he following?" Nate asked through gritted teeth.

"Not sure, but I think so," I said.

Oscar ran back to the corner and peeked around, then sprinted back to us. "We're good," he said.

"I'm so damned slow," Nate groaned.

"You're still faster than he is," I said. "And we're only a couple of blocks away. Keep going."

We moved as quickly as we could, but I saw Alpha at the intersection behind us before we got to the next turn. He looked around, spotted us, and started moving our way. I'd seen him run a short distance before, and it was more of a waddling speed-walk, which made me pity him even more. He'd forever lost the wonderful feeling of just *running*. We turned another corner, staying in the middle of the street so we'd be easy to see.

"I wonder why he didn't get back in his car and drive around to find us," Oscar said.

"Good thing, though," I said. "He might have found Evie."

Nate was doing his best, but he was starting to slow down and lean on me even more, causing me to go slower, too. Oscar took over holding on to Nate, since he was much stronger.

The dark hulk of the YMCA loomed up ahead of us at the end of the street. I left the guys behind and sprinted to the doors. I thanked Jin and her wall of doorknobs as I pulled out my lock-picking kit and chose my tools; the lock was a familiar one, an industrial model that was one of the easiest kind to open. And it was nice to have a streetlight nearby to show me where the door handle was, as opposed to having to pick another lock in the dark.

I had the door open by the time Oscar and Nate made it to me. Looking over their shoulders, I could see that Alpha was less than a full block behind. We had a couple of minutes' lead on him, tops.

We went down the darkened hallway, passing a number of closed doors. Nate was more hopping than running, but he was still keeping up.

We followed the signs on the walls, around a few corners to the back of the complex. I looked through the windows set into the back doors, then pushed them open. We all stepped out to the concrete deck surrounding the big outdoor swimming pool.

Oscar tried to help Nate around to the far side of the pool, but Nate shook him off. "I'm fine," he said. "Get yourselves set up." Nate started hobbling around the side of the pool, and Oscar ran back to me.

I grabbed my grappling hook and rope back from Oscar and gave him the loose end of the rope. I ran over to the right side of the pool area and snagged the hook on a metal brace that was holding a life preserver. Oscar pulled the rope tight and tied it off on a similar hook on the other side of the enclosure. It stretched across the entire pool deck at knee height.

The pool had a lightweight cover over it, a sheet of plain gray canvas. I thanked our lucky stars. Oscar ran around and cut some of the ropes holding the cover in place with his utility knife. The cover floated on top of the pool, barely connected by a few lines.

I searched around the area and found the electrical panel. I pulled it open and looked at all the switches and dials inside, not sure what to flip to turn off the lights around the pool.

To hell with it, I thought, and pulled the claw hammer out from where I'd stuck it in my belt. I took aim and smashed a few likely looking spots, and eventually the lights both around and inside the pool winked out. I was probably lucky that I didn't get electrocuted.

I stuffed the hammer back and grabbed my night-vision goggles, which were still slung around my neck.

"Smooth," Nate said in my earpiece.

"I guess I need a few lessons on electrical boxes," I said.

Before I put the goggles back on, I looked around the pool deck. In the darkness I couldn't see the black rope we'd just strung from wall to wall, which was good. The entire pool area was a dead end; the only possible escape route was the door we'd come in through. Now that all the lights were out, it was really hard to see the pool itself; the cover floated on top of the water and matched the surrounding concrete almost perfectly. I crossed my fingers that the plan would work and put my goggles back on.

Everything took on a familiar green glow. I could see Nate at the far side of the pool from the doors, the weird reflective nature of the tactical suit making him a fuzzy blob instead of a distinct human shape. He was standing as well as he could but swaying a little from pain and exhaustion. I couldn't see Oscar for a minute, until he waved. He was pressed up against the wall of the main building, so as soon as Alpha came through the door, Oscar would be slightly behind him. He had his tranquilizer gun in hand.

I drew Nate's gun and took up a similar position to Oscar, on the opposite side of the door.

We stood. And waited.

"Jeez, he's slow," Nate muttered.

Evie got back on the line. "Tire's fixed, on my way to you now."

"Got it," Nate said. She didn't ask any questions, but doubtless she'd heard us discuss the plan in her earpiece as she changed the tire, so she knew what we were up to.

"Does this plan fall under the category of irony?" Oscar asked.

"What do you mean?" I asked.

"Well, Commander Alpha trapped Nate with a pool table. Now we're set up to trap him with an entirely different kind of pool. Is that ironic? Or just a weird coincidence?"

"I don't know," I said.

"I've been fuzzy on the actual meaning of irony since that Alanis Morissette song," Nate said.

I heard some crashing deep in the YMCA. Undoubtedly, Alpha was smashing open every door in order to find us. The place was an even better choice than I'd thought, because the building itself slowed him down.

"It just goes to show: that musical was right," Oscar said.

"Which one?"

"*The Music Man*. Trouble with a capital *T*, and that rhymes with *P*, and that stands for pool," he said.

I laughed probably a little more hysterically than was normal. But it was a good release of tension.

I felt a slight rumble in the wall behind my back, and we all shut up. Alpha was close. I took a deep breath.

The rumble got bigger, and I could hear footsteps pounding at a speed-walking pace.

The door from the main YMCA building smashed open, shattering the glass window panel.

Wow, this guy must just hate doors, I thought. I saw Oscar take aim and fire. Since the pistol had a silencer, all I heard was a tiny chuff sound. Oscar ducked behind a stack of flotation boards and peeked back out.

"I know you're out here, Doctor," Alpha said. "And that you have friends with you." He looked around but clearly couldn't see very well in the darkness.

"I've been waiting for you," Nate said, his deep Doctor Oracle voice floating from across the pool.

I aimed and took my shot. I know the dart made contact, but Alpha didn't even flinch. So much for this formulation of the tranquilizer. It probably just made him feel a little sleepy. Or angrier.

"There's nowhere else to run," Alpha said. He took another step forward toward the pool.

"I don't intend to run," Nate said. "I intend to take you *down*."

Alpha erupted into laughter. "On the contrary, my dear doctor, I have you trapped. It's you who's going down." He took another cautious step forward.

"I feel bad for you, Tyler," Nate said. Alpha stopped walking.

"Don't call me that," he said.

"Here you've gone to all of this trouble, and it's just going to end poorly for you," Nate said. "All you'll have to show for the whole thing is a hole in your mom's floor. Do you think you can patch that up by the time she gets back from Branson?"

"Don't talk about my mother," Alpha said.

"Then again, she probably expects something like this from you, doesn't she, Tyler?" Alpha took another step forward, grinding one of his huge fists into his other hand. He was getting close to the edge of the pool. Even with my night-vision goggles on, it was hard to see where the concrete ended and the canvas pool cover began.

"Shut. Up," Alpha said through clenched teeth.

"Just another screw up," Nate said. "Just another classic Tyler maneuver. She'll probably shake her head and think to herself, 'Of course he screwed this up. What else did I expect?'"

Alpha twitched and growled.

"Or," Nate said, "she'll just think to herself, 'All these years, all that strength, and he's still getting himself hauled up flagpoles.'"

Alpha let out a yell and ran straight toward Nate, ready to start pummeling. His knees hit the rope we'd strung across the pool deck. The rope stretched a little bit, and the cleats it was hooked to made a groaning sound, but it held.

Commander Alpha windmilled his arms, yelled in a highly undignified manner, and fell headfirst into the floating canvas pool cover, which promptly slipped aside and sent him sinking into the deep end of the swimming pool.

Nate was off like a shot, limping around the side of the pool, and I ran over to meet him. Oscar and I helped Nate over the rope, then we made our way through the broken door at top speed.

"He'll be out of there as soon as he can walk his way across the bottom," Nate said.

"Then get your arses in gear," Evie said over my earpiece. "I'm right out front."

We piled out the front door of the YMCA and found the van ready and waiting, engine running and side door wide open for us. As soon as we were inside with the door shut, Evie drove off like a bat out of hell.

Nate, Oscar, and I pulled off our goggles and hoods. I looked at Nate; he was pale, sweaty, and shaking. He reached down to the big zippered cargo pocket on his pants, opened it, and pulled out the Midnight Star diamond. He passed it to Oscar to put away for safekeeping and slouched down in his seat.

I looked out the back windows of the van. The YMCA was already out of sight, and there was no chance that Alpha could catch up with us. Even if he'd taken down the license plate number on the van, it would be back to the rental car company shortly, with its rental records wiped from the system thanks to Evie's computer savvy.

Within an hour, we were back in the air on our way to the island. Someone could restock the equipment in the Seattle warehouse space on a later day; now we just wanted to get Nate back to Dr. Adams so she could patch up his broken foot.

"He's going to come after us harder than ever now," Nate said.

"Probably," I agreed.

"We'll just have to deal with it as it comes," he said. "Keep on doing what we're doing but keep an extra-vigilant eye out on what he's up to."

"So this is what it's like to have a nemesis," Evie said. "I suppose it's about time we specialized."

"I wonder what kind of trouble he's going to be in with the Green Lady," I said. "Since he lost her favorite diamond."

"I've heard she can be pretty vicious when she puts her mind to it," Oscar said.

"Not surprising," Nate said. "Look how Catalyst turned out. If they are related, they'd be a perfect pair."

Nate settled back in one of the reclining seats to try and relax, and the rest of us did the same. I didn't fall asleep, but I was able to get some good thinking done. I thought about how happy I was to be going back to the island, safe and sound with everyone around me safe and sound as well. And I thought about how, even though the night had been stressful and nerve-wracking, it was also thrilling.

Mostly, I thought about how I'd finally found what I wanted to do, and I'd made it in just under the wire before turning thirty.

I thought that my mother would be proud.

As the island came into view out the window, I checked in on Nate. He was awake and looking out the window. I sat down next to him.

"You did great back there," I said.

"Yeah, I didn't feel so great doing it, though. That's not how I want to do business, dragging someone's personal tragedies through the mud," Nate said.

"You said what you had to say to get him to rush you."

"Doesn't mean I have to like it," Nate said.

"No," I said, holding his hand. "But you can learn from it."

Nate sighed. "I wonder if Alpha can?"

EPILOGUE

I pushed my cart through the long, luxurious hallway of the eighth floor of a high-rise condo building in downtown Portland, Oregon. It was well past quitting time, and most women in my position would be ready to head out and settle in with a good book, a glass of wine, and maybe a bubble bath.

An older man in an immaculate suit stepped out of the storage room in front of me.

"Miss Anderson, I've been waiting for you," he said.

"Yes, sir," I said, tucking sweaty, flyaway black hairs back under my cap. "Mr. Ambrose. What can I help you with?"

"Rita has come down with a sudden case of food poisoning," he said. "She's been taken to the hospital."

"Oh no," I said. "I hope she's all right."

He waved his hand dismissively in the air. "I suppose she will be. But we have a problem."

"What can I do to help, sir?" I asked.

He looked down his nose at me thoughtfully and paused for a long moment. I fidgeted with the white cotton gloves that were part of my uniform. "You've been doing a good job here, Anderson."

"Thank you, Mr. Ambrose."

"We'll need you to head up and clean suite 2201. We don't have any overtime to offer, but rest assured that a job well done will be noticed."

Jackass, I thought. "Absolutely, sir," I said.

"Excellent," he said, and turned to go.

"Mr. Ambrose, sir?" I said.

"Yes?"

"I don't have access to the twenty-second floor," I said.

"Ah, yes," he said. He pulled a key card out of his breast pocket. "This will get you where you need to go. Be sure to drop it off with security on your way out tonight."

"Yes, sir," I said. "Thank you for the opportunity, sir."

He turned and strode down the hall to take the guest elevator back to his office. I turned back the way I had come and pushed the housekeeping cart back to the service elevators. I pressed the button and waited for the elevator to slowly grind its way up to eight.

When the car arrived, I got on and pressed the button for the fourteenth floor. I rode up in silence, so I could hear the creaks and rattles of the old service elevator. It was a dinosaur compared to the luxurious glass elevators the condo owners used.

At the fourteenth floor, the doors opened and a man dressed in service coveralls got on. He had a green cap on his head, a thick mustache under a bulbous nose, and he carried a large toolbox in his hand. His name tag read "Mario." He stepped to the back of the elevator, and I swiped the key card through the scanner and pressed the button for twenty-two.

"Having a good day?" I asked.

"Never better," he said.

I looked him up and down and raised one eyebrow. "That's a Mario name tag with a Luigi cap."

"This was the only name tag available. But you're right, I don't think Mario is really *me*. I'm totally his taller, more handsome brother," he said.

"Definitely," I said. "I've heard that poor Rita is having stomach problems. I hope she'll be okay."

"In about three hours, I bet she'll be right as rain."

"Good to know, *Luigi*."

The elevator shuddered as it reached the top floor of the building. I pushed my cart up to the door of penthouse 2201. The plumber walked the other way, toward the door of penthouse 2202. He reached the door and pulled an aerosol can out of his toolbox. He shook the can, plugged a straw into the nozzle, and put the straw through the thin crack underneath the door.

He sprayed the entire contents of the can, then threw it back in his toolbox. I pulled a cardboard box out from the bottom of my cart, the sides emblazoned with a toilet-paper company logo. Opening the box, I took out two small gas masks from under rolls of toilet paper. We each put one on.

I pulled my lock-picking set out of the pocket of my apron. He bowed and doffed his Luigi-green cap to me, waving his gloved hand out toward the door. "After you, Princess Peach," he said.

"Luigi's girlfriend was Princess Daisy," I said.

"And this is why I love you," Nate said as I leaned over to pick the lock.

ABOUT THE AUTHOR

Missy Meyer was born and raised in Seattle, Washington, but moved to Florida in order to work for the world's largest mouse. (She's also had an amazing variety of jobs, including singing improv comedian, bank teller, webmaster, pizza chef, accountant, camp counselor, and casino dealer.) She draws the web comic *Holiday Doodles*.

Missy is married to Scott Meyer, the guy behind the web comic *Basic Instructions* and the author of *Off to Be the Wizard* and the Magic 2.0 series of books. They currently live near Orlando, Florida, with their two cats.

ACKNOWLEDGEMENTS

Thanks go out first and foremost to my husband, Scott. Without his encouragement and support, this book would not exist. Also, big thanks to Rodney Sherwood, Kate Jaeger, Cheryl Platz, and Matt Patin for their valuable help, feedback, and support.

And a huge thank you to everyone who has purchased this book!

Made in the USA
Columbia, SC
21 November 2019

83578408R00167